EDGEWISE

A Novel

Jan Stites

Niangua Books

ISBN: 1-4392-0487-X
ISBN-13: 9781439204870
LCCN: 2008907748

Visit www.amazon.com to order additional copies.

To the memory of Sandra Athena Stark,
to whom I owe my firstborn
and
To Bert Felton, husband and sailor extraordinaire:
you float my boat.

One

There must be some mistake. Simone stood before a chain link fence tipped with spiked points. Plywood barricaded some windows; the piercings in the wood looked like bullet holes. Black bars striped other windows, either to keep local people out, or patients in. At her feet: shattered glass. This wasn't a hospital; it was the set for a horror movie.

Oakhill Hospital Day Treatment Center, the sign had originally read, but the *i* had been spray painted to read *Oakhell.* This was not the part of Oakland she had expected, the region of prosperous hills. She was in its crime-infested flatlands. Probably not just the hospital's windows but its patients were bullet bait. What was she doing here?

She picked up one of the glass shards from the sidewalk. It stank of whiskey. She considered slashing her wrists. Then she wouldn't have to worry that she was not going back to her classroom to teach any time soon.

She stared at the hospital's four trailers, grouped in a loose square, all of them the brown of dead flowers, bare and squat and drab. Fog drifted over them, as if the hospital were smoldering after a patient riot. She had nowhere else to go. Sighing, she smoothed the loose blouse she wore over leggings because she was tired of men staring at her breasts and started picking her way through the broken glass to the front trailer, its door the only part of the hospital not barricaded behind the fence. Locked.

She knocked, waited. The door opened to an Asian man wearing jeans and a pink T-shirt emblazoned with a chest-sized Tweety Bird.

"Hi," he said, smiling. "Can I help you?"

"I'm supposed to be visiting the program."

"You are?"

"Yes."

"No. I mean, who are you?"

"Oh. Sorry." *Way to go, idiot.* "Simone Jouve."

"No problem. Welcome. I'm Jun Gambia, one of the counselors."

Tweety Bird gestured to a gate in the fence that barricaded the complex. "Members enter there."

"'Members'?" Simone asked.

The man smiled, or didn't; Simone wasn't sure. "General meeting starts in five minutes. I'll explain our outpatient program right after the meeting. Just wait out in back with the others. The gate combination is three-two-one." He closed the door.

Simone went to the gate. A small brown bird with a black head like an executioner's hood that she hoped wasn't an omen perched on the fence, watching her try to work the lock. She forced herself to take a deep breath. She could do this. After lining up the right numbers, she entered the compound.

A huge black man, arms flailing, lumbered toward her, yelling words—all Simone could make of his rant was *aliens* and *Jesus* and *Eddie Murphy*. Panic gripped her. She stepped back. He kept coming, his eyes on her now. She stepped back again, but he was almost within striking distance. She pivoted, ready to run and scream. The flailing man veered away from her, heading back behind the front trailer. She could still hear him, still smell his sweat.

Heart pounding, she lingered at the gate, hoping someone sane would appear. No one came to save her. Finally she walked hesitantly forward. As she neared the corner of the front trailer, she detected murmuring voices behind it and followed them, emerging into the glare of a dusty courtyard that held a scattering of round concrete tables with concrete benches, a volleyball court, and a basketball hoop.

Some two dozen people seated at the tables turned and stared at her. Their conversations stopped as if her presence had flipped a switch. They were black, all of them. Expressionless, they scrutinized her. Smoke curled from their cigarettes, dispersing into the fog. Simone yearned to be that smoke.

"Hi," she made herself say in a full voice. She slid onto the concrete seat of the nearest table; the two women sitting there regarded her as if she were three-headed. "I'm Simone."

The woman across from her scowled. Her hair stuck out from her head. Her purple sweatshirt stretched against her sides. She wasn't fat, Simone decided, just big, a fullback of a woman.

Simone refocused her attention to the other woman at the table, who was slight with curly hair and an unsettling grin. She gave the woman her best first-day-of-school smile. "Hi." The woman's face barely changed. Simone felt more alone than she did when she was by herself.

"All right, y'all, who's gonna cover my bet?" demanded the big woman in the purple sweatshirt.

"What odds you giving, Satch?" asked a skinny woman with long, pointed earrings seated at the next table.

The woman named Satch ran her eyes over Simone and snorted. "Three to one against."

"Ten."

"Five," Satch said. "Bet's a dollar."

"What are you betting on?" Simone asked.

"Count me in," said the woman with the large earrings, their tips touching her shoulders.

"What are you betting on?" Simone asked again.

"Got a dollar say you ain't coming back tomorrow. White folks visit. Don't come back."

Simone swallowed quickly and glanced at a table where a balding man, the joints of his glasses bandaged with tape, was cradling three brown teddy bears as if they were his triplets.

"You staff?" another man asked her, his languorous eyes on the smoke rings he was blowing.

"Shit, no," Satch said. "She come in the nuts' entrance, just like us. I seen her come round the corner." Her eyes bored into Simone. "What you doing here?"

Simone wasn't about to mention her crying jag in front of a roomful of tenth graders, or what her thighs looked like under her leggings, or her principal's declaration: "I can't allow you back in the classroom. Get help." She shrugged.

Satch narrowed her eyes and curled the corner of a lip crowned by a dark brown mole. "Got to have qualifications to join this club. You schizophrenic? Bipolar? OCD?"

She wasn't any of those things. But she had to say something, and it might as well be true. "I guess I'm just really tired."

"Tired?" Satch said, glaring at her. "Oakhill ain't no spa. Don't got no hot tub."

"I know. I didn't mean..." She really *was* tired, too tired to finish her sentence.

"Tired!" Satch said. "What right you got to be *tired?"* She waved at the cadre of faces behind her. "We all tired."

At first Simone made herself hold Satch's gaze, but finally she looked away and, in relief, let her eyes follow a tall, umber-skinned woman wearing a batik pantsuit and matching red beads in her braided hair.

"Good morning, everybody." Batik Lady nodded to Simone, who wanted to kiss her feet in gratitude for the greeting.

"Hi, Muslimah," said the teddy-bear man, tucking his head down like a bashful child.

Muslimah smiled at him then turned to Satch. "I'm glad you're back," she said.

Satch kept her eyes on the table. "Had the flu."

"Have you seen a doctor? You seem to get that flu a lot," Muslimah remarked.

Simone detected the slightest hint of reprimand.

Muslimah straightened the file folders in her hands. Satch didn't respond. "We'll talk later," Muslimah said. She crossed the courtyard to the far trailer.

Simone saw her chance. "Did you get a flu shot? I teach, so I'm around a lot of sick kids, but since I started getting flu shots I never get sick."

"Fuck you, bitch!"

Simone's gut cramped.

"If you so damned healthy, why you here?"

"She was just trying to help," said the slight woman with the unsettling smile.

"Yeah," agreed the man with the teddy-bear triplets.

"White folks always be telling black folks how to live," Satch said. "And I *know* you ain't coming back, 'cause Oakhill ain't white enough."

A car screeched down the street, the sound keening into Simone's eardrums.

"Noooo!" screamed the slight woman. She clamped her hands over her ears, scrunched shut her eyes, and screamed again, rocking back and forth. *"Noooo!"*

Satch instantly moved into action; she took the screaming woman in her arms and glared again at Simone, as if she'd done something to cause the screams.

"Noooo!" The woman kept screaming.

The teddy-bear man buried his face in their fur.

Simone's heart beat fiercely. She reached out her hand to touch the woman, to help comfort her, but Satch's scowl stopped her.

"I got you, Viola," Satch said gently to the screaming woman. "You safe." Her dark, blazing eyes never left Simone's.

The huge man reappeared, his arms flailing wildly.

"Noooo!" The woman kept screaming.

Simone covered her mouth—the screaming was a siren summoning her to scream along and never stop.

Tweety Bird came out the first trailer door and dashed over to Viola, taking her hand. "Feel my hand, Viola," he said. His voice was barely audible over the yelling but so steady that Simone decided he was talking to her, too. Her pulse ratcheted down to triple digits. "You're not on the sidewalk. You're safe."

"Noooo!"

Another woman, this one with straightened hair flipped up at the ends, stood and clutched her hands to her chest. "I'm having a heart attack!"

Was she? Should Simone do something? Everyone else was ignoring the woman. She must be crazy. They were all crazy. Muslimah hurried over. Satch released Viola, whose screams eventually subsided into tears. The two staff members put arms around her and escorted her inside the trailer. The woman having the heart attack jutted out her lower lip, clasped her shoulders, and sat down.

Simone felt like she was breathing air through a pinched straw. She stood and squeezed her arms around herself. She might dissolve in front of a classroom, but she had a life—and a car that could take her away.

"Figure I'm gonna win my bet," Satch said, studying Simone with a withering smile. "Leaving now and ain't coming back tomorrow, huh?"

Simone fled out the gate.

Two

Simone cut through every yellow light, threading her way back through the Caldecott Tunnel, back to the sunshine and her home in safe Talaveras, fifteen miles east of Oakland. She stabbed the lock to her condo and felt the relief of the paroled prisoner when she slammed the door shut behind her. Then she hurled her purse against the wall. No way she belonged at Oakhell. She would call Kathleen, her principal, and demand she be allowed to return to her classroom where she belonged. Her students were twenty-first-century kids; they understood stress. It was 10:13. The students would be changing classes for two more minutes, Kathleen patrolling the halls. In five minutes she'd call.

She paced the one room that, with the bathroom, constituted her home. Breathing hard, she realized the place smelled like rotten broccoli. The reason sat on the stove. The plants in the kitchen windows drooped, begging for water. Dirty dishes tottered in the sink, and trash erupted from the wastebaskets. She'd been a neat person ever since she was old enough to demand her diaper be changed. How had she let her place get so filthy? Even the ceramic mask collection on one wall looked dirty. She would clean that very day. Everything. Even if it took all night. It was not like, at age forty, she had other evening plans.

If only Michael hadn't moved out, hadn't moved to Los Angeles to become a rich and famous screenwriter. She would have gone with him, even though it would have meant giving up her teaching job, not to mention this freshly bought condo, but he hadn't wanted her. She had watched herself turn thirty-eight, then thirty-nine with him, convinced that if she just loved Michael a little harder he would happily marry her.

She needed a plan. She would spend at least four nights a week researching potential suitors on Match.com or meeting up with them for drinks. And she would throw herself into her students, who liked and needed her. If she didn't have children of her own, at least she had that. When Carl, one of her best students, had cried over his first low grade on Monday, he had somehow triggered her own hysterical tears. One minute she was in the hallway comforting him, assuring him he was bright and talented and didn't have to be perfect, and the next she was collapsed at her desk sobbing. She didn't understand that, but it didn't really matter because all that mattered now was what she did from here on.

She grabbed the phone to call her principal, Kathleen, who sounded as if she was speaking from the distant end of a long pipe. Though she seemed reluctant, when Simone mentioned filing a grievance against her, Kathleen agreed to see her that afternoon. Simone then put in a call for the benefits counselor to get a referral for a therapist in order to satisfy Kathleen's demand she get help. Unfortunately the benefits counselor, who had referred her to Oakhill, was out for the day, but she wouldn't need to tell Kathleen that. If only her skirt hadn't slid up when Meghan had had to guide her to the office. If only Meghan and Kathleen hadn't seen all the lines she'd cut on her thighs.

After several hours of triumphant cleaning, Simone redid her fingernails, choosing polish to go with the powder-blue dress, which would brighten her eyes and make her look like the accomplished professional she was. In the bathroom she re-applied eyeliner with a surgeon's care. She made herself look frankly at the razor blade she'd last used to cut herself two days before. It rested in a small pool of water in the seashell-shaped soap holder.

Cutting was something else she had to change. Gingerly she rubbed her finger across the cold blade and considered using it, one last good cut. No. She slid the blade into the discard slot of the small blue ten-pack she'd bought the previous week and took it with her to her car. She hefted the lid of a rusting trash bin and tossed in the box of blades. As the lid dropped, she felt her chest expand. Oakhill was a phenomenally effective program: she'd been there less than an hour and she was practically cured.

Simone stopped as she entered Kathleen's office. Meghan was there, too. Meghan seemed to shrink away from her; Simone was stunned to realize her best friend seemed afraid of her.

"Sit down," Kathleen said. The principal wore a yellow dress that clung like it had been sewn from whipped butter. "I asked Meghan to join us as the school's union rep."

Simone glanced at Meghan, who took the seat beside her in front of Kathleen's desk. Meghan's eyes were half-hidden behind the wavy blond hair that framed her slim face. Simone tried to read her expression, then addressed Kathleen, professional to professional. "I apologize again for my behavior the other day." Today was Wednesday. Was it really only Monday she'd lost control in front of her students? "It was unacceptable. But as you know, I've been teaching for fifteen years without a problem. I'm lining up a therapist. I want to come back."

Kathleen folded her hands beside a picture of her family of four—irksomely gauzy and perfect, like one of those photos displayed in photography studio windows. Simone had trouble imagining Kathleen taking the time to have children. Maybe she leased them.

"I'm prepared to file a grievance if necessary."

"It wasn't just one incident," Kathleen said. "I told you before about the concern expressed in recent weeks by your colleagues, students, and their parents, a concern I've shared." Kathleen leaned toward her. "It goes beyond that. You skipped yard duty Monday morning, before the…incident. Again. That's the fourth time in two weeks."

Yard duty was a contractual responsibility. Given teenagers' propensity to think themselves immortal and act accordingly, it was essential. Simone's mind reeled. How had she let herself forget four times?

"I sent you a reprimand. You failed to respond. Furthermore, you skipped the last two mandatory faculty meetings, with no explanation, and you haven't posted your grades on our website. Not to mention your breakdown in front of your students. You're welcome to file a grievance, but…"

Shame flushed Simone's cheeks. She clinched her hands, hidden from Kathleen's view by the desk, and clawed her skin, trying to slow her downward spiral. The union would back her. It had to. She looked at her friend, who gave a single shake of her head that made Simone's stomach drop.

"As I told you before, you need to take a voluntary leave of absence for the last seven weeks of the year," Kathleen said. "That way you'll have time to get yourself together."

Yes, Kathleen had insisted she seek help, but had Simone really missed the part about seven weeks? This couldn't be happening. She had no sick leave; she'd donated it to needy colleagues, her buddy Meghan among them. So much for good karma on that good deed. If she wasn't teaching, she wouldn't get paid. The benefits counselor had said it could take two months before disability kicked in. And if she couldn't make the stiff payments, she'd lose her home. "I can't afford to take a leave of absence."

"You can't afford not to." Kathleen surveyed her with eyes that could be measuring distances. "You need to get help. Summer school starts June twenty-fifth. If you're better by then, you can come back."

"You don't understand." Simone gripped the edge of Kathleen's desk. "I went to the hospital. I can't go there. I can't." She heard her voice break.

Kathleen stood up, as did Meghan. "I have a meeting at the district office."

Simone stood, too, her legs trembling. "What if I refuse to take a leave?"

"If you refuse, I'll institute dismissal proceedings." Kathleen's voice was straightforward, cold.

Simone willed her legs not to buckle.

"The two of you can use my office. I have to go." Kathleen left. Steadying herself against the desk, Simone tried to collect her thoughts, but her brain was on a merry-go-round. She turned to Meghan. "Why didn't you defend me? Isn't that what a union rep does?"

"You broke the contract in several ways." Meghan's eyes fell toward Simone's thighs, then rose, but not far enough to meet Simone's stare. "Besides, are you saying you don't need help?"

"But at the only place I can afford to go, the people are crazy!"

"There must be other options. You've got insurance."

Simone covered her face.

"Simone?" Meghan said.

She made herself meet Meghan's gaze. "I chose to take the money rather than insurance. It's the only way I could afford the condo."

"You dropped your insurance?"

Meghan was wide-eyed, aghast. Her husband was a corporate attorney. *She* would never have to choose between insurance and a mortgage. "Look," Simone said, "I'm just strung out from not sleeping. I'll see a doctor and get something for sleep. I'm getting a therapist. I'm a good teacher. You know that, Meghan!"

"You're a terrific teacher. The students love you. Kathleen said they get tons of requests to be in your classes. But a person doesn't hurt herself just because she's tired."

Meghan was a math teacher. In her world, things added up or they didn't. Simone didn't compute. "I'll find a therapist. But if I'm going to pay for one I've got to be working." She projected her voice a little to keep a quiver out of it. "Help me get my job back."

Meghan raised her eyes to Simone's. "Kathleen already put through the papers for your leave."

"With your approval?"

Her friend blushed and looked away.

That night Simone swam laps in the condominium complex pool, smacking the water so hard on each stroke that she sent a shower of stars into the glare of the pool lights. Fifteen minutes. Twenty. Nonstop. Thirty-five. Fifty. Back and forth, the crawl stroke, over and over. Sixty-five minutes. Eighty. Finally she could no longer lift her arms over her head and stood in the shallow end in the stink of chlorine.

She remembered swimming underwater with her mother when she was little, both of them pretending to be sharks. Simone had "attacked" her father, but the man whose knobby white legs she'd grabbed turned out to be someone else. A stranger who yelped. She remembered her mother laughing underwater, could picture the bubbles that rose from her mother's grin, making Simone laugh, too, until she accidentally inhaled water, choked, and shot to the surface gasping.

Could she swim three laps underwater now? She sucked in as much air as she could, then shoved off from the side, kicked hard, pulled herself through the water with spent arms, aimed for the light at the far end, reached it, spun around, kicked off, swam frantically, the air seeping from her body, reached the end, turned, swam the third lap, ran out of air halfway to the light, kept going. If she didn't make it, if she drowned, it wouldn't be so bad. It would be easier than having to breathe. Her lungs sent sirens to her heart. She kept kicking and pulling. Touched the light. Staggered to her feet. Stumbled backward. Breathed, or tried to. The night went dark. The stars disappeared. She lay in the water, face up, not awake, not passed out. After long moments of taking in chlorinated air, she pulled herself upright.

She climbed from the pool, lay on the deck breathing hard, then trudged back to her condo. Dripping, she slipped out of her suit and dropped it on the hallway's tile floor. Drowning or not—it didn't seem to really matter.

She sat down hard on the sofa, wrapped an afghan around her still-naked body, and shivered anyway. Trickles of water slid down her face, her breasts, and found their way to her thighs, where they slid across the lines of her cuts. She covered her face with her hands and tried to picture happy, splashing ocean surf. She kept seeing blades.

Her head ached. She needed to sleep—she had slept only three or four hours a night for weeks—but the swimming had electrified her. She rushed to fix herself warm milk and then chamomile tea. The tastes calmed her but didn't make her sleepy. She clicked on the television. The night began, and it felt long already. She gazed at the screen, which swirled in a blur until finally she switched off the set. Weariness assailed her. As she lay on the couch in the dark, she listened but heard no clock, no passing cars, no calling voices, not even her own shallow breathing. She felt like an astronaut floating alone in the vast silent blackness of space, tethered to her ship by a single line. How easy it would be to sever that line and just drift off.

If only she hadn't dropped her insurance or lost it in front of her students and Kathleen. If only Michael had stayed. Or taken her. She would have to return to the horror that was Oakhill for two months to satisfy Kathleen. If they didn't let her return to school after that, she'd just do what she did tonight: swim underwater until she ran out of breath for good.

As for how she would pay her bills for the two months until summer school began, she couldn't borrow against her condominium because she had no equity. She would have to apply for disability and in the meantime cover her expenses with cash advances from her credit cards, though she had no idea how in the long run she'd pay the exorbitant interest rates. She thought about her father, but it seemed inappropriate to ask him for money at her age. Besides, she hadn't told him of her problems and didn't want to burden her only parent.

Pathetic. Tears blurred the dark. She flung off the afghan, charged into the bathroom, turned on the nightlight, and stared at her image in the mirror for long, lost moments. Who was this bony-faced stranger? She spat at it. It spat back. Saliva seeped down her reflection. It wasn't enough. She opened the medicine cabinet and took out her fingernail scissors.

She didn't feel anything as the sharp tips sank into the soft flesh of her cheek. Blue eyes stared back at her, unblinking. Blood oozed out in a single drop. She pressed the scissors harder. The tips hooked her flesh; it resisted. She forced the scissors downward, ripping a short thin line. A little longer. Make it a little deeper. She studied her handiwork as if she were applying makeup. Then she rubbed her fingers along the jagged seam until blood rouged her cheek. It was better than tears.

There you go, bitch. How does that feel? she heard a voice within her say. *And where have you been for the past forty years?*

THREE

Simone eased the Oakhill gate closed with a suppressed *clink*. The fence's spiked points cast elongated shadows in the bright sunlight. She felt as brittle as dry brush and paused. She worked to focus on the raw, comforting ache of her cheek. Oakhill's members had good reason to regard her with suspicion, even hostility. They didn't know she wasn't one of the bad guys, that she made it a point to challenge her students' racism and to confront and assess the prejudices she knew she had grown up with and had worked to set aside. She just had to maintain her customary cheerfulness and be patient. Sooner or later they would come around, even that muscular, sneering woman named Satch. Simone would be able to put in her time here, and maybe even learn something about the lives and trials of people different from her. Summoning up her best smile, she rounded the corner.

Most of the other members seemed frozen like actors on a movie set waiting for someone to holler "Take!" The only movement Simone saw was hands, with cigarettes moving to and from faces. Cigarette butts dotted the ground like bird droppings.

A laugh barked out triumphantly.

"Hope you feeling rich, Satch."

Satch turned and saw Simone. "Shit!"

Simone strode forward, still smiling. "Good morning, everybody!" No one answered.

The woman Simone had made richer was wearing hoop earrings that could double as bracelets. The style looked chic on her. The earrings swung as she held out her hand to Satch. "Got my five dollars?"

Satch reached into her pocket, took out a five-dollar bill, and slapped it in the woman's palm. Simone felt oddly guilty for showing up.

The huge babbling man wafted by again, but today he held his hands in front of him as if they were handcuffed. Someone else sat huddled on the ground in the distance, rocking slowly back and forth.

"Hey," Simone said to Teddy Bears. He blinked at her behind his taped glasses. He hunched his shoulders higher, a turtle pulling into his shell. "How are the bears today?" she said.

He glanced at her, then lowered his shoulders. "Katrina and Big Pa just fine. But Big Ma done got herself a cold."

"That's too bad," she said. "I hope the other two don't catch it."

"What you do to your face?" Satch demanded.

"Played with a stray cat. Turned out it had a temper." She'd rehearsed her answer in the car.

Satch just shook her head. Simone smiled at Satch, smiled at Teddy Bears, smiled at Screaming Woman, smiled at everyone there. Maybe she could be helpful here. These people didn't seem to have much cheer in their lives. The Heart Attack Lady came out of the trailer sipping a cup of coffee, and Simone decided that was just what she needed: deliberate cheerfulness required caffeine. She went inside the trailer, entering a kitchen where an immense woman—she must have weighed three hundred pounds—was rubbing a sponge over a table in long, repetitive strokes and half a dozen other people sat with slumped shoulders and haggard faces. The room reeked of lemon-scented soap.

"Hello," Simone said.

"This table filthy," the woman said, the table anything but filthy.

"Welcome back."

Simone whirled. Dressed in a red T-shirt with Goofy logo and a small peace earring, with a short ponytail and dimples deep enough to wade in, the counselor was a welcome sight. *Jun,* she remembered. *Rhymes with The One.* She felt herself relax a bit. Only now did she realize how tense she'd been, Oakhell's token white girl.

"I like your shirts," she said.

"Thanks." Jun glanced down at Goofy as if seeing him for the first time. "I own controlling stock in Disney."

"So you're here researching a movie?"

"You got it. How about you?"

"I thought this was a good place to launch my presidential bid."

He smiled and held up the coffee pot, a silent invitation.

The only cups were Styrofoam, hostile to the environment, but she wasn't ready to start campaigning just yet, not here, not now, not with the one person in the room who didn't regard her as first cousin to the Imperial Wizard of the KKK. Simone held out a cup, her trembling hands betraying her to Jun and herself.

"Nervous?" Jun asked. His smile revealed a crooked incisor she found sexy.

"A little."

"Good. That's a sign of sanity." He steadied her hand with one of his. "What happened to your cheek?"

She saw it through his eyes, picturing how it looked in the mirror that morning: an angry red welt. "I picked up a stray cat."

He pursed his lips and seemed to think this over. "Well, drink up. I made it myself."

The coffee was so thick she thought she could ladle it into a taco.

"Think it will wake you up?" he asked.

"I think I could use four quarts of this to change my car oil." She glanced at the people slumped at the three long kitchen tables. "Maybe you should give some to everybody."

Jun smiled. "This is the fourth pot."

Only then did she notice that almost everyone seated gripped coffee cups.

"So what's the agenda?" she asked, truly curious.

"General meeting starts momentarily in the front room," he said. "We check in, then sign up for fifteen-minute small groups with whichever therapist you choose."

"That's impressive. You can fix people in just fifteen minutes?"

"You'd be surprised how long fifteen minutes can seem."

A woman with arms clearly carved by lifting weights came down the hallway. Her closely cropped hair framed peacock-green eyes that dazzled Simone. She felt guilty about her relief at seeing another white person. "Jun, could you announce general meeting?" the woman asked, then walked back down the hallway.

"That's Evelyn," Jun said. "She's the director."

He called out the door to the people outside. Simone followed the others to a large room at the front of the trailer.

Everything in it—chairs, walls, rug, blinds—was less beige than blanched. She took a seat by the door, which she chose to think of as the emergency exit. Some two dozen people trudged into the room like her students on the eighth day of California's STAR testing. Muslimah, the elegant counselor who yesterday had challenged Satch, entered last, the cowpoke rounding up the stragglers.

The woman with the cleaning fetish stood in front of the room. She uncapped a purple marker and laboriously printed the day's date on a dry-erase board: Thursday, April 14. By the time she finished, it was almost Friday.

"I'm Regina," she said. "We're gonna do check-in now." She spoke in a rote but serious voice. "Tell how you felt the night before, how you feel today, then tap the person next to you. Marvin, you start."

"I'm Marvin," Teddy Bears said. He hugged the bears. Patches covered the knees of his pants. "Felt sad last night, feel the same today." He tapped Satch.

"I'm Satch. Felt real good last night. Morning started out fine. Now I'm mad. Real mad."

Simone chanced a glance. Satch glowered at her.

The next few members droned about what they had done, had eaten, had said, until Jun reminded them just to talk about their feelings—but how could they, when they didn't seem to have any, when they spoke in voices as devoid of color as yesterday's fog? When it was her turn, Simone threw all the enthusiasm she could command into her own "I felt a little down last night, but I feel better today."

Sirens sounded outside the windows, a police car and an ambulance piercing the quiet. People stirred uneasily in their seats. Simone watched Screaming Lady—Viola—twitch. Satch took her hand. Some of Simone's students, juiced with their teenage hormones, had unusual fears she often talked out with them. Surely she could find a way to help this woman, too.

After everyone had finally, finally checked in, Regina swept her eyes across the table. "This is Simone's first day, so she needs a buddy. Who will volunteer?"

Simone pasted her smile back on. She sensed the other members glance at her, glance at Satch. She felt the hostility radiate from Satch and poison them all. The silence stretched like funeral-home visitation hours for a hated dead person. She felt her smile wilt, retract.

"Come on, people," Jun said.

Silence.

"Marvin? Thanks," Regina said.

Simone flicked her eyes to Marvin; he was holding up the arm of one of his teddy bears. She didn't know whether to laugh or cry. If she had a friend here, it was stuffed.

Regina then announced they were going to sign up for small group meetings and explained for Simone's benefit that any member could call a group to discuss whatever he or she wanted and that all members were encouraged to attend others' groups to give support or offer feedback.

Simone wanted one of Jun's groups. She raised her hand tentatively, then lowered it. She debated raising it again but opted not to because she didn't want to seem like a hot dog, requesting a meeting her first day. She watched silently as various members scheduled groups with Jun; with Muslimah, who today was dressed in a red-and-gold caftan; and with Evelyn, the director.

Footsteps sounded down the hallway. A woman swirled into the room in a whirlwind of bright colors: red, yellow, turquoise.

Straight black hair, hazel eyes. Simone thought her skin to be the color and smoothness of maple syrup. She wore a short skirt over tights and a frilly blouse, and seemed primed to grab a partner and samba. Alev, her name was; she said she felt happy. She spoke with a hint of a Latin accent as she asked for a group with Jun. Simone tried to blunt her jealousy.

When the groups had all been scheduled, the meeting ended; Jun approached Simone. "I'm your treatment coordinator," he said.

"What does a treatment coordinator do?"

"Oversees your care, helps you through the rough patches, generally keeps tabs on your progress. I've got a small group right now, then we'll do your intake interview. You might want to sample a group."

He entered one of the rooms off the hall. She hesitated to follow, but a nudge on her back made her glance around; Katrina, the smallest bear, was pushing her forward. Marvin peered out from behind the bear and smiled, and Katrina prodded her again. They entered a small, windowless room featuring eight folding chairs and one easy chair. Alev swept in behind them and took the chair closest to Jun, her knees occasionally brushing his. Simone felt like a sixth grader competing for the attention of the one boy who'd hit puberty.

Satch came in next. Damn. Behind her was Viola. She was still wearing a smile, one that seemed the echo of a voice long silenced.

The room smelled riper than a locker room—courtesy of Satch, Simone surmised—mixed with some kind of grapefruit-scented hair gel that was almost as bad.

"What's coming up for you today, Viola?" Jun said.

Viola perched gingerly on the edge of her chair, as if she feared it might explode. When she spoke, Simone had to lean forward to hear because her words sounded as if they'd been run over by a semi.

"I just keep remembering that day," Viola said. "Over and over again."

"I know it's hard," Jun said gently.

"Don't know how to stop thinking about it."

Jun glanced around the room, inviting people to speak. Most stared at the floor. Viola's trauma, whatever it was, seemed familiar turf to this crowd. Simone's mind raced, trying to find something helpful to say to Viola, who appeared forlorn despite her strange smile. "Have you tried using positive imagery?" she asked. "When you start remembering the negative, visualize something positive to block those thoughts."

"That's a big help!" Satch snapped. "Don't be thinking about what happened, girl," she said to Viola. "Just think 'happy' thoughts." Satch spat out the words.

"That's enough," Jun said to Satch.

Satch could use a little positive imagery, Simone thought.

"It was last November," Viola began, looking at Simone. "My baby looked so pretty in her blue dress."

She started telling her story, her dulled voice punctuated by that creepy smile. She told about how she was taking her three children out to get ice cream. Aisha was skipping ahead while Viola had linked arms with her two other children. "It was real foggy and kind of cold, but my kids love ice cream."

Simone sensed she didn't want to hear what Viola was about to say.

When she heard tires screeching, Viola said, she didn't do anything right away. But then two gangbangers took off running, which woke her up. She knocked her two closest children to the ground, covering their bodies with hers. "I screamed

Aisha's name. I was trying to make her take cover." Her daughter, she said, stopped skipping and turned toward her.

"The bullets were real loud." Viola didn't blink, didn't pause. "There was so much blood." Her voice was bewildered. "How could one little girl hold so much blood?"

Viola closed her eyes, and Simone thought she could reach out and touch the woman's tears. But Viola wasn't crying, though she wasn't smiling anymore either. *Positive images?* Simone cringed.

"Hell," Satch said, looking from Simone to Viola and back to Simone. "Just gotta start thinking happy thoughts, girl. Oughta go buy yourself a Happy Meal."

"Stop it, Satch," Jun said. "Simone didn't know."

"Then she shouldn'ta said nothing."

Simone couldn't begin to comprehend Viola's pain. No wonder the woman looked at her with eyes like burnt embers. "I'm sorry," she said. "I'm really sorry."

"Are you okay?"

Simone turned from the chain-link fence to see Alev, the woman whose bright clothes gleamed like the colors of a carousel.

"I feel bad about Viola," Simone said. The meeting had ended at last, and she'd bolted.

"Me too. But we can't change what happened." She extended her hand. "I'm Alev."

Simone took Alev's hand, each finger ringed. It was reassuring to press real flesh. "I'm glad to meet you." She envied the woman's petite stature, her small but rounded breasts. "I said some stupid things to Viola."

"You were just trying to help. Besides, Viola didn't seem to mind. Just Satch. She's a real bitch, huh?"

Relieved, Simone squared her shoulders. She enjoyed the warmth of the sun that seemed to massage her back. "I've met friendlier people. Why's Satch here, do you know?"

Alev tossed her head, her round, orange-and-gold earrings tinkling like tiny cymbals. "She's on probation for something. Assault, maybe. Or murder."

"I'm probably her next victim. Do you think flak jackets come in fuchsia?"

Alev didn't grin. "That woman's just jealous of both of us. We have good figures and gorgeous hair. Hers looks like a Brillo pad. What do you think of Jun? Sexy, huh?"

Heat flushed Simone's face.

"When I leave here," Alev said, "we're going out for dinner and dancing. He asked me last week." She raised her hands as if holding a dance partner and performed five sexy steps of a samba.

Of course Jun would choose Alev, Simone thought. What man wouldn't? By comparison she was a sixth-grade wall-flower.

"Are you ready?" Jun had come up behind her.

"For you," Alev said, "I'm always ready."

He smiled vaguely. "I'm here for Simone's intake interview."

"You lucky woman," Alev said. "See you two later. No hanky panky." Her skirt swished against Jun's legs as she sa-shayed away.

Jun led Simone to a small trailer across from the larger main one. The easy way he moved, with a slight spring to his step, made her picture him bouncing gracefully on a trampo-line. Inside the small trailer, four cubicles were lit by flickering fluorescent lights and separated by low partitions. A watercolor of mountain stream and pebbles brightened Jun's cubicle. "Did you paint that?" she said.

"Yeah."

"It's really beautiful."

"Thanks."

They both regarded the painting, and Simone wished she were there, inside the painting, walking alongside the stream. Viola and her children should have been there, too. But she had to put Viola from her mind or she knew exactly what she would do when she got home.

A silver-and-blue bicycle helmet sat on the desk. "You ride?"

"It's how I commute. About ten miles each way. Want some coffee?"

She didn't, but she didn't want to hurt his feelings. "Sure. Where did you get the name *Jun?*"

"My mother's Filipina." He gave her a mug. "I have to warn you. Four cups of this will put hair on your chest."

"Oh? And will I be able to pee standing up?"

"That takes ten cups."

He gestured her to a seat beside a large steel desk that was incredibly ugly.

"Put some wheels on that thing and you'd have a Hummer," she said. He chuckled, delighting her. "How long have you been at Oakhill?"

"I'm a rookie," he said.

"Drafted in the first round?"

"I'll be honest. I've only been here three months."

Although it was hard to be sure, she thought the smile wrinkles at the edges of Jun's eyes suggested he might be near her own age. The right age. "So what did you do in your previous life?"

"House painting. Freelance art. But I decided I needed a steadier income, and I like helping people. So I got my MSW."

"I guess three months in the field is plenty of time to learn the tricks of the trade."

He gave a wry smile. "I hope so. You're only the second case I've coordinated."

"The first one still alive?"

"So far."

She wondered if his first was Alev. "Well, I'll try to go easy on you."

He set the coffee on the table. "From what I know, you need to go easy on yourself. When you first called, you said you cut yourself?"

"It's no big deal. They're just superficial."

"Any cutting is a big deal. When did you start?"

"About four months ago." No man in his right mind would be attracted to a woman who carved herself, and he was the most appealing man she'd met in a long time. She would have to negotiate this topic with panache.

"And the reason you cut yourself is?"

"I really want to be a mother. But not a single parent. For some reason I keep dating men who, if they were forced to choose between marriage and electrocution, would take it under advisement. I think I'm angry at myself for making poor choices." He would have to like her forthrightness. He didn't wear a wedding ring.

"I see. What happened that made you cut yourself the first time?"

"Nothing different, really." She frowned. That was the mystery. After Michael moved last June, she'd been adrift, more than she was before she met him. She dated several men in the ensuing six months, but no one excited her until she met Spence in January through Match.com. A former Peace Corps volunteer, Spence told her he'd been arrested six times for political protests over issues dear to her. They'd emailed and had four long phone calls before their first date. Their only date. "I could love you, Simone," he'd said over dinner, a statement that both alarmed and thrilled her. When she phoned him after their date, he failed to return her call. He must have come to his senses. Not long afterwards she'd begun cutting. But one date was hardly enough to explain why she'd turned to razor blades.

"Where do you cut?"

She could picture her blade as vividly as if she held it in her fingers, its gleaming silver reflecting the light from the bathroom bulb, edge smeared red. "My thighs."

"And your face?"

She looked away.

"Why?" he asked.

She couldn't answer. She had to shrug.

"Can you tell me why?" he prodded.

"Sometimes I get so tense that I feel like I'm just going to rip open. Cutting calms me."

"What kinds of things make you feel you have to cut yourself?"

She folded her hands as if in prayer. "Nothing in particular. Rage maybe?"

His dark eyes told her he thought that was too quick and easy an answer, like saying all circus clowns were secretly sad.

She knew he didn't understand what she meant, but she wasn't sure she knew herself.

"Tell me about your family. Your parents."

"Oh, we had a great family. My friends envied me." There'd been so many good times. "Once when I was a freshman in high school, the school board was going to eliminate the music program." She told him how her mother secretly organized the band and chorus students to assemble quietly at the school board office—she could still see their blue uniforms with the gold trim that to her looked like the notes that rose from their instruments and voices. Her mother had flung open the doors and led the students down the aisle. The band triumphantly played "Seventy-Six Trombones" followed by the chorus, which sang "The Sound of Music." People in the audience gave them a standing ovation. The board voted to keep the music program. "The other students kept telling me how much they wished they had a mother as 'cool' as mine."

"She sounds like a lot of fun," Jun commented.

"She was."

"Was?"

"She died in a car accident when I was sixteen."

"I'm sorry."

Jun's dark brown eyes seemed to light on her, their touch barely perceptible, like a moth's.

"Mom was a painter, too," she said. "She liked the Impressionists, liked anything French."

"And your father?"

"He taught European history at the state college until he retired two years ago." No tragedy here to bring down Jun's moon. "He's a wonderful man. When I was little, he'd pull me in my red wagon the six blocks to an ice cream parlor for a butterscotch cone."

"That's an unusually happy background for someone who mutilates herself."

She flinched. *Mutilates* sounded like such a brutal term. She preferred to think of it as cutting.

"Was your family really that perfect?"

His obvious skepticism reminded her of her own when a student who never handed in homework swore he'd left his completed essay on the kitchen table. "Nothing's perfect."

"Tell me about the imperfections."

She imagined herself in the painting sitting with her feet dangling in the water. "My parents didn't always get along," she offered. "I'm not sure how much they loved each other by the end."

Jun jotted down a note to himself, and Simone worried he was jumping to the wrong conclusions. "Even though they had problems, they both loved me a lot. I'm not Miss Childhood Trauma. Whatever problems I have are my own doing."

His face was neutral. He wrote something.

She worried she'd insulted him. "Childhood issues are fine for other people, but I don't think they're relevant to me. I just need to stop being self-indulgent. And I need to learn how to meet a man who doesn't think a wedding ring is shock therapy." She grinned to show him she was kidding about the shock therapy.

He chewed on the top of his pen, then opened a file folder. Her name was affixed to the folder on a small orange label. "I've glanced at the forms you faxed," he said, scanning something in her file. "You don't seem to have any discretionary income."

"I'm on leave from school. I don't have any sick leave, so I'm not getting paid. I'm going to apply for teachers' disability, but at the moment my only income's from Visa." She smiled.

"That's rough," he said. "Fortunately we have a dole to cover the cost of our services for people without coverage or resources."

Simone chewed her lip. The word *dole* conjured up images of large families and dirt-streaked faces. "I can pay some," she said.

Jun raised his eyebrows. "Our services cost six thousand a month."

"Six *thousand?*" Simone felt faint.

"Not to worry. After all, the program's taxpayer-funded, and I'm sure you pay taxes. Okay?"

She did a lightning-fast assessment of her options as Jun filled in a line on her form. Without help, she'd be unable to come to Oakhill. Maybe she should go backpacking instead. Reconnect with nature and herself. That's what she did after Michael left. After other relationships failed, too. Solo backpacking trips always increased her self-confidence, which might be more beneficial than Oakhill. Then again, she took her Swiss Army knife when she backpacked. What would keep her from using it on herself? "Okay," she said.

"Good. By the way, we have a psychiatrist on consult. He'll want to evaluate you for meds, antidepressants probably."

She didn't take drugs, not even aspirin. Besides, she'd seen enough students messed up by Ritalin to know psychiatric medications were heavy duty. "Are they optional?"

"Yes," he said. "But I urge you to try them."

She smiled; she didn't feel like getting into any of the reasons she didn't want medications with Jun. He probably thought she was damaged goods already.

"As for our program, you know we have small groups in the mornings. Then we have lunch followed by volleyball, which is optional. After that, four days a week we have men's group and women's group, process group, art therapy or drama therapy, depending on the day. Drama is a small group, limited to a few members. I'd like you to join our drama-therapy program. A new group starts next week. You might find it helpful in sorting things out."

"Fine," she said, though she didn't have a clue what drama therapy was and didn't want to know what he thought she needed to sort out.

"There's one last thing." He took a piece of paper from her file. She couldn't see what it was. "I've typed up a contract. It states that you agree not to cut yourself while you attend Oakhill, no matter how tense you feel. That includes when you're not on the premises."

It seemed to Simone that her whole body was drawing back, that snowmelt water was flowing through her veins. She wrapped her oversized shirt around herself. Jun handed her the contract. She had to unfold her body and force herself to take it. When she did, the words blurred together. Yes, she wanted to stop cutting. But what if she needed to, just once, a thin line, a sliver really. The cut on her face burned, which was comforting. She was suddenly angry at Jun.

"I'd also like you to affirm the contract with me every day before you leave."

"What do you mean, *affirm*?" She hated how that word sounded.

"Every day before you leave, you repeat your promise to me. You affirm it. It's like renewing your marriage vows."

Jun held out a pen. She didn't move. He waited. Reluctantly she took the pen from him.

Go ahead, the voice inside her urged. *You can always cut yourself. They'll never know unless you tell them.* She took the silver pen and scribbled her name, careful to make her signature illegible. Then she handed the contract back to Jun, who grinned.

"Is there anything you'd like to ask me?" he said.

"I know what happened to Viola. But why did she start screaming yesterday?"

He rubbed his cheek for a moment, considering something. "Well, since you know about her daughter and she's discussed her condition in groups, I'm not breaking confidentiality. Viola suffers from Post Traumatic Stress Disorder. Things like a car screeching or fireworks can trigger flashbacks."

"Will she get better?"

"Let's hope."

"Is there anything I can do to help her?"

"You need to focus on helping yourself."

"Compared to hers my problems are chicken feed."

He gestured to her face, which burned where she'd cut it. "Viola never did anything to deliberately hurt herself." He rose and they walked back to the main trailer. "Are you coming to another small group?"

Risk facing Satch? She would rather stick her hand down a garbage disposal. "I think I need a little fresh air."

Simone entered the trailer into a hubbub of scraping chairs, crackling brown bags, the popping of soda cans, voices hovering, and occasional laughter. The smells of chips, meat sandwiches, perfume and body odor suffused the room. At the closest table, Alev sat across from Jun, happily chattering, making him smile.

No one would notice if she left, she thought. She took her lunch from the refrigerator where she'd stashed it that morning and observed the room. The only stool left was beside Regina, the woman who'd led the morning meeting, predictably wiping off the table in front of herself with a paper towel. The open stool was in a corner directly behind Satch. Simone scooted the stool as far forward as she could go. She thought she could feel Satch's shoulders just inches from her own.

Readying a smile, Simone turned to Regina and extended her hand. "Hi, I'm Simone."

Regina leaned away. "Hands got lots of germs."

"Right." Simone lowered her hand.

"Ain't never known no Simones."

"It's French."

Regina kept Lady MacBething the table.

"Better be careful," Simone said. "I used to be purple until I took too many showers. Look how I ended up." She held out her pale hands to demonstrate.

Regina grinned and stopped cleaning. Simone, surprised, felt like a therapist. The other woman opened a brown bag and took out cupcakes, chips, cola, and candy bar.

Simone opened her own container of tofu-and-carrot salad. Though she wasn't a vegetarian, she minimized how much meat she ate, didn't want high cholesterol or too many calories. It had taken her a year of dorm food, which had been easy to push away, to slenderize a body she'd let get pudgy in high school. She might not be Prada-thin—for one thing she was top-heavy—but she ate carefully.

Regina peered at the tofu. "Look kinda like somebody barfed it up."

Simone regarded her salad. She put the lid back on.

"Gotta eat something," Regina said. "You skinny. Want some of mine?"

"No thanks."

Satch stood over Regina. "Don't want to be too friendly with no white girl. We ain't her type."

Simone flushed. *No, you aren't my type,* she wanted to say to Satch. *But that's not because of your skin color. It's because you're not nice, or fair.*

"Don't hurt nobody to be friendly, Satch," Regina looked up and said.

"Well, just remember, sister, you fixing to buddy up to that white girl, gonna find you ain't got many friends." Satch shouldered her way out of the trailer.

Regina got up and began washing her hands.

After lunch Simone watched a volleyball game in which Jun and a young man with dreadlocks played against Satch and a man whose orange shirt, green suit jacket, and protruding stomach made him look like a pregnant leprechaun. Satch played with grim focus, spiking the ball at every opportunity, lunging for every shot that came anywhere near her. Her athleticism impressed Simone. She decided to wear tennis shoes the next day so she could join in the game. The possibility of beating Satch pleased her.

She went back inside the trailer to go to the bathroom, and found Viola sitting alone in one of the small group rooms. Just looking at her made Simone feel guilty and stupid. Simone went past her to the bathroom. When she came out, Viola was rocking and smiling. She reminded Simone of a Christmas tree in February, still festooned with tinsel but highly combustible. "Are you okay?" Simone asked.

"I keep trying to figure out the timing," Viola said at last. "If we'd waited to get ice cream."

"I'm sorry for what I said in your group. I didn't know about your daughter."

"I don't let my kids leave our apartment alone," Viola said. "Don't go anywhere alone. If Satch didn't come get me, I wouldn't be coming here."

"Is there anything I can do?"

"It was my fault. I shoulda never let her get ahead of me."

Viola's voice was eerily flat. "It wasn't your fault," Simone said. "You didn't pull the trigger." Simone smelled a body.

Satch, trickles of sweat seeping down her skin, stood in the doorway. "Hey, girlfriend," Satch said to Viola.

"If you need a ride or anything, I'm in the Contra Costa phone book. S. Jouve, Talaveras."

Simone walked to the door. Satch stared at her for a long moment. She stared back. When Satch moved aside, Simone wanted to sprint past her, but she forced herself to step slowly. Outside, seated by herself at a picnic table, she felt a little better than she had when she'd arrived, but a long way from feeling comfortable. That was probably a good thing. The day she felt comfortable at Oakhill was the day she really would need a mental institution.

Four

"Louis, my last relationship, sang like Elvis on helium," Simone said in her first small group the next day. "He wrote country music, the kind that wails about how your baby left you..."

Jun's eyes stayed on hers and Simone felt heartened, despite the fact Alev's shoulder occasionally brushed his. Alev's perfume—Shalimar?—seemed to suck up the available air.

"...and your house burned down and you lost your job..."

Across from her, Satch sat in an orange velour sweatshirt, fingernails and toenails painted to match, her arms folded across her breast, her whole face scowling.

"...and your dog ran away..."

Thankfully the rest of the members present—Alev, Viola, Regina—looked amused.

"...and you tried to do your own laundry but shrunk all your shirts. I think country music just naturally belongs in Laundromats." She smiled at Jun to show she knew she sounded silly, but wasn't absurdity fetching? He seemed content to listen and smile his dimpled smile. The orange Daffy Duck T-shirt he sported today deepened his brown eyes.

The smiles from everyone except Satch fueled her, and she went on to introduce them to Daniel, an inventor she went out with about six years back. "He hardly ever washed his hair. He liked the greasy look. It was like making love to a can of

Crisco." But hygiene hadn't stopped her, she thought to herself, hadn't made her end the relationship. It was Daniel who had broken it off, complaining that she nagged him about his hair. The only romance she'd actually ended was with Peter, who listened well and helped her grade her students' papers, cooked a delicious risotto, and was an attentive lover. It seemed odd she'd found him boring. He wouldn't be entertaining enough to discuss here.

"Shit," Satch said. "You here 'cause you got man problems?" Satch squinted at her as if she were a gray bug on a gray folding chair. "Bet you got a nice car, a big house."

Simone sat back. Satch's anger twisted her stomach.

"Satch, stop or leave," Jun said. "We don't allow personal attacks."

Satch stood up. "Folks here got real problems." She started toward Simone, her hands forming fists. "Schizophrenia. Rape. Murder."

Simone froze. Jun rose and began herding Satch toward the door.

"Why she here, Jun?" She pointed around Jun at Simone. "'Cause she white?"

Simone thought of the four other people she had heard share their problems this morning, people dealing with incest and alcoholism and homelessness. She had tried to offer some lightness, but Satch was right.

"She just here 'cause she white and can't satisfy a man."

Jun opened the door.

"This bullshit, man. That bitch don't belong."

Jun pushed Satch out.

If Simone's face burned any hotter it would torch the room. Satch was right again. She couldn't satisfy a man, not emotionally. They all left her. She would try to flatter them, to make at least one love her. The minute one left she glommed on to another. Many dates turned into one-night stands. Some men became emotionally abusive. Some delighted in humiliating her, like Greg, who'd said he wanted to be able to kick her ass and have her welcome him back. She had. She must have had over sixty sexual partners. She was a whore for love.

"Lunch," someone called in the hallway.

Jun pulled the door closed. "We can go a little into lunch." He sat. "How are you feeling, Simone?"

His eyes crinkled in such a caring way that Simone wanted to cry. She dug her fingernails deep into the back of her neck and pinched her skin until it hurt. Until it soothed her. "I'm fine."

"After what Satch said, why would you be fine?"

"Satch is Satch."

"Meaning?"

She heard his skepticism. "It means that Satch is entitled to her opinion."

"She just said some things that would be hard to hear."

"I teach. You don't always get rave reviews."

Anyway, Satch was right. Simone's problems did pale compared to probably everybody else's at Oakhill. She could feel Jun's probing eyes trying to force her into saying more. She stared at the black legs of the beige chairs and their vague shadows on the brown rug.

"Simone, you need to stay here for a minute," Jun said. "Everyone else can go to lunch. We'll be there shortly."

The others filed out quietly. Simone felt like she'd devoured a swarm of yellow-jackets. If she moved too fast, said too much, wanted too much, they would explode into a frenzy of stinging.

"Look at me," Jun said.

She raised her head and used the trick she taught students terrified of giving speeches: she focused on Jun's forehead, the black hair falling near his eyes.

"Something happened. Something came up for you."

"Not really."

"And I'm a flying walrus." His lips were pressed tight in a straight line, as far from a smile as from a frown. "Why do I feel like I'm the only one in this room?"

Because you are. She and her yellow-jackets had flown away.

"We can sit here all day. Talk to me."

She wouldn't light. But she had to give him something. "I was thinking about some of my former lovers." *Lover.* What a tawdry word. Like *whore.*

"What about them?"

"Nothing in particular. Just remembering some things. Good and bad."

"That's an area you could explore in drama therapy next week."

"Thanks for the suggestion." Whatever drama therapy was, she had plenty of drama in her life already, even if her own story wasn't as award-winning as some of the others.

"Let's go to lunch."

She rose, grateful. Only when she was safely past Jun and seated between Regina and Alev with her back to Satch did she return to her body.

"What did you talk about, you lucky woman?" Alev said.

"Nothing, really. He just wanted to know how I felt about Satch."

"Don't you be letting Satch get to you," Regina said, breaking her potato chips into near-perfect quarters. "She like a mosquito. Keeps on circling and circling 'til she got a chance to bite. You let her see it hurt, she bite you again."

"Thanks for the advice."

A man walked into the lunchroom, conspicuous in his height and whiteness. He walked on the balls of his feet as if aching to sprint. His black hair was tousled and sprinkled with white. Two snakes were tattooed around his neck, their heads flared over his Adams apple.

Simone turned to Alev and raised her eyebrows.

"A new member," Alev said.

"What's his name?"

"Rick. He hasn't said much."

A few of the other women were openly staring at Rick. Didn't they mind he was white, or did being a man make all the difference? She would be friendly; she knew how difficult the first day could be. She walked over to him. "Hi. I'm Simone."

He glared down at her from what seemed the highest ledge of himself. "All you have to do is laugh in a woman's face and she'll love you. Hah!"

Simone stepped two steps back.

"Volleyball," someone announced.

Rick turned around without another look at Simone and walked outside. Simone thought that she should set him up with Satch. A psychiatric hospital probably wasn't the best place to connect with a man, anyway.

Simone debated skipping volleyball and skipping out of Oakhill for the day, but she'd dressed to play, wearing Nikes, black leggings, and a loose, turquoise shirt.

"Hey, come on, let's play volleyball," she called to the other groupies, who were mostly sitting around the picnic tables, smoking and talking and ignoring her. Marvin turned his teddy bears around, which Simone realized he'd done so they could have a view of the game, an insight that made her decide she was losing her own sanity.

"Come on!" she motioned to the spectators with her hands, urging them to the court. They just sat there like cigarette metronomes: inhale—puff—inhale—puff.

Shrugging them off, Simone joined Jun, Rick, and Satch, who wore orange shorts and a purple T-shirt. Jun said he and Simone would take on Rick and Satch. A thrill shot through her: he'd chosen her for his team. Jun took the back of the court and assigned her to the front. She stood near the net facing Satch, who was in the front position on the other side, close enough to touch.

"Gonna beat you, white girl," Satch said softly. "Gonna beat you real bad."

Simone shook her shoulders, loosening up. She told herself that she was athletic, that she would outplay Satch, that they would win this game.

Rick served first. Jun blocked the shot, but he didn't get the ball over, so she clobbered it back across. Rick hit the ball to Satch, who set it up high for him, and he spiked it. Simone leaped to block. The ball spun off her fingers and fell out of bounds. Her fingers stung. She'd forgotten how hard a volleyball could be.

Satch did a quick victory dance, shuffling backwards like Michael Jackson, and grinned. "Good shot," she said, her smile mocking. Simone wanted to be angry. Instead she felt irrational fear.

Rick prepared to serve.

"Try to set me up next time," Jun said to her.

Anytime, Jun, she wanted to say. On the next serve she tried to set him up, but the ball bounced off her wrist. "Sorry," she said in a small, breathless voice.

"No problem," Jun said, but he was wrong. There was a problem. She was the problem. If she couldn't play right, if she messed up the game for everybody else, she wouldn't play at all. Nobody wanted a loser on his team.

"What's the matter, white girl?" Satch murmured, loud enough for Simone to hear her, soft enough for Jun not to. "Scared of the ball?"

Satch's mockery unnerved her. Again fear crowded out her anger. While Satch looked cool, unmoved, sweat seeped down Simone's face and under her arms. She wondered if she should fake a sprained ankle.

Rick's serve went long. Jun hit two serves across the net to equal the score. On Jun's third serve Rick set up Satch, and Simone leaped to block the ball, but it dribbled off her fingertips and out of bounds.

Triumph burst across Satch's face. Simone wanted to bloody it. "Good shot," she said instead. If she couldn't impress Jun with her playing, maybe she could score a few points for good grace.

Satch rotated to the back of their court, and Rick moved across from Simone. Satch served. Simone positioned herself carefully and hit the ball up for Jun, watched it rise and turn against the hot blue sky, watched Jun spike the ball back. Neither Satch nor Rick could reach it. They'd broken Satch's serve.

"Yes!" Simone thrust her fist high.

Jun smiled. "Good set," he said.

Satch seemed mortal now. Simone faced the net and crouched, breath to breath with Satch, ready for more.

The game seesawed back and forth, each side scoring a point or two before losing the serve. When Rick served, the ball went over Jun's head but stopped short of Simone's feet. She dove for it, sliding across the asphalt. Her knees ground into the rough surface. She just managed to hit the ball up. Jun walloped it back across. Rick lunged for it but clipped the ball into the net. Simone got to her feet. Her right knee throbbed; blood trickled down her calf. Jun knelt to check it. She felt like a proud little girl.

"It's no big deal," Simone said. "Really."

"We need to put something on that," Jun said.

"I will. Let's finish the game." She wanted to keep going, to outplay Satch, to win. A bloody knee would be a victory badge.

"That's it for today," Jun said. "Come with me."

He patted her shoulder, and she was thrilled. *I'd follow you anywhere, Daffy Duck.*

In the portable, Jun had her sit while he got the first aid kit. She settled herself on one of the folding chairs, welcoming the feel of the cool metal against her sweaty skin. She felt happy, waiting for Jun to touch her.

"It hurt?" Marvin came from outside, cradling his three bears, glancing down his taped glasses at her bloody knee.

"Not much. How's the family?"

"They're fine." He made a bear paw pat her shoulder.

"Hey Marvin," Jun said, setting the first aid kit down on the table.

"Hey." Marvin made the bears wave good-bye and went back outside.

Jun signaled Simone to prop her leg on another chair and opened a bottle of peroxide. "Ready?"

"Go ahead," she said, with melodramatic flourish. "You'll never make me talk!"

He smiled, touched her knee, and poured. The pain felt cool and keen, like Jun himself.

"Leave your knee up for a few minutes," he said. "I've got to put the volleyball equipment away."

Simone savored the memory of his touch.

"Hey, Si-moaney." Satch peered in the portable. "You don't like it when I talk to you, do you? I scare you, white girl?"

"I don't like bigots whatever color they are," she retorted.

Satch sneered. "See you Monday. 'Less you too scared to come back."

Satch's words sank in. Monday. She'd forgotten about the looming weekend, about the hospital being closed, about not seeing Jun. At that moment, facing another empty weekend, she would take back any of the men who hadn't loved her, even William, who used to ask her to fetch him coffee when he was sprawled on the couch watching TV and she was busy grading papers. She winced at the memory of her mute compliance. She would have done anything to be loved. Anything.

Whore.

At the closing meeting she didn't really hear anyone, just kept picturing the blue boxes of blades on drugstore shelves.

Slut.

After the meeting Jun approached her. She was too busy looking at him to hear what he said except "…Friday…be gentle…"

She would stop at the store on the way home.

His hands cupped her shoulders. "Talk to me," Jun said.

She forced a smile. "Sorry. I was tuned to a different channel."

"I'm concerned about you."

"You're the one wearing the Daffy Duck T-shirt. I'm fine."

"You looked pretty upset in the check-out meeting."

"No, I feel steady on my feet. Really."

"Why do I feel like I'm talking to a shadow?"

"Only the Shadow knows."

"What plans do you have to stay safe this weekend?"

"Oh, rock climbing, hang-gliding, wing-walking."

"Simone, I asked you a serious question.'

"Okay. Okay." Maybe he had no sense of humor except when it came to T-shirts. And she didn't want to make him mad. "I'm going to be with friends." That was a lie. Her only real friend had been Meghan. She pictured Meghan's blonde hair, her artful jewelry, contemplated calling her. But no. Meghan had betrayed her and sided with Kathleen. If it weren't for Meghan, she wouldn't have to be at Oakhill. Their friendship was over.

"Good. You need to look me in the eyes and affirm your contract."

Resistance welled up in her. He was trying to take away her options. He didn't have that right! Still, the contract was only words. Blades could slice right through them. She looked away. "I affirm my contract."

"Good. Now look at me and say just what it is you're promising."

He scared her. She hated him, hated this place. She swore she wouldn't come back, not ever, not even for a day.

Whore.

She looked at his eyes as if she were regarding two inanimate dabs of brown. "I promise not to cut."

"That wasn't so hard, was it?" he said.

"No, you didn't cut my leg off without anesthetic."

"Huh?"

"In this book of Civil War stories I was reading, they used to cut wounded soldiers' legs off without anesthetic and burn the legs for warmth."

"Maybe you should read something lighter for a while." Jun wasn't smiling. He was trying, but she realized he didn't know the right things to say. If he asked her if she planned to cut, she'd tell him yes. Then maybe he could stop her. But he didn't ask.

"Would you like a hug?" he said.

In a millisecond her eyes scanned the space. All the other members had disappeared. So had the other staff. She and Jun were adrift in a sea of beige. He could hug her; he could take her. He could make love to her, right there on the blanched carpet. She tried to swallow.

He put his arms around her. Leaning into the discernable heat of his chest, she felt harbor. If only he would hold her until Monday.

He released her. "Remember your promise and take gentle care of yourself this weekend. I'll see you Monday."

She turned away, reminding herself she had bones that could move her forward. She assembled herself enough to walk outside.

"Simone?" Alev stood on the sidewalk, bouncing on her heels, ebullient. "Guess what I did before I left!"

"What?"

"Snorted coke. In the bathroom. I feel great!"

She watched Simone expectantly. Simone wasn't sure what she was supposed to say. She felt so tired. "I don't think you should do that." Was doing coke was any worse than cutting?

"You should try it," Alev said.

She tiredly tried to summon up the words of all the police officers who had come to talk to her students. "I wish you wouldn't," she said. "It isn't safe. You could overdose accidentally or do something dangerous without realizing it. Drugs obscure your judgment."

Alev smiled, happy. That made one of them.

"You want to come over to my place? It's close," Alev said.

Simone considered the invitation. Alev might be a cokehead, but she'd have stories to tell about Jun that might be useful. She could scope her out, too, suss out her feelings for Jun. And it would be safer not to be alone.

But she didn't want to limit her options. *Slut*. "Thanks, but I can't. And you really ought to lay off the coke, Alev. It can mess you up pretty bad."

Alev embraced her. It was as if she'd recognized a sorority sister. "Thanks for caring. See you Monday." She practically skipped down the sidewalk.

Simone started toward her car, passing a yard full of scraggly weeds and a singular poppy. She stopped to touch the blossom—pumpkin-orange, silky—and exhorted herself to allow the beauty of spring to shield her from her own harsh winter. But it seemed as apt as poetry that the poppy was closing in the fading afternoon light.

Five

The minute Simone stormed into her front door she regretted she hadn't stopped to buy blades. But she had other, less bloody ways to cut something. She jerked open a drawer of her file cabinet and took out a stationery box filled with photographs of her former lovers. No, she thought. *Lovers* was too kind and intimate a word. These were pictures of her johns. She took off the lid and rifled through the snapshots. Nick. Greg. Dylan. Scott. David. Jackson. Josh. Harold. Daniel. Louis. Kurt. Lawrence. Etc. Men with flat, wary faces who didn't know what to do with their mouths when she aimed her lens at them.

One picture in particular arrested her, a snapshot of herself and Michael that an agreeable stranger had taken on a backpacking trip to Yosemite, the rounded crest of Half Dome visible in the distance. Michael was grimy from four days of camping but grinning, wearing his favorite green chamois shirt, the one she'd bought him for their three-month anniversary. It brought out the green of his eyes, the way she hoped she herself would bring out the love in them. But despite two years—two crucial years—of her best efforts to cut through psychic Plexiglass, he hadn't loved her back. One more man who hadn't wanted her.

Too bad she didn't have a picture of Spence. She tossed the photos back in the box, carried it to the kitchen, dumped the pictures onto the counter, then made a neat stack of them.

When she had a small tower, she reached for the carving knife sticking out of a wood block. The large blade caught the light from the window, refracting it onto the wall. Simone ran her finger lightly along the edge and considered using it on herself, on her wrist, lengthwise; it would have to be lengthwise. But when she decided to do that—if she decided to do that—she would do it in the bathtub so no one would have to clean up the mess. She plunged the knife through the stack of photographs, piercing all of them. She had to hold the pictures down with her left hand to extract the blade. She thrust the knife into them again. When she yanked it out, the pictures scattered as if fleeing for their lives.

It wasn't enough. She skewered all the men onto the tip of the knife and took them to the fireplace, where she fashioned them into a pile. Striking a long match, she set the pile alight. She knelt beside them, watching the flame burn, watching the ashes float, watching the smoke of so many wasted years disappear up the chimney. It seemed religious, like something monks would do appease the gods.

She stood up and felt irritatingly unchanged. It hadn't erased her many transgressions. She looked down at the blade between her feet.

The last time she'd cut, when she was watching the blood seep to the surface, she'd heard a voice within herself that sounded like a man's, like a gang leader's. *There you go, bitch. How does that feel and where have you been for the past forty years?* She understood it now. It was her own voice, hardened by years of betraying herself for so many unloving men. She fumbled with the buttons of her sleeve, uncertain of her intent.

When the phone rang, she decided it had to be Jun, that he somehow knew of her peril, and she lunged to answer. "Hello?"

"Hi, doll."

Her father. She exhaled, deep and long.

"Haven't heard from you for six whole days. I was beginning to wonder if you'd eloped with the man of your dreams and you were even now drinking rum punch on a beach in Tahiti."

She smiled despite the sleeve flapping around the hand holding the phone. "I did elope. Twice. But we went to Bali Hai, not Tahiti."

He sang, as she'd hoped he would, the opening lines to "Bali Hai" from *South Pacific.*

His melodic tenor cheered her. Many of her best memories from her childhood were of the two of them singing duets. Once they'd gone to the drive-in to see *The Music Man.* They already knew the soundtrack. The film broke. Cars honked. People spotlighted the screen. It was fifteen minutes before the crew got the film going again; she and her father sat on the hood of their pink Rambler station wagon, perspiration painting their faces and gliding down their chests, singing song after song from the score. Her mother would have stayed home to paint, singing along with recordings of Edith Piaf. Her father's family came from France, and her father taught European history at the college, but it was her mother, with an Irish background, who'd been enraptured by everything French.

"How are your barbarians treating you?" her father asked.

When she last saw him three weeks previously she still had her job, and she hadn't told him she wasn't teaching, hadn't wanted to worry him. "They're fine. Say Dad, can we get together tomorrow?" She heard the neediness in her own voice and hoped he was too blithe to note it.

"What's wrong, doll?"

"I just really need to talk to you." She sensed his hesitation and crossed her fingers.

"I've got a big date tomorrow night," he said.

Since his retirement two years previously, he always had dates. She wondered how he found it so easy. "Oh. Well, that's okay."

"How about a picnic lunch at Cezanne?" he suggested.

The park—located halfway between Talaveras and Sacramento, making it a forty-five minute drive for each of them—wasn't really called Cezanne, but her mother had dubbed it that because the light and colors reminded her of a Cezanne painting. "You don't have to."

"For you, anything. You've always been the most important woman in my life." He always liked saying that. "Would you like me to provide the cuisine?"

"That's okay. I'll get it."

"Great, the park entrance at noon. *Au revoir, chérie,"* he said.

"Au revoir."

Simone hung up the phone. She looked at the knife. It looked like a knife now, and that was all. She knew it would wink at her again. She would water her plants. She picked up the pitcher and watered Estella, her spider plant, touching the slender arching leaves. Jamie, one of her favorite students, had given her the plant for Christmas. Simone pictured the girl: dyed black hair, black lipstick, and black eye shadow that encircled her eyes, making them seem like targets. She regretted that she hadn't gotten to tell Jamie good-bye or to assure her one more time that—at least in Simone's class—she didn't have to wear dramatic make-up to be seen.

The next morning she scrubbed her hair with cantaloupe-scented shampoo. When she'd finished her shower, she applied her makeup carefully: black eyeliner and blue shadow to highlight the eyes that looked like her father's, tinted cream for color on her cheeks, and lip gloss the color of raspberries. She wished she were applying makeup for a man other than her father, but at least she wasn't spending the day alone. She plucked a few errant hairs from her eyebrows, then brushed her long hair a hundred strokes, just as her father did to her every night when she was a child. He used to say the brushing made her hair so shiny he could use her as a flashlight.

She decided on a loose blue Save the Whales T-shirt. Surprised that her shorts all seemed too big, she chose the best-fitting pair, tan ones, and notched her belt tighter than usual. A good meal with her father would help fill her out. She grabbed an ice chest and picked out an assortment of foods from the local deli, cringing as she charged it all. Her father would have provided either peanut-butter sandwiches or fast-food fried chicken, the extent of his culinary abilities. Her mother had had gall bladder surgery back when Simone was too young to cook, and her father had alternated peanut-butter sandwiches and fast-food fried chicken until her mother hobbled back to the kitchen in self-defense. Cooking had been the one domestic task her mother had been willing to perform. She rarely cleaned, though Simone's father railed against the sloppy house, insisting cleaning was her mother's "job."

As Simone steered her Echo onto the ever-clotted Highway 680, she wondered if she should tell Jun that the tension between her parents had played some kind of subliminal role in her own mistaken choices of men. Her inability to fall for a man who wanted marriage no doubt stemmed in part from the mess that was her parents' relationship. She would tell Jun she wanted to get beyond that barrier. Maybe he would be the one to leap over the barrier himself. Driving amid the vibrant green hills, Simone felt herself relax, her shoulders loosen. She wondered what Jun was doing, whether he was painting, whether he was alone or in the company of a woman. Not Alev, she hoped. Jun had better taste than that. Satch must be spending the day mugging people. White people. Simone told herself she had to let go of her discomfort with Satch's anger. She had wasted years trying to defuse other people's anger. Satch wasn't worth the energy.

In the Cezanne parking lot, she got out, opened her arms, and turned around embracing the hills. Then she circled the wooden tables, choosing one that was partially shaded. She spread a red-and-white checkered tablecloth over the bird-soiled top, set the picnic basket on a bench, and glanced at her watch. She was thirty minutes early.

Two hummingbirds buzzed past her, diving at each other like fighter planes. Amazed by their aerial abilities, she watched avidly until both darted away, then leaned back against the picnic table and raised her eyes to the sky. The sun had leached out the blue, leaving behind a milky color. She inhaled the still-moist spring of the earth. One long-ago spring day, her mother had come to the park with Simone and her father—one of the rare times she joined their outings. She'd painted these rolling hills the drab brown of summer. Flying over them, however, was a teeming mass of birdlike splotches of colors, from lapis lazuli to ochre yellow to indigo red. The painting suggested a life full of both drudgery and delight, which now, as Simone thought about it, suggested her mother, too.

There was so much she didn't remember. After all, astonishingly, it had been twenty-four years since her mother's death;

Simone couldn't even recall the exact blue of her mother's eyes. Closing her own, she saw the door to her mother's attic art studio, reachable from below by pulling stairs down with a rope. When her mother was painting she raised the stairs behind her. Not that she needed to. Simone knew—even when she was as young as six or seven and just home from school, bursting to chatter about what they'd done that day—she was never even to call her mother if the stairs were raised. When her mother did emerge, if she was in a good mood she would fix hot chocolate or brownies or popcorn. If she came down dusty and grim, Simone would do her best to coax a smile out of her. She was methodical about it, writing down every joke, every riddle she heard, learning to mimic famous people and family acquaintances.

"Hey, doll."

She opened her eyes. Her father, also early, stood over her, his hair snowy in the sunlight. His smile made her instantly feel better. Then she saw him register the cut on her cheek. "What happened to your face?"

"A stray cat."

Her father extended his hand to help her sit up. "You've always been a softie for strays. You look especially beautiful, *ma chérie.*"

"And you especially handsome." He was dressed in khakis and a red polo shirt, his white hair full and soft, freed at last from the oil slick of Brylcream he used to use. He seemed to her to have become dashing.

"Thank you. Now tell me what was so urgent."

How could she tell him the truth about the cut on her cheek, or the other cutting, much less what happened at school, or the hell of Oakhill? All she wanted was his presence, not his questions. "I...well...this is hard to tell you, but..."

He rubbed his hand over his chin. "What?"

She wasn't sure if the fear was in his voice or her own, but whichever it was made her uneasy. "I'm not sure. I was upset." Maybe the cutting mattered less than her resolve not to do it again. "But I'm better today. I'm sorry to make you come for nothing."

"It's always a delight to see you, doll. You know I'm here for you. Any time. Heck, I'd give you a million dollars if I had it." They hugged. He'd always made her feel loved. When she was sick, he'd brought her presents. Every day. He had attended every school function, every piano recital, which considering she never practiced, must have been excruciating.

They gazed at the surrounding green hills. A bird performed a little aria unseen from a branch above them.

"Nature's symphony," her father said," the sweetest music I know. Great choice of spots."

"Thanks. I paid extra for the bird."

A fluttering of wings and it was gone.

"Some things just don't know how to take a compliment," he said. "So how's your love life?"

Her only love life was her fantasy romance with Jun. "Not exactly blossoming."

"I don't understand it. You're beautiful and sexy. You ever hear from Michael?"

"I've told you, never. Maybe I'll see him on TV, on the Oscars. Or hauled in for setting fire to Malibu."

"You should try an Internet singles service."

She had. It's how she'd met Spence, the man who'd said he could love her over dinner but disconnected his phone after she left him a message. Or maybe it had stayed broken for two weeks, or maybe he'd been kidnapped by Scientologists. "How's yours?"

He grinned like a boy with a date to the junior prom. "Fantastic! I met a woman my age at a singles' lunch yesterday. Claire. We didn't have much time to talk, but I liked her instantly. I'm taking her to dinner tonight, and I'm really excited."

Simone shook her head. "Dad, you get excited when a pretty waitress brings you the check." She smiled.

He kept beaming. "Not like this. We only had about half an hour to talk before the event speaker started, and Claire had to leave early, but I knew immediately she was something special."

"Did you think Mom was special when you met her?"

He didn't hide his surprise. His shoulders went back as if he was about to salute. "I suppose."

"What made that change?" If she understood what had soured her parents' relationship, maybe she could avoid souring her own.

"Your mother was a selfish woman. I didn't realize that at first."

"Selfish how?" Simone kept her voice TV-interview steady.

"She put her own interests first. She was a lousy wife and mother."

Simone knew well why her father thought this. He railed against her mother's isolation in the attic when Simone was little and home from school. But she recalled her mother leading Simone's whole Scout troop in a Conga line around their campsite, recalled her wearing a Groucho Marx mask to shop: bulbous nose, furry eyebrows, thick plastic glasses. She also remembered the summer she got too sick with measles to read; her mother had read her *Little Women*, and they'd cried together over Beth's death. She wondered if she and her father were remembering the same person.

"She was a lot of fun," she said.

He looked begrudging. "At times."

She'd spoiled his high. Simone reached across the table and took his hands, the fingers roughened by gathering wrinkles. The two of them had held hands at her mother's funeral, which had been attended by three hundred people her mother knew through scouting, PTA activities, and school-related volunteer work. "What do you think Mom was going to the store for that day?"

He dropped her hands. He didn't ask what day she meant. "What difference does it make? She was in an accident." He stood. "Simone, honey, you know she's dead. She's been dead for twenty-four years. I don't remember all the details. Come on and join us in the twenty-first century. What's past is prologue."

"But you taught history. It's all about the past."

He crushed a napkin in his hand. "Societal history is different. It's meaningful. Digging into personal history is just an exercise in masturbation. Now, excuse me. I'm a man who needs a can." He got up and walked toward a small brown and yellow concrete building.

Obviously she'd upset him. He'd never been comfortable talking about her mother's death. She should never have brought up the topic, especially not when they'd gotten together at her request; she should have known it would hurt him. She began cleaning up the scraps of trash around the table, including a Trojans wrapper and a Heineken Beer can. Her father had taught her to leave an area cleaner than she'd found it.

He returned with a somber look. "Your mother had been drinking that morning. Surely you knew that."

The birds stopped singing. Clouds slid instantly against the sun. Simone felt hit in the mouth with a rock. This was a new bulletin, not part of their usual call and response over Simone's mother. She squinted at her father. "Are you saying she had a drinking problem?" She couldn't recall her mother ever stumbling around or acting drunk.

"Occasionally."

"Why don't I remember that?"

"It wasn't a big deal. She didn't drink often. I don't want to talk about this anymore."

She felt bad for unsettling him, wanted to give him back his bounce, but she couldn't think of a thing in her current life that would please him. She certainly couldn't tell him about Oakhill; that would only upset him further. Telling him that she was in danger of losing her job was out of the question. And asking him for money, which she'd pondered doing, meant hearing him ask why. She thought back to the previous October's school-wide survey by the school paper. "I was picked most popular teacher by the students," she said, omitting the timeline.

His whole face changed. "That's terrific! It's about time they noticed the obvious. After all, it's in your genes." He winked.

They sat and ate. She enjoyed the artichoke dip spread on sourdough bread, though she was careful not to overeat. While they ate they chatted, mostly about politics: global warming, family planning, the worldwide AIDS epidemic, the kind of topics that had dominated their dinner-table discussions and about which her father had sharp opinions made sharper by reiteration. He had been the host of the family talk show, her mother the largely silent sidekick.

When they'd eaten and cleaned up, her father rose to his feet with a theatrical groan. "I need to be leaving to be back in time to get ready for my date. You know how bad traffic can get."

"Sure thing."

He hugged her tenderly, for a long moment, then put his hands on her shoulders. "You have so much going for you, doll. Live in the present. I need you."

She felt a familiar surge of pride. They'd always been so close, much closer than her friends and their fathers.

Once when she'd been about ten, he'd had a particularly harsh argument with her mother. Unable to bear their hurled barbs, Simone had retreated outside. Eventually her father came out and plopped down in the chair next to her on the porch. She tried hard to think of some joke or riddle to cheer him, but her mind felt vacuum-emptied of words.

He stared at the house across the street. "If it weren't for you, I'd kill myself," he said.

For the first time in her life Simone experienced a glimpse of her own power. Her father's life was in her small hands, and she vowed never to let him down. She had relearned that lesson again and again about men: they acted powerful, but behind their eyes they were desperate. Cheering them had been her life's mission, in a way. No more. Her father, yes, because he was her father and she couldn't bear to lose him, but she would stop trying to cheer up every man she dated and start trying to cheer herself. For her father's sake as well as her own.

Back at their cars, he turned to her. "You should go to a singles' event tonight. Don't sit at home moping. Be good to yourself, okay? And be careful with stray cats."

"Okay."

"*Bon.*" He kissed her undamaged cheek. "See you soon."

Six

When Simone entered the hospital kitchen on Monday, Regina was cleaning a table while Satch opened and shut cupboard doors, releasing a small puff of dust that hovered briefly like a winter breath. "Shit," Satch muttered. She slapped shut the last cabinet and turned to glare at those in the room. "Some asshole done gone and ate my crackers."

"Check in the refrigerator," Simone suggested.

"Fuck you."

Curiously, the insult barely stung. Several people drifted out the door. Simone knew it would be smart to leave, but she wasn't in the mood. She'd done nothing wrong. "What exactly did I do that made you hate me?" she said, genuinely curious. "I didn't ask to be white."

Satch rotated to face her. Hands on her hips, legs spread apart, chest thrust out, her stance struck Simone as strikingly masculine. "Ain't just 'cause you white," Satch said. "You go around acting like you work here. Always smiling."

"So you'd like me better if I was miserable?"

"If you was real."

"Like you?"

Satch turned her back. Simone looked over at Regina, in a red-and-yellow flowered muumuu that emphasized her enormity, rubbing a sponge in endless spirals over one of the three tables.

"Hey, Regina," Simone said. "If you get that table any cleaner they're going to perform surgery on it."

Regina straightened and put her hand to her head, streaking white suds across her brown brow. She looked at Simone as if she were speaking Hawaiian.

Simone started for the coffee pot; Satch started for the door. As they passed, Satch brought her broad shoulder hard against Simone's. Pain shot through Simone's back. She stumbled backwards into Regina—just as Jun was coming in the door. Regina steadied Simone, who felt a furious surge of adrenaline.

"What the hell's going on?" Jun said, his face crimped in anger. "We have zero tolerance for violence!"

Regina released her and went to the sink to wash her hands. Satch looked at Simone, then Jun, with what Simone decided was chagrin. "Reckon I..." Satch began.

"I tripped," Simone interrupted.

Satch raised her eyebrows and stared at her.

Jun looked from one to the other. "Well there better not be any more 'tripping.' Is that clear?"

"Yes," Simone said.

"Yeah. Sorry," Satch said to Jun. She glanced at Simone once more before going outside.

Satch could have smiled, Simone thought—after all, she'd just saved her from yet another reprimand from Jun. What good did surliness do anyone? Simone prided herself on the very cheerfulness Satch seemed to despise. She'd read somewhere that the best way to spread happiness was to be the image of it, and since spreading happiness was what life was all about, she felt her smiles to be a moral obligation. Her students smirked at her when she said this in class, but they were freshly minted teenagers, snared in their own intrigues. Satch was an adult and should have some sense of the common good.

Jun raised the coffee pot. "Want any?"

Hand shaking from unspent adrenaline, she picked up a cup. "You okay?" he asked.

"Haven't had enough caffeine yet."

He steadied her hand with one of his and filled her cup with the other. His touch swelled her adrenaline even more. She wanted to wrap his short ponytail around her fingers and pull his lips to her mouth.

He released her. "Drink up."

She gulped the coffee.

"How do you like my latest brew?"

It tasted like burnt rubber smelled. "I think you could pave roads with this stuff. Maybe you could have a second career."

"I was going to become an optician, but I didn't want to make a spectacle of myself."

His grin spread to her. "I like that," she said.

"Good. Oakhill's number-one directive is that you must laugh at my puns, no matter how bad."

"And drink your coffee?"

"That's asking too much. Before I forget, our consulting psychiatrist will see you today some time between eleven and eleven-thirty, so don't schedule a group then."

"Okay."

The door slammed.

"How was your weekend?"

"Great."

Suddenly Alev was beside them, her eyes on Jun. "You're not proposing, are you?" Alev asked in a teasing tone, her colorful earrings jingling as she flipped up her long hair.

Simone remembered Alev had told her she and Jun had plans to go dancing and felt a guilty rush of jealousy. Was Alev just imagining Jun's interest?

"I asked," Jun said, "but she turned me down."

"Are you crazy?" Alev said to Simone, smiling.

"That's debatable," Simone said, smiling back.

Jun glanced at his watch. "Time for general meeting." He went to the door and called to the groupies outside.

Alev fanned her face to show she was hot for Jun. Simone knew just how Alev felt. A spectacle indeed.

When time came to schedule groups during the general meeting, the available slots were filled before she could be called on. She'd intended to request a group with Jun, but she had no topic in mind and told herself that one day without a group wouldn't change anything anyway.

"Come to my group?" Marvin asked her after the meeting.

"Sure," she said, delighted to be invited. Within three minutes of her standing around with yet another cup of coffee, two other members asked her to their groups as well. Her upbeat attitude and the positive feedback she offered were paying off with almost everyone.

Satch and Viola joined her for Marvin's group with Jun. Nobody spoke, waiting for Marvin to begin, but he just kept silently clasping his bears to his chest.

"I'm really glad you called a group," Jun said, his shoulders tantalizing beneath his Tweety Bird T-shirt, his voice gentle but nudging. "What's coming up for you today?"

Marvin shut his eyes. He still didn't speak. The silence stretched longer and longer.

"Why don't you tell people why you came to Oakhill," Jun said.

"Don't nobody want to hear about that." Marvin kept his eyes on his fuzzy brown bears.

"I do," Simone said.

"Yeah," Satch said. "Why you here, Marvin?"

The overhead lights made Marvin's bald head gleam. His taped glasses slid down his nose; he pushed them back up with his index finger. "Here 'cause I stabbed myself in the stomach," he said. "Wanted to die. Almost did."

Simone felt her stomach shrink at the thought of being stabbed like that. She cut herself only superficially. Putting the point and blade of a knife into your stomach was so much more violent. She couldn't imagine this man who sat cradling teddy bears doing such a thing. "Why did you do that?" she said, trying to keep the horror out of her voice and sound therapeutic.

Marvin stuck out his lower lip. "'Cause I hurt Noni."

"Who that?" Satch asked.

"My grandma. I live with her."

"What you do?" Satch said.

He bit his lip and looked near tears. "I was hearing voices. Called me nigger, told me I was bad. I thought the voices was coming from Noni's dishes." He inhaled and sniffled. "Broke 'em all."

Simone had never encountered anyone who heard voices. This childlike man was one of them. At least she'd known the voice that called her *bitch* when she cut her face was coming from inside herself.

"Noni stepped on a dish," Marvin continued. "Cut her foot real bad. Neighbor took her to the ER. I got a big knife and stabbed myself." He nodded. "Deserved it for hurting Noni."

"But you didn't mean to hurt her," Simone said.

Marvin rubbed his forehead. "Don't matter. She old. And I be tired of voices talking at me."

"You didn't have no medication?" Satch said.

"Had some. Didn't do no good."

"How you doing now?" Satch asked.

"On new meds. If the voices come back, gonna kill myself for real," Marvin said, chin up.

"Can't lose hope," Viola said. "You got to hold on to hope, Marvin."

"Not gonna hurt Noni again. I'm bad."

"No you ain't," Satch said. "Schizophrenia like the flu. A disease you got. Ain't who you is."

Simone looked directly at Satch and saw a surprisingly compassionate frown on her face. "Satch is right," she said. Satch's eyes flitted toward her before returning to Marvin.

"Why don't you tell people how you spend much of your weekend," Jun said.

Marvin sat up straighter. "Take my bears to the hospital. Play with kids."

"You play with kids on the cancer ward," Jun said. "Right?"

"Yeah."

"Wow," Simone said.

"Take guts to do that," Satch said.

"More than I have." Simone couldn't imagine how she'd be able to stay upbeat if she spent weekends with dying children. She gave silent thanks she wasn't schizophrenic. Her voice hated her, but at least she agreed with it.

The psychiatrist was late. He finally appeared just in time to make her miss the closing meeting. Bearded, gray-haired, rubbing his shadowed eyes, Dr. Roulizi looked like he needed to be strapped upright in his seat. He asked her a few questions about her cutting, eyes studying a file in front of him. "You need antidepressants," he said.

"You've spoken to me for five minutes," Simone said lightly. "It feels like a mechanic who looks at a nick in my fender and tells me I need a new car."

A smile raised his lips. "I've been at this a long time, Ms. Jouve. People who cut themselves benefit from anti-depressants."

"All of them?"

"Most."

"Well, I've stopped cutting."

"Congratulations. But stopping cutting's a lot like quitting cigarettes. The urge isn't likely to just go away."

"Maybe not. But that doesn't mean I have to act on it."

His eyes fell surreptitiously to his watch. Simone was keeping him from something. A cigarette maybe.

"Why are you so opposed to antidepressants?" Dr. Roulizi asked.

"I rarely take medications of any kind. Besides, compared to other people here, I don't think I'm depressed."

He leaned back in his chair and put his hands behind his head as if he had all day. "So if you've stopped cutting and you're not depressed, why are you here?"

"My boss insisted. And I thought I could use a tune-up."

He leaned forward. "Then think of antidepressants as spark plugs. But it's your decision."

"I've decided." Americans were too quick to pop pills. Mostly she needed a breather, a respite from loud students and useless men. Oakhill would give her some perspective at least.

He closed her file. "Let Jun know if you change your mind."

Simone stood, relieved the issue had been settled so simply. "Thanks for your time." Leaving the room, she glanced back to see Dr. Roulizi chewing on a red-and-white plastic straw. An oral fixation, she decided. Maybe the man needed meds.

As Simone walked out of Oakhill savoring a hug from Jun, a car slowly passed her, exhaust loud, rap music making the air throb. The singer's voice and the pounding beat made her think of a boxer repeatedly punching his opponent's face. She quickened her pace.

Viola was standing at the curb, arms crossed, hugging herself, frowning, beside a much-dented Chevy with badly oxidized red paint, its hood up. Satch was hammering a wrench against something under the hood. Simone's chest tightened. She couldn't leave Viola stranded, even if Satch was there. She stopped. "Can I help?"

"Motherfucker ain't running."

She hated to say it but she had to. "Do you all need a ride?"

Satch straightened, wrench in hand, her big face grim.

"I need to get home to my babies," Viola said.

Satch slammed down the hood of her car. "Guess we do."

"Thanks," Viola said.

Simone felt trapped. She wanted to push twenty-dollar bills in their hands and call them a cab, but that would be irredeemably white. She waved toward her car. "I'm just down there."

Viola walked beside her, Satch behind.

"Got to take Viola first," Satch said.

"Okay. Where to?"

"The projects," Viola said. "It's not far."

Satch passed them as they neared Simone's car and put her hand on the back door handle, making it clear Viola was to ride in front.

Viola gave directions to the Crestmont Projects. She told Simone about her about her children, Darius and Shona, eight and five. Simone asked about their school—"I keep them home from school. My neighbor's a retired teacher"—and about technology—"Darius keeps changing the tune of my cell phone so when it rings I never know it's mine." From the back, Satch was a mushroom cloud of silence.

The Crestmont Projects were mustard-yellow, three-story apartment units that seemed to list to one side like a prison guard who'd had too much to drink. Three men clustered in a courtyard in front, their eyes prowling.

"Don't want to be showing your white face to them," Satch said from the back seat. "I'm gonna take Viola in. Lock the doors."

"Thanks for the ride," Viola said. She turned to look at the men, her eyes wary.

"Any time," Simone said.

Satch snorted and got out with Viola, took her arm, and led her around the men, giving them a wide berth. The men watched. One called something, but the women ignored him and hurried on.

Simone kept the car in drive, her foot primed to flick from brake to gas, willing Satch to return. Violence hovered about the men—though maybe that was her stereotypical projection of the Crime-Infested Projects. Then she remembered Viola's murdered daughter. She wanted Satch back fast, but didn't, too, because it would mean riding together, just the two of them in spiked silence.

Satch sauntered right by the men on her return, head high. Someone said something that sounded like "hot mama." She unlocked the doors as Satch approached and got in the back.

"Where do I go?" Simone said.

Satch stared out the side window. "Straight three blocks. Left two. Right four."

Simone pulled away, trying not to peel out in insulting fear. The car's silence felt stifling as summer heat. She counted the streets, made the turns.

"Here," Satch said finally.

Simone braked in front of a seven-story, grimy white stucco building. Most of the surrounding houses and apartment buildings looked equally dingy, but trees along the sidewalk blossomed white, while jasmine covered much of what Simone thought was Satch's building. It was not the prison stockade she had imagined Satch inhabited. "This is it?"

"Uh-huh." Satch got out. Closed the door. Looked at Simone. "Thanks," she mumbled.

Simone watched Satch walk down the sidewalk and was about to pull away when she saw a lanky, good-looking man exit the building. "Hey, baby," she heard him say. He threw his arms around a suddenly smiling Satch. The man's skin reminded Simone of the color of a kiwi peel. Satch said something to him, and he glanced toward Simone and laughed. Then he grabbed Satch's wrist and pulled her into the building.

How could Satch be in such a bad mood so much of the time at Oakhill when she had that delicious looking man to come home to? Envy swept over her. She pulled away and headed back to her empty condo.

SEVEN

"Hey, Marvin," Simone said the next day after lunch. "I bet the bears would like to play volleyball. Come on, Regina, be on my team."

"Careful what you asking for," Satch said, walking past her. "Might get it."

Simone had no idea what Satch was talking about. "Hey, Viola, come on out." Somebody had to be in charge of recess.

It was volleyball as played in the Cuckoo's Nest. Marvin served with Katrina; the ball dribbled off her paw. The man Simone still knew only as Leprechaun wielded his two hands like a bat, sending the ball soaring over the trailer roof. One man swung at the ball only after it had already bounced. A woman kept ducking. When the ball came at Yvonne, she jumped back and announced, "I'm having a heart attack!" Rick, the man who'd said that if you laughed at a woman she would love you, wasn't laughing now: he drilled the ball into the net so hard he dropped two players on his own team to their knees.

Though the combined score totaled only eight points, Jun called the game at the usual thirty minutes.

"Thorazine patients the worst," Satch said, coming up beside her. "That's why I warned you."

It took Simone a minute to realize Satch was explaining something to her, not accusing her of it. "Thorazine patients?"

"You real new to this," Satch said. "Thorazine slow you down, like Robert. You see how he swing after the ball hit the ground?"

Simone smiled.

"Don't want no schizophrenics on your team if they be taking Thorazine. Go for the bipolars, long as they in a up cycle. 'Course some of 'em, like Lonnie, don't have no control, but at least they awake."

Satch ambled over to Viola, leaving Simone standing there trying to understand why she'd suddenly been so friendly.

Muslimah sat the female groupies around the kitchen table. "Who would like to start us off?" she said.

No one spoke. Simone felt odd to be around only women.

"Come on now," Muslimah said. "It's just us women. Regina, you look upset. Why don't you start?"

Regina fidgeted with the fabric of her muumuu as if it were a knot she had to untie. Tears began trickling down her puffy cheeks.

"What's going on?" Muslimah asked.

"My stepdaddy, he died last night," Regina said finally. She kept fingering her dress, kept her eyes on the floor.

"I'm sorry," Simone said.

"No!" Regina shouted. "Just wish he'da died a nasty death. Man hurt me." She'd started at a shout but ended at a whimper. Simone felt herself flush.

"Tell us about it," Muslimah said.

Eyes on the floor, Regina spoke in a shaky voice. "First time I was just five," she began. When her mother went to work, her stepfather came to Regina's room. "Man smelled of booze. Scared me. Said if I screamed or told Mama what he did, he was gonna kill me and Mama too. He was real big. Forced his huge ugly self in me. It hurt real bad. I bled all over them sheets."

Simone flinched in horror. She'd heard about such things courtesy of Oprah and Dr. Phil, but they happened to strangers.

"Man raped me for six years. One night my mama caught him. Beat him with her fists. Made him leave. I thanked Jesus, but then Mama slapped me. Said it be my fault 'cause I was too cute. Never hugged me no more. So I started eating so nobody'd think I was cute. Still do. Now I'm just a big old fat woman. No man ever gonna want me."

Simone wrapped her arms around herself. That Regina could say what had happened to her, and how she'd been hurt by it, amazed her. But if Regina could bear witness to what happened, and knew how she had dealt with the hurt, then why hadn't she healed? For a panicked moment Simone felt that gravity had disappeared.

No one spoke. Regina hunched over.

"Ain't no big old fat woman," Satch said. "You a woman. That's all."

"It wasn't your fault," Simone said. "Not any of it."

"Your mama a real bitch, girl," Satch said.

"Please don't cuss," Yvonne said, her hand at the frilly blouse that covered her neck. "It's rude."

"So is rape," Simone said.

"You been raped?" Regina asked.

"Not exactly," Simone said before she could think. Spence hadn't hurt her. Yes, they'd had sex, but he hadn't even climaxed. He'd apologized. *I could easily fall in love with you, Simone.* Her experience was nothing like Regina's. She glanced at Satch, who looked right back with eyes so dark they seemed like a deep well she could fall down. Simone looked away.

"I been raped," said a woman with a face that seemed to slant. "Couldn't afford to live no place but one of them rat motels. Didn't have no screens. He came in through the window. Smashed my face. Put a knife to my throat. If I'd had a gun, I woulda shot his balls off."

"My cousin made me have oral sex. I was ten," Viola said in a voice so soft it sounded like it had been brushed with cotton.

Simone wanted out. Her feet weren't connecting with the earth. Her nerves were exposed wires.

"My husband messed with my girl," said another woman. "Motherfucker's in jail. Hope somebody messes with him."

The women all considered this, like sisters comparing stories of tornadoes they'd survived. Simone wanted to hurl a stick of dynamite onto the table.

Satch turned to her. "What you mean 'not exactly'? You been raped or you ain't?"

Simone cleared her throat. "I mean my experience was nothing like what these other women suffered."

"Uh-huh."

"That's enough," Muslimah said. "Nobody appointed you Keeper of the Truth, Satch. You have secrets of your own."

If Simone hadn't known black people could blush, she knew it now. It seemed like somebody was pouring black coffee over Satch's face.

"What happen to you?" Regina asked.

Because Regina was asking, Simone felt she had to answer. "A date thing. He brought me roses. And we had a lovely dinner. We went to look for stars. He said he was going to..." She swallowed, put her feet on the floor. "But he stopped when he knew I wasn't enjoying it. He didn't even climax. He was very apologetic afterward."

Satch snorted.

That sound made Simone explode. "What the fuck do you know about it? What the hell do you know about how I feel?"

"You lying or you denying," Satch said.

"All right ladies, chill," Muslimah commanded. "We're here to give each other support."

Simone caught Regina watching her. "I'm so sorry for what happened to you," she said to Regina. "And the others, too." She looked around the circle at everyone but Satch, saw the raw red pain that darkened and twisted around them like a deadly shawl.

Spence hadn't climaxed. He'd apologized. It hadn't really even hurt. It had not been a big deal. It had not.

EIGHT

When time came to schedule groups the following day, Alev was called on before Simone and took Jun's last slot. Simone decided to call a group with Evelyn, Oakhill's director, hoping the woman would be as nurturing as Jun. Simone had thought she'd talk about the voice that had called her *bitch* when she first cut, if she could do it without mentioning the cutting. Six members crammed in the small room for her group. To her surprise Satch, in purple pants and orange top, joined them.

Evelyn's tautly muscled arms stuck out beneath short sleeves. With her khaki pants and closely cropped gray hair, she looked like she could model for an L.L. Bean catalogue—the men's pages.

"Heard something you oughta know," Satch said.

Simone braced herself.

"This is Simone's group," Evelyn said. "The topic's up to her."

Satch's smile was mocking. Simone couldn't let herself chicken out. "Go ahead, Satch."

"Told my auntie about the man what raped you. Say she saw on *Oprah* about rape. Say some rapists don't never come. And they talk real sweet."

Simone blinked and looked at Evelyn.

"There is a pattern with certain rapists sometimes labeled Smooth Talkers," Evelyn said. "They rarely climax. They say a lot of flattering things."

I could love you, Simone. Rarely climax.

Simone was in a red Bronco on a dirt road. Smoke from Spence's cigarette floated around his face. *I'm going to rape you.*

"What you think of that?" Satch said.

Take your clothes off.

"Figured you'd want to know," Satch added.

Do it. Now!

Someone coughed. Simone reminded herself she was not in Spence's Bronco. "Thanks for trying to help," she said to Satch, a little too firmly. "But I already knew I was raped."

"You said not exactly. Said it weren't no big deal," Satch retorted.

"Compared to the stories we heard yesterday? I wasn't a child. I wasn't hit, it wasn't at gunpoint. I mean, don't get me wrong. I didn't enjoy myself."

"Rape always a big deal 'less you dead," Satch said.

"Thanks for pointing that out. I mean obviously it is, on one level. I just meant I got off easy compared to a lot of women." She glared at Satch. "You know, I'd like to repay your interest in my problems. I'd be happy to come to your group in the event you decide to focus on your own."

Satch shut her mouth.

"What's coming up for you right now?" Evelyn said.

"Nothing."

"You look angry." Evelyn's green eyes bored into Simone's.

"Not really. I don't let myself get angry."

"Why is that?"

"Anger is stupid. It pushes people away."

"What people?"

"Any people. I learned that in teaching. I mean, students who act up respond far better to humor than to anger." She glanced at the others.

"You real pale," Regina said.

"I'm always pale." She grinned.

"Why you making jokes?" Satch said, her face scrunched in a frown.

"Because I want to."

"Why?"

The heat rose in Simone's cheeks. "If you don't have a sense of humor, Satch, you go crazy."

"You can make yourself crazy, too," Evelyn said, "if you use humor to avoid your feelings."

"I know exactly what I'm feeling."

"Which is what?" Evelyn said.

Simone looked at Satch, who looked at her right back.

"Simone, look at me please," Evelyn said.

Simone inched her eyes over to meet Evelyn. Jun would never attack her like this.

"Are you angry with Satch?"

"No."

"Why?"

"She was just trying to help." Simone kept her gaze on Evelyn, which was easier than looking at Satch.

"Are you angry with me?" Evelyn said.

"No."

"Why not?"

"Why should I be?"

"Well for one thing, I keep pushing you."

"Isn't that your job?"

"You should be angry," Evelyn said.

"You want me to be angry at you? That's crazy. I thought *I* was supposed to be the crazy one." Simone chuckled. Lonnie sat on his hands and swung his feet. Marvin shifted a bear from one knee to the other. Alev plucked at her sleeve. Viola's smile had turned upside down. Regina watched her with an expression of concern so sympathetic that for about two seconds Simone felt like crying. She bolted to her feet.

"Where are you going?" Evelyn said.

"I need to pee." Simone rushed to the bathroom. She slammed the door and punched the lock. She ran her fingers over the wooden door hoping to find a splinter. When she didn't, she bit down on her hand until it hurt. Fully clothed, she sat on the toilet seat, watching the tooth marks slowly fade.

After lunch, Jun directed Simone and six others to sit in a circle on the dingy beige carpet. "Drama group meets twice a week," he said. "We start by doing games and exercises so you get warmed up and trust each other. Trust is essential to our work. Then later we role-play scenes that you suggest." He went on to lay out the ground rules: they couldn't miss sessions, confidentiality was required, and they were to be supportive of each other. "Okay," he said, "stand and form a circle."

They did. Jun stood in the middle.

"Link hands."

Simone reached for Regina's hands, and the dry palm of a guy named Willy, dreadlocked and spaced out.

"Okay, now," Jun said, "I'm going to lean in different directions and let myself fall. It's up to you to catch me so I don't hit the floor. This is how we start building trust."

Before Simone could sniff in derision, Jun relaxed his body completely and fell toward her. She and Regina and Willy caught him easily and pushed him back so that he fell forward, then to one side, then to the other, elastic as one of his cartoon characters. "Now, whose turn?"

Willy volunteered. Like Jun, he fell easily. So did Viola. Simone felt her body tense more with each successful collapse. Satch kept her body stiff, as if hedging her bets, and Simone felt a small rush of connection between them. Next came Rick, who shook his head. The snakes on his neck seemed to tremble. She liked him for refusing.

Regina stared down at the floor when Jun asked if she wanted a turn. "I be too fat. Can't nobody catch me."

"You're not too big, Regina," Jun said. "We'll catch you. Trust us."

Regina nudged herself into the center. She signaled the others to close up the circle so she wouldn't have far to fall. Though she didn't go limp, she did lean enough that Simone felt they were at least steadying her. Finished, Regina grinned as if she'd just been asked on a date.

Simone was next. The circle expanded again. She felt her palms sweat. She didn't move.

"You can do it," Jun said.

Vines seemed to grab at her feet.

"That's okay," Jun said. "When you're ready. Now, I'm going to pair everyone up."

Simone's partner was Satch.

"Okay," Jun said, "the younger one of you says, 'I want it' and the other says, 'You can't have it.' This is practice for expressing emotions. Go ahead and start."

Simone stared at Jun, trying to say *This is ridiculous.* Jun stared back: *Trust me.* Simone watched a moment as the other pairs began saying their lines. "I guess I'm older," she said.

"I want it," Satch said.

"You can't have it." Simone hated the small sound she made.

Satch stepped closer. "I *want* it."

"You *can't* have it!"

"I *want* it!"

"You can't have it!"

Satch lowered her voice and again stepped toward Simone, taut, deadly.

Simone wanted to step back but refused.

"I want it!" Each word from Satch was a curled fist.

Simone straightened up and threw every inch of herself into her words. *"You can't have it!"* she shouted.

The room went silent. Everyone stared.

Satch stepped forward until only a thread could pass between them. Her fists were clenched, her face tight with rage. "I want it, white girl!"

"Nooo!" Simone screamed. *"Nooo!"* She felt she was only her scream.

Jun stepped between them, nudging them apart. Simone breathed fast and shallowly, saw her fists clenched like Satch's. After a long moment Satch stepped back and uncurled her hands.

"Very convincing," Jun remarked.

Simone wrapped her arms around herself. Jun led the others in applause but Simone couldn't hear it. She shut her eyes and saw Spence. The words she had said to Satch that she hadn't said to him rose in her throat with the taste and power of bile. *I'm going to rape you,* Spence had said. What she'd done next was so appalling she didn't dare contemplate it.

At day's end she tried to slip past Jun but he blocked her. "Contract?"

It was only one word, but it squeezed her lungs like fists. "Contract."

"And that means?"

"That I won't hurt myself tonight."

"Good. You look like you could use a hug."

She wasn't sure she wanted him to because it might take a crowbar to pry her loose. "Okay," she said. His arms encircled her and she leaned into his chest, his shoulders. He felt at once strong and soft, and she wondered how he could be both. When he released her, she felt the absence of his warmth.

Walking to her car, she passed a pink garage door graffitied with the words *Real Niggaz,* beneath which someone had scrawled *eat pussy*.

The splinters of a whiskey bottle littered the sidewalk ahead of her. She walked to them and stopped. The largest piece held a torn label: *Johnny Wa-*. Streaked with grime, glinting in the sun, the shards beckoned her. Simone squatted. The stink of whiskey assaulted her nostrils. She fought the impulse to grab a piece and rake it across her thighs. The glass looked so pretty the way the sunlight made it sparkle.

"Look like you fixing to lick that thing," came a voice behind her. "Ain't no popsicle."

Satch was grimacing down at the broken bottle. Her words lacked hostility.

"Yeah, well, good night," Simone said.

Satch didn't respond and didn't move, not until Simone got up and stepped over the glass and covered the remaining distance to her Echo in long strides. She looked back to see Satch watching her. Simone fumbled with her keys, got the door open, closed it and pushed the locks, asking herself if she was trying to keep the danger out or in.

The light blinked on her message machine, a surprise. Simone pressed the play button as she admired the white-and-yellow blossoms her spider plant had sprouted just that day.

"Hi, it's Michael."

Michael! She practically stood on tiptoes.

"Sorry I haven't been in touch."

She'd forgotten how deep his voice was, but supple, too.

"Just wanted to let you know I'm getting all kinds of interest in my script. Been going crazy revising it."

Michael didn't have dimples exactly, not the way Jun did, but he did have creases enclosing his smile like parentheses.

"I'm meeting with a potential investor up your way in a few weeks. Thought we could have dinner. I'll call you when I know the date. Take care."

Simone sank to the sofa. What did it mean that he was calling her? Maybe he was lonely, felt incomplete the way she did, had discovered he needed her. Perhaps he would even invite her to join him in L.A. She told herself to get real, that he'd only proposed dinner, that he hadn't even left her his new number. But after months of silence even a whisper thrilled her.

The first time they'd met, Simone had been backpacking alone, setting up camp at Lake Aloha in the Desolation Wilderness near Tahoe. Michael had ambled into her campsite, sheepishly asking to borrow a pot because he'd forgotten his own. He'd ended up staying for a dinner of dehydrated spaghetti reconstituted with boiling water into a mush that tasted like spiced dirt. They had talked and laughed long into the night. At 2:00 a.m. they'd gone for a swim, skinny dipping in the cold mountain lake, floating beneath a conveniently spectacular meteor shower, as if the gods were heralding a brand new couple.

Simone sprang to her feet and whirled around her home, laughing, until she got so dizzy she had to steady herself against the wall.

Nine

"Simone?"

Jarred awake, she didn't recognize the voice on the phone. Groggily she glanced at the clock: 5:45. She hadn't gotten to sleep until well after midnight.

"This Satch."

"Satch?" Other than in drama, she and Satch hadn't spoken in the week since Michael had called.

"From Oakhill."

As if she knew other Satches. "You sound awful," Simone said. Satch's voice had plunged from baritone to bass. Her sinuses sounded clogged.

"Got the flu. You gotta pick up Viola."

"A viola?" Simone tossed aside her flannel sheet, hoping that baring herself to the cool morning air might clear her mind.

"You say you pick her up if she need a ride."

Viola. "Sure. You're not going to Oakhill?"

"Too sick." Satch's voice sounded somehow stretched, as if it were being cranked out of a pasta maker.

"Give me her address again?" Simone flipped open the yellow notepad she kept beside the phone and scribbled the directions Satch gave her.

"Apartment 205. Got to go to the door."

"Okay," Simone said.

Simone could hear Satch breathing, forcing air in through constricted nasal passages so that her nose faintly whistled. Simone pictured the Crestmont projects, the listing buildings, the prowling men. "I guess it'll be safe enough?"

"Oughta be. Homies still sleeping." Satch hung up.

Simone replaced the phone, astonished that Satch had called her. Of course Simone had given Viola a ride before, and most of Oakhill's members traveled by bus; they were too poor to own cars. Probably she was the only taxi service that Satch could think of. She hoped Satch was right about the "homies." *Oughta be* safe?

Yawning, she scooted back under the covers of her sofa-bed and observed the ceramic masks on the opposite wall, the way the early morning sunlight streaked their blunt features. She was doing so much better. She'd been right, that romance—even the barest hope of romance—had been what she really needed. Since Michael's message she hadn't experienced the slightest desire to cut. She hoped he'd call about dinner soon.

Simone had been at Oakhill for almost three weeks already; at the rate she was improving, Kathleen would have no reason to refuse to let her teach summer school. Maybe when she left Oakhill—in another week or two if she continued to do so well—Michael would want to go backpacking with her. And if he didn't, perhaps Jun would. Flinging aside her covers, she practically bounded out of bed, eager for the day ahead.

Two hours after Satch's call, Simone stopped her forest-green Echo in front of the Crestmont Projects, relieved to see that Satch had been right about the *homies*: the front of the projects was deserted.

She started down the sidewalk, stepping over filthy syringes and used condoms, walking around dark splotches she hoped were colas but feared were blood. Movement caught her eye. She stopped. From beneath a staircase emerged three young men in jeans so big their crotches hung almost to their knees. They wore black bandannas around their heads, and they walked with that lame lope she associated with rap videos. They spread themselves across the sidewalk. They probably carried guns beneath their bulky black-and-silver Raiders jackets; they looked ready for the shoot-out at the OK Corral.

An image from the Rodney King riots flashed through her mind—angry black men smashing bricks against the head of a white truck driver. She paused, then reminded herself that there was no riot here, she wasn't male, and her own positive attitude would protect her. She walked toward the young men, smiling.

Their faces were grim, and they kept their accusatory eyes on her. She felt as though she were walking into the wrong end of a pair of binoculars, getting tinier by the moment.

They loomed ever larger, a barricade across the sidewalk. She stopped in front of the youths. Their eyes like cold charcoal remained fixated on her.

"Good morning," she said as cheerfully as she could. Good diplomacy, she thought; she'd probably be appointed Secretary of State.

Not one of them smiled. Not one of them moved.

"So, what do you think of the Raiders' chances this year?" she said. No response. Why did they bother wearing the damned jackets if they didn't care about the team? "Go Raiders!"

"Most crackers like the 49ers," one of them said, his eyes skeptical.

"The 49ers are sissies," Simone said quickly. "The only nation is the Raider Nation."

The boy who questioned her smiled cautiously.

"Why you here?" the second boy said. "You a cop? A social worker? Gonna take away somebody's kid?"

Though the boy's words were hostile, his litany sounded rote, like somebody's one hundredth "Hail Mary."

"No. I'm just giving somebody a ride to the hospital. She wants to go."

"Who?" A third, older boy stepped in front of the others, a scar on his cheek erratic and menacing.

"Viola."

The boy's face softened slightly. "They killed her baby."

"Yeah," she said. "They did."

The third boy signaled the others; they split and allowed her to pass between them, but they stood so close together her shoulders brushed their jackets. If she were going to be a regular visitor, she'd buy all the Raiders regalia she could afford.

"Thanks," she said. "Enjoy your day." Boy did that sound inane; she was grateful they didn't shoot her just for that.

"Don't be coming around here at night," one of them said to her back. "Not everybody as friendly as we is."

She turned back to them. Only one still looked hostile. "Thanks for the warning."

Climbing the stairs to the second floor, she wondered what it would be like to try to teach those young men. She walked along the concrete walkway that surrounded each floor and knocked at apartment 205. A yellow curtain moved in the window next to the door. A little girl gaped at her. Joining her, a wide-eyed boy shouted loud enough that Simone could hear him, "Mama, it's a *white* lady!"

The front door opened the width of the chain lock as Viola peered out.

"Hi," Simone said, still determined to be cheerful. "Satch is sick. She asked me to pick you up."

Viola opened the door, pulled Simone in and locked the door shut. Her two children watched Simone intently. The girl, about five, had short curly hair like her mother's and a zestful smile. The boy looked about eight. A Raiders cap hooded eyes that watched her as intently as had the young men's. Though she gave him her most open smile, he gave her nothing back.

"Hi," she said in her best happy voice. The little girl giggled and took hold of Viola's leg. The boy put his hands on his hips to show her he couldn't be fooled by cheap smiles. From white people.

Their apartment was neat and decorated with framed prints of African women and children. The aromas of bacon and something sweet—syrup, maybe—hovered around the room. *Thump.* Simone jerked. Something had hit the wall in an adjoining unit. A television set brayed from an apartment on the other side. The walls seemed about as substantial as ice cream cones.

"Simone, these are my children," Viola said, putting her hands proudly on their shoulders. "Shona and Darius." She was dressed as always in black.

"Morning." Simone smiled at them again. "I really like your names."

"You get on now," she heard someone say. A gray-haired woman wearing flamingo pink pants and shirt with a silver cross around her neck approached from a back room. "Who are you?"

"This is Simone, Eunice," Viola said. "She's from the hospital."

The woman studied Simone. "You a doctor?"

She wanted to say no, that she was just one of the nuts, but she wasn't sure how that would be received. "No. I go there, like Viola."

"Where's Satch?"

"She's sick," Viola said.

Eunice sighed. "Well, y'all get going."

"Nice to meet you," Simone told her then waved good-bye to the kids.

Viola picked up Shona and gave her a huge hug; they rubbed noses, the child laughing. When Viola set down her daughter, she turned with mock solemnity to her unsmiling son. "Am I gonna get a hug?" Darius seemed to be thinking it over. Simone turned away in case her presence made it difficult for him. She envied Viola her children. She opened the door and turned back just as Viola released him. "Be good," Viola told her children. "And study hard."

"Y'all go on." Eunice waved them away.

Viola closed the door behind them. "Eunice teaches my kids. She's real good with them."

Simone didn't ask why Viola home schooled her children. She didn't have to.

"Thanks," Viola said when they passed through the gate at Oakhill.

"No problem. I can take you home, too."

"If it's not too much trouble."

"No trouble at all," Simone assured her. Viola gave her an odd look and went on up the stairs.

Buoyed by the sense of pleasure she felt from having helped Viola, Simone grabbed a basketball and went out to shoot baskets in the bright morning sunlight. She enjoyed running around, shooting lay-ups and long shots, hitting few of either and not caring.

She didn't see Jun until he walked over to the court, dressed in his orange Daffy Duck shirt, his short pony-tail curled under. Everything about the man made him seem masculine. She wanted to cup his pecs with her hands, undo his pony-tail, and run her fingers through his hair while she nibbled on his ear lobes.

He watched her a moment. She faced him.

"I've never seen eyes as blue as yours," he said. "Cobalt blue, if I were painting them."

"Thanks."

"You know what a chicken crossing the road is called?" he said.

"A dumb cluck?"

"That's good. I was thinking poultry in motion." She laughed. "Let's shoot some hoops."

She passed him the ball. He dribbled between his legs as if to avoid an opponent then went in for a successful layup and threw the ball to her.

When she'd been playing alone, she didn't care how badly she played. She did now.

"Basketball isn't really my sport," she said. "I'm much better at football."

"Oh? Tackle?"

Telling him of her abilities as wide receiver would sound boastful. Most men shied away from immodest women. "Water girl."

"Go ahead and shoot," he said, smiling. "There's nothing breakable around."

Oh yes there was, she thought. Her heart. She shot. Missed the net. Missed the backboard.

Jun retrieved the ball. "Try again. But bring your right hand up higher."

She tried. She missed.

He got the ball. Before she knew it was happening, his arms were around her, his chest muscles pressed against her back, his hands touching hers. His warm breath caressed her neck, sending bubbles of pleasure all through her.

"Feel how I've positioned your hands on the ball. Got it?"

"Yeah," she said. She focused on the feel of his callused hands.

"Okay, now we're going to push up and forward."

With his help, she made the basket.

"All right!" Jun said. He clapped her a high five. Maybe she could keep missing shots, she thought, keep his arms around her. She retrieved the ball and tossed it to Jun.

"Show me." Alev was a swirl of vibrant color and energy.

Jun tossed Alev the ball. "Put your left hand under and your right hand up here," he said, demonstrating how to hold the ball without putting his arms around her. "Then push in one smooth arc."

Simone let her eyes linger on Alev. She was thin all over. Not slender but thin, coat-hanger thin. Her somewhat loose clothes cloaked her thinness to a degree, but her arms jutted out like pipe cleaners, and beneath her skirt her legs seemed like two bones walking. Gaunt cheeks. Dark hollows beneath her eyes. Alev was anorexic, Simone realized. She had to be. And a coke addict. There was no way she had a date with Jun. No way at all.

"Keep practicing," Jun said. He still hadn't touched Alev, who'd sunk two shots. "I've got to make a phone call."

Jun smiled at Simone as he passed. She recalled the feel of his arms around her and felt like someone was tickling her with a feather.

In her group, Simone regaled Jun, Regina, Viola and Marvin with school tales: how she dressed in Goth clothes, make-up and attitude early in the year to challenge stereotyping and conformity, how she assigned teenagers for whom peer pressure is life itself to walk down the halls singing Christmas carols in April.

Nobody in the group had said much. She hadn't given them a lot of opportunity.

"I'd love to see you in action," Jun said. "With a teacher like you, I would have enjoyed school."

Simone was gleeful. She could tell him more. "Once—"

Jun held up his hand. "It's been a while since you discussed anything serious. How are you feeling?"

"Great! Coming here has really helped."

"You do seem relaxed," he said, "and you're very entertaining."

She smiled.

"But I get the feeling your walls are so high a catapult couldn't get over them. You may think those walls keep you safe, but really they just keep you cut off from the support people want to give you around your real issues."

"You be like a little kid," Regina said, "going around all happy but scared, too, like you talking to keep the bogeyman away."

"Regina's right," Viola said.

Surprised by their comments, unable to think of what to say, convinced she simply was doing better, Simone felt relieved when Alev thrust open the door, entered without knocking and announced, "It's time for my group."

Simone started to get up to use the bathroom.

"Please stay," Alev said, a sharp edge to her voice.

Glad the groups were only fifteen minutes, Simone tightened her bladder muscles and sat back down. As several members came and others left, she wondered whether the source of her growing discomfort was her bladder or Alev's obvious anger.

"You stole Jun from me!" Alev said when the door closed.

Simone drew back on her seat, a sick feeling in her stomach despite the fact she was sure Jun would never have been attracted to Alev.

"And when Jun started to put his arms around me this morning, you made him come help you instead."

Stomach knotted, Simone replayed the events of that morning in her mind, trying to remember if there was any truth to Alev's accusations, if she had said or done anything—however inadvertently—to make Jun decide not to put his arms around Alev. She was sure she hadn't, but she felt an inexplicable, sickening sense of guilt.

Jun said something about being a counselor and caring for everyone.

"You loved me until Simone came," Alev said. "You did."

Though Jun insisted Alev was mistaken, Simone felt within herself a growing urge to cut.

Alev rushed from the room. It was several long moments before Simone realized that Jun was addressing her, assuring her she'd done nothing wrong. His words fell like winter's first snowflakes, soft and lovely—but quick to melt.

Ten

That afternoon Viola remained seated in the car even after Simone had gotten out. Simone glanced around the projects to see if there might be someone threatening, but the only people outside were two teenagers kissing as they crossed the dirty concrete lawn in front. "Is something wrong?" She peered in the driver's window.

"Got to check on Satch."

"Can't we call her from your place?"

"No."

Viola didn't say anything else, so Simone got back in the car. "I don't understand," she said. "What can we do if she's got the flu?"

"Isn't the flu."

"What is it?"

Viola just stared grimly out the window. Even though what she wanted to do was drive to the nearest drugstore to buy razor blades, Simone headed the car in the direction Viola pointed, curious to learn for herself the exact nature of Satch's illness. They drove for two miles and pulled up alongside Satch's four-story building. Jasmine covered much of one wall, its sweet aroma so intense Simone could practically feel her nasal passages closing.

Viola looked around, seemed to satisfy herself it was safe, and got out of the car. They entered the unlocked lobby. The hallway wallpaper of red roses was yellowed in patches, as if a dog had peed on it. Dirt balls and trash scraps littered the torn rug. A roach scurried toward them. Simone sidestepped. She loathed roaches, couldn't bear the thought of stepping on one of the vile bugs, so she gave it a wide berth. Satch would stomp the thing. If Simone were a roach, she would definitely avoid Satch's apartment. Given the fact she was supposedly smarter than an insect, she had to wonder what she was doing heading toward it.

They took the cramped stairway to the third floor, where a sax floated out a song of heartbreak and love, its notes so pristine Simone was sure even Regina wouldn't want to polish them.

Viola stopped. "Number 314," she said. "Just knock."

"Aren't you coming?"

"No. Thomas knows me."

Thomas was presumably the handsome boyfriend she'd seen before.

"Number 314."

The fact Viola didn't want him to know she was there unsettled Simone. She knocked tentatively on the designated door. No one answered. Viola signaled to knock again.

The light-skinned man she'd seen previously opened the door, a saxophone around his neck. Jewel tones flecked his hazel eyes. "Good afternoon," he said. "What can I do for you?"

"You play beautifully."

"I try. You are who?"

"Sorry. Simone Jouve."

"Thomas."

Only then did Simone register he was blocking the door. "I came by to check on Satch. I'm from the hospital."

He scanned the area around her. "You a social worker?"

"No. A patient. Could I see her?"

Thomas gave an apologetic shrug. "She's not feeling too good. She had a little wreck. The airbag inflated. It messed up her face some. I told her she didn't need to be embarrassed, but..." He smiled as if to say, "What can you do?"

Thomas turned slightly to glance over his shoulder. Simone glimpsed Satch, her face swollen and battered. Satch covered her face with her hands. Stunned, Simone wondered if Thomas beat her. The thought made her catch her breath.

He again blocked her view. "She'll be fine in a day or two. Come back then, and I'll play you a concert." Leaning in the doorway, he resumed playing.

Golden notes settled around Simone. She didn't know what else to do, so she turned and rejoined Viola. They left the building, Simone's mind spinning.

Inside the car, Viola crossed her arms, her mouth downturned. "Women always like him. If he'd asked you out, you'd have said yes."

Simone waved her hands to dismiss Viola's words. "No way. I mean, he's good looking, but he's Satch's. He said her air bag messed her up."

Viola exhaled dismissively. "You saw Satch's old Chevy. Think it's got airbags?"

"He beats her, doesn't he?"

"Last few times, he said Satch tripped and hit her face. Nobody's that clumsy."

Simone tried to understand how the swaggering, aggressive woman she knew had been reduced to the bruised, defeated one she'd seen and why Satch of all people would stay with a man who beat her.

"Wanted you to see for yourself. You got to help."

"I have to help?"

"Yes."

"Shouldn't we call the police?"

"Won't do any good. Satch won't file a complaint against Thomas."

"Why?"

Viola glanced outside the window, started to speak but stopped. Bags ringed her dark eyes, and Simone wondered if Viola was able to sleep at night. "How about getting a Temporary Restraining Order?" she said.

"Cops don't care if you call and say somebody's violating a restraining order. Especially not a black woman."

Simone leaned her head against the window. The flowering jasmine looked so pure. Why couldn't the world be as simple? "Will he hurt her again?"

"What do you think?"

Simone didn't want to think. She didn't want to be there.

"Thing is," Viola said, "Thomas works some nights for UPS. Sorting packages."

"Some nights?" Viola nodded. Simone glanced at her watch. It was five o'clock. "Should we come back later?"

"Got a church social tonight. Promised Eunice we'd go."

"Well, I've got plans." She did. She had plans to cut herself to relieve the guilt that had burned in her since Alev's accusations. But she couldn't just leave Satch at Thomas's mercy. "I guess I could come back, get her and bring her to your place."

"You can't. Thomas knows where I live. My kids—"

"Maybe I could take her to a battered woman's shelter. There must be some of those around."

"She won't go. Thinks he'd just find her anyway."

Simone inserted the key in the ignition. "If she doesn't want to do anything about this, there isn't a lot we can do."

"Her aunt," Viola said. "You got to take her to her aunt. She lives in Alameda. Satch won't leave on her own, but maybe she'll go if you take her."

"She's got a car. She could drive herself there."

"Thomas takes it when he works. You got to help. It's getting worse. Satch respects you."

"No way. Satch hates me. I'm the last person she'd listen to."

"Got to try. You got a car."

Simone stared back at the building. Dark swaths of dirt smudged the wall not covered by flowers. She tried to picture Satch cowering, but her imagination wasn't that vivid. Still, she'd seen Satch's face. "What time does Thomas leave when he works?"

"I'm not sure. After dinner."

The idea of hanging out in Oakland to help a woman who'd made her days at Oakhill so difficult had about as much appeal as jury duty. So did the possibility of returning for Satch only to discover this wasn't one of Thomas's nights to work. She wondered if he ever hit anyone besides Satch.

"Please," Viola said.

"I'll try." Simone started the engine to take Viola home. They rode past boarded-up store windows scrawled with graffiti, Laundromats where customers slumped in chairs, liquor stores reinforced with iron mesh and steel bars. "Does she love him?"

Viola just stared out the window. Simone wondered what Viola saw. It seemed she'd left Simone, even though her body remained in the car.

After dropping Viola off—no one lurked in front, thankfully—Simone stopped at the first drugstore she passed and bought a blue box of single-edged razor blades. In her car she ripped off the plastic wrapping and slid the top blade partially out. Should she cut herself here? She glanced around. A beer truck sputtered in so close its burly driver barely edged his way out. A stylish woman exited the store and lit up a Virginia Slims. She stood on the sidewalk, tapping her foot and watching the smoke drift skyward. Simone decided to wait until she was safely ensconced in her home. She stuffed the small box of blades in her purse and drove to a better part of Oakland, the Grand Lake area.

Objectively speaking, she had found Thomas appealing until she'd realized the truth. Was there a link between Thomas and Spence, the man who'd wooed her then forced her to have sex? Both men exuded a polished self-confidence, a kind of charisma for lack of a better word. Her attraction to Spence probably came initially from the way he'd courted her with roses and compliments. Her attraction to Thomas was based at least partly on the soulful notes he coaxed from his saxophone. Maybe she'd just confused the man with the music. Maybe Satch made the same mistake.

She ordered frozen yogurt at a store around the corner from the theatre then wandered among the overflowing shelves of new and old titles at Walden Pond Books. Why had she let herself get roped into helping a woman who would just as soon flush her down the toilet? She told herself she was building good karma and imagined narrating the scene to Michael. Maybe he could use it in a script.

At eight o'clock she drove back to Satch's, wishing she'd asked Viola to describe Satch's car because she didn't remember it. She stopped in front of Satch's building and surveyed the area but saw no old Chevy. In the lobby she listened for the notes of a sax; the only music she heard was the thumping of rap from somewhere above. She started up the stairs, picturing Satch greeting her with gratitude.

When she reached Satch's apartment, Simone realized the music was coming from inside. She relaxed, convinced that a man who could play the sax like Thomas wouldn't be listening to rap, though it did seem to be the perfect music to accompany a beating. *Ta-boom, ta-boom.* She put her ear to the door but heard nothing else. Hoping for the best, she knocked. There was no response. She knocked again, louder. Still no response. "Satch," she called, kicking the door. "It's me, Simone. Open up."

Finally the door inched open. Satch's right eye was swollen shut, her lip split, her cheek purple. Simone winced.

"What you want?" Satch said in the angry voice Simone knew so well.

So much for gratitude. "Is Thomas gone?"

Satch nodded.

"Viola wanted me to take you to your aunt's."

Satch's one open eye lit up for a moment, then dimmed. "She ain't there. She in Texas. Visiting her daddy."

"Oh."

They looked at each other across the threshold. Simone couldn't just leave her there. "Isn't there somebody I could take you to?"

Satch shrugged like she didn't care, but Simone thought she saw tears in Satch's eyes before she looked away.

Nobody? Satch had nobody? This realization made Simone wish she'd gone on back to her cozy home because she felt trapped. She nudged the door open, pushing Satch backward, and stepped inside. The music assaulted her. "Get your toothbrush and whatever else you need. You've got to get out of here."

"Done told you. Ain't got nowhere to go."

"Fine. You can come with me for tonight. Tomorrow you'll probably be thinking more clearly, and we can make a plan then."

"Come with you?" Satch asked, a look of incredulity on her face. "Where?"

"To my place. You can share the sofa with me. It makes into a bed."

Satch didn't budge.

"You can come with me now, or you can stay here and wait for Thomas to come home and use you as his punching bag. It's your choice."

Satch turned, stood still for a minute, then walked away. Simone didn't know if Satch was planning to come back, but she thought it best to just wait and see.

The smell of roach spray permeated the apartment. The kitchen floor was probably dotted with corpses of the disgusting vermin, on their backs, their tiny feet jutting into the air. There was an orange-and-brown-plaid sofa in this room, a brown shag rug, a high-tech stereo with several large speakers, and a CD collection that filled shelf after shelf after shelf. On top of the television sat a round pink music box. Simone lifted the lid. The central figurine was a young black girl, petite, long-limbed, posed on her tiptoes, turning slowly to the notes of "Unforgettable You," a song Simone loved. She wondered if Satch had bought the music box or if Thomas had given it to her.

She sensed Satch's presence, hastily closed the lid, and set the music box back on the television, feeling a sense of guilt for having violated Satch's privacy.

"You bring a limousine?"

Did Satch provoke her beatings? "Yes, and a chauffeur. And I live in a mansion. With a butler. But you can sleep in the servants' quarters if you'll be more comfortable."

Satch exhaled loudly. Only then did Simone register the Safeway bag in Satch's hand, stuffed with something, Satch's pajamas presumably, the bag crumpled, one edge torn, a woeful suitcase that for some bewildering reason made Simone want to cry.

Eleven

"Welcome to my mansion."

Simone opened the door to her condominium and moved aside. If Satch was surprised by the smallness of her home, she didn't show it. She scanned the combined living area through her one eye that wasn't swollen, turning her head to be able to see it.

"Not quite the mansion you expected, huh?" Simone said.

"Shit. Ain't got to share with no roaches. No sirens. No shouting. No shooting. Seem like a mansion to me."

Simone saw her point. Her home was a haven, at least from external dangers. "Would you like some juice or something to eat? Or some ice for..."

"Naw." Satch's eyes lingered on a fuchsia with pink blossoms. "Having all them plants be a white thing."

"Why?"

"Hard enough just staying alive."

"Hey, you're the one living with a man who beats her." Satch's glare made Simone wish she could take her words back.

"Thomas my business. Where I'm gonna sleep?"

Simone motioned to the sofa. "It's a sofa bed. Opens up into a queen. We can share."

Satch's good eye opened wide. "Share?"

"Unless you'd prefer the bathtub. You can shower or whatever first."

Satch took her Safeway sack with her to the bathroom, the bag crackling as she passed. Simone opened up the sofa bed and pulled an extra pillow from the closet. When Satch emerged, she smelled of Simone's honeysuckle soap. She'd changed into pink shorts and a red T-shirt that clung tight, emphasizing her bulk. Her face seemed to be swelling and purpling more by the minute. It must hurt, Simone thought. She half envied Satch her pain, though her own desire to cut seemed to have subsided. "Are you sure you don't want some ice? Or aspirin?"

"Naw." Satch walked over to Simone's CD collection.

In the bathroom, Simone stashed the box of blades amid the extra linen, changed into a large T-shirt and added sweatpants to keep her cuts hidden, washed, then returned to the one large room that served as everything but bathroom.

Satch held up a John Denver CD, which had been left by a previous lover. "If you listen to this shit, ain't no wonder you in a nut house."

"What put you there? Rap music?"

"Naw. The cops. On probation."

Was she imagining it or was Satch puffing with pride? "For what? Serial killer?"

"Yep. You might not live 'til morning."

"I can think of worse fates." Simone turned the light off and lay down on the bed, snuggling beneath a comforter.

Satch remained standing.

"Do you plan to spend the night like that?" Simone asked.

Satch took the extra pillow and stretched out on the carpet.

"Suit yourself," Simone said.

She listened to Satch's steady inhales, her long exhales. Did Satch regard her wounds as evidence of failure or as badges of honor? She ran her fingers over the cuts on her thighs, familiar and comforting and the source of a strange pride, proof of a toughness she respected.

She turned over, her back to Satch, and tried to sleep, but it eluded her as usual. Since she couldn't fix warm milk or watch television without waking Satch, she tried meditation. Satch began snoring, the sounds deep and repetitive. Simone pictured herself in a small boat, bobbing in the waves, lulled by a foghorn, until sleep overtook her.

When Simone woke Saturday morning, she felt a back touching hers. She scooted to the side, surprised she hadn't wakened when Satch moved into the bed. It was odd to be sharing; she'd slept alone for so long. She got up and went to the bathroom, where she took a long, hot shower. By the time she finished, she heard music coming from the other room, loud music. Satch was playing Simone's Tina Turner CD *Private Dancer*, playing it loud, at six o'clock on a Saturday morning. What on earth was the woman thinking? Simone put on her robe and returned to the living room.

Satch faced the window with her back to Simone, moving to the music. She swiveled her hips like a belly dancer and her arms like cobras, graceful and hypnotic. Tina sang about doing whatever a man wanted. Satch grabbed her hair with one hand and jerked her head back, turning it side to side as if someone were slapping her. When the song ended, Satch covered her face with her hands.

Simone didn't want Satch to know she'd witnessed her, what—dance? violation?—so she retreated to the bathroom and made a show of thumping a wall to let Satch know she was finished showering. When she walked into the main room, Satch turned toward her.

"You ain't looking too good," Satch said.

Satch's face was purple and swollen, though at least now her eye partially opened. "Have you looked in a mirror?" Simone asked.

Satch shrugged. "Music too loud?"

"A little."

Satch didn't apologize or show the slightest remorse, but she did take out the disc and return it to the CD rack. "You like Tina Turner?"

The question sounded more like a challenge than an inquiry. "Very much. Aren't I supposed to?"

"Don't know. Tina Turner and John Denver. Maybe you schizophrenic."

"I like musicals and Tracy Chapman, too. Maybe I'm a multiple personality."

For half a second Simone thought Satch was going to smile, but she didn't. Simone opened the refrigerator and realized she hadn't gone shopping for a while. "Guess it's time for a run to the store."

"I eat most anything."

"How about sugarless jelly and olives?"

Satch grabbed her purse. "Gonna go with you."

Simone pictured the supermarket, its parking lot filled with BMWs and Mercedes, its aisles filled with customers wearing designer clothes. Parents and students from her school shopped at that store. If anyone she knew saw Satch, they might raise questions she didn't want to answer. Then again, if Satch wanted to come, what was she going to say, that black people weren't allowed? "Fine."

"Got to wash up," Satch said.

Satch took about fifteen minutes and came out dressed in bubble-gum-orange velour sweats. Simone's heart sank; she'd hoped they'd get in and out of the store without being noticed. Satch was about as inconspicuous as Simone would be in Satch's apartment building wearing a white hood.

On the way to the store, Simone chastised herself. It shouldn't matter what anyone else thought. Besides, she had her own wounds; they just didn't show.

"You eat cereal?" Simone asked as they entered the store and took a basket.

"Sometimes."

Simone turned the basket up the cereal aisle and selected her usual: Grape Nuts. "The official sponsor of Oakhill Hospital," she said to Satch, which—to Simone's amazement—startled a smile from Satch, who took the cereal and made an over-the-shoulder shot into the shopping basket.

"Wow," Simone said. "Good shooting."

"Used to play with Michael Jordan," Satch said. "Taught the man all he know."

It was Simone's turn to smile. "I taught Tina Turner to sing."

"John Denver more likely."

Bakery goods were across from the cereal. Simone selected sourdough English muffins while Satch chose a pack of doughnuts, chocolate ones with bits of candy sprinkled on top.

Satch headed down the beverage aisle; Simone went to stock up on yogurt. She reached for the Yoplait just as someone else did the same. It was the last person she wanted to encounter: Kathleen Ginger, Principal.

"Simone," Kathleen said as their hands nearly touched. She ran her eyes up and down Simone as if x-raying everything. "How are you?"

"Couldn't be better. And you?"

Please don't let Satch show up, Simone prayed.

"Excellent. And I'm glad to hear you're doing well. I'd like to chat, but I have guests coming. Take care." Kathleen pushed her cart on down the aisle.

Simone wondered if she should be concerned that Kathleen hadn't mentioned summer school but told herself the grocery store wasn't the place for a job interview. She took the yogurt out slowly, wanting plenty of distance between herself and Kathleen.

When Satch caught up with Simone, she was laden with Pepsi, white bread, American cheese, and chips. They reached the check-out stand just as someone pushed a cart behind theirs. Simone could tell who it was by the lavender scent of her perfume. Since Satch was standing beside Simone and taking things out of their basket, it was obvious they were together. Kathleen covertly inspected Satch: her bruised and swollen face, her messy hair and orange fingernails that matched her sweats.

Simone was at a loss what to say. "Hi, this is Satch, we're at a nut house together" was too risky. "Hi, this is my friend Satch" would be brave but inaccurate. She settled for "Kathleen, this is Satch."

Kathleen's eyebrows arched. "Are you a teacher, too?" The sharp focus of her eyes belied the cheeriness of her voice.

"No," Satch said, "a movie star."

Simone almost strangled on her own surprise and laughter.

"Oh?" Kathleen said. "Have I seen you in any movies?"

"Naw. I always be the corpse. This my make-up. Pay a lot, though."

Simone turned her back to Kathleen to try to deflect further questions. Satch finished loading the basket and took a card from her Safeway bag: a food-stamps card.

Simone took out a credit card and slapped it down on the counter on top of Satch's, hoping Kathleen wasn't watching closely. The young cashier appeared totally confused.

"I'll pay," Simone said.

"I got it." Satch pulled her card out from under Simone's and handed it to the cashier. "You pay last night," she said, and looked at Kathleen. Her voice dropped an octave and came out suggestively. "Simone always like that. That girl'd be paying for everything if I let her."

Satch smiled at both of them, took her card back from the cashier, and picked up the groceries.

"She's just kidding," Simone said. Kathleen kept right on staring. "See you soon."

No response. She could feel Kathleen's puzzled eyes following them all the way to the car.

Satch jumped up in the seat beside her, grinning.

"Do you know who that was?" Simone said, not sure if she felt more like laughing or crying.

"Yeah. A bitch."

"Yes, but an important bitch. She's my boss."

Satch turned deliberately to look out the window, and Simone was sure she was trying to hide a smile.

"A movie star, huh?"

"Uh-huh."

"Will you give me your autograph?"

"Depend. Got to stop talking and start driving. I'm hungry."

When they got home, Simone listened to the crisp sounds of the cereal she crunched and wished Satch would speak, but Satch seemed absorbed in picking the pink sprinkles off a doughnut. The lengthening silence made Simone uneasy.

"So how did you get the name Satch?" she asked.

Satch kept her eyes on the doughnut. "Satchell Paige my daddy's hero. Satchell play baseball in the old Negro League. Daddy say Satchell so good, if he'd been white they'da named a candy bar after him. Guess Daddy thought I was gonna be a boy. When I come along, named me Satch anyway."

The doughnut smelled of sugar and chocolate. Simone wanted to rip it out of Satch's hand and stuff it in her own mouth, but the last thing she wanted was to gain weight. "Can I ask you something about what you said last night? I mean, you don't have to answer."

"Don't gotta do nothing but die some day."

"You said you were on probation at Oakhill. What for?"

Satch didn't reply at first. "You remember them cops killed the unarmed black man a few months back?"

"Yes." Simone vaguely remembered the incident. Three Oakland police officers, two white, one black, mistakenly thought an unarmed black man was reaching for a gun and riddled him with bullets. She was pretty sure he'd been a minister who left a wife and three children behind.

"Pissed me off," Satch said. "He'da been white, them cops never woulda shot him." Satch tapped her fingers on the table. "Folks protested. Weren't nobody doing nothing illegal. Cops started swinging their clubs. Turned it into a riot. I broke a few windows. Hit a couple cops." Satch sat back in her chair, drank more Pepsi. Burped. "Judge say I got an anger problem. Go to jail or to Oakhill. So I'm at Oakhill. Don't do no good though."

"You don't think Oakhill's helping?"

"Don't think I got no anger problem. 'Sides, therapy just a bunch of folks blabbing. Don't do nobody no good."

Simone's heart skipped a beat. "It might help if you called groups."

"Uh-huh."

They sat in silence a moment, both dabbing up crumbs.

"Did you think of someone I could take you to?" Simone asked.

"Naw. Just drop me at my place."

She wanted to. Spending the day with the unpredictable Satch would be about as much fun as chopping onions. Still, she couldn't just dump her back at her home. Viola had said the beatings were getting worse. "Why don't you stay here." She tried to sound positive, wondering what she would do with Satch Sunday when she went to her father's for their monthly lunch.

"And do what?"

"I don't know. Rent movies or go for a walk or something."

Satch took another swig of Pepsi and washed it around her mouth as if she were preparing to gargle. "There a pool here?"'

"Yes..."

"Good."

"I don't..." Simone didn't want to explain that she only swam at night, when no one could see her handiwork.

"Don't wanna be seen with me, huh?"

"That's not it."

"Just like at the store. When that nasty woman come up, you got even more white."

"It's not what you're thinking."

"Uh-huh."

If Simone gave in, her scars would be exposed to Satch and anyone else at the pool. If she refused, she'd be a racist, and

Satch would probably tell everybody at the hospital all about it, Jun included. "Don't you want to go for a drive?"

Satch folded her arms across her chest. "Naw."

"Let's hike at the park then swim later. Did you ever swim at night? It's the best."

"Figure ain't nobody gonna see me at night, huh?"

Goddamn it, Simone thought. "Fine," she said. She'd keep a towel wrapped around her waist until she got in. Surely the marks on her thighs would be invisible in the frothing water. She got up to change.

"One thing," Satch said. "I don't got no suit."

Simone's suits were all size seven; Satch was probably a sixteen. Not sure what she was searching for, Simone ransacked her dresser. Satch peered over her shoulder and rifled through a stack of tight-fitting sweaters and shirts. "Got clothes make you look hot. Why you don't wear 'em?"

"They're not comfortable."

"So why you buy 'em?"

Simone shut the drawer. "Temporary insanity." She rummaged around the floor of her closet and came up with Michael's red sweatpants. For a moment she hesitated, wondering if she should save them to give him at their upcoming dinner, but she worried he might see her holding on to them as desperate, which it probably was. "Cut-offs okay?"

"Fine." Satch turned away and took a Pepsi from the refrigerator.

Simone found it satisfying to attack Michael's sweats with her scissors, cutting off most of each leg, every click of the scissors a reminder of her independence. Another former lover had given her a large yellow tank top that she never wore because it made her feel like a banana. She thought it would fit Satch.

The phone rang; she answered it.

"Hi, it's me."

Meghan. Simone hadn't spoken with her since Meghan refused to back her with Kathleen. She didn't speak now.

"Simone, I miss you."

Meghan's words sat in the air for a long moment then settled around her like an old, familiar coat. She'd missed Meghan, too. When she'd turned forty in November, Meghan had baked her a chocolate cake in the shape of a heart, frosted it red and swore this would be the year Simone met the man of her dreams. And she had. Too bad he was her therapist.

"How are you?" Simone said and turned her back to Satch.

"Fine. How about you? Are you taking good care of yourself?"

The warmth in Meghan's voice made Simone long for the easy intimacy they'd once shared. "I'm fine."

"The students miss you."

What was she supposed to say to that? She'd still be teaching them if it weren't for Meghan. "I miss them too."

"I feel bad about what happened," Meghan said. "But seeing all those scars… I care about you, Simone. I'm sorry if you feel I betrayed you."

She *had* felt betrayed, but at that moment she didn't know what to feel.

"Are you getting help?" Meghan asked.

She sounded genuinely concerned. Simone could feel her resentment dissolving. "Yes." She walked into the bathroom and shut the door. "I go to a hospital outpatient program."

"Good. I was afraid to call, afraid you might still be angry. But I think about you all the time."

"I *was* angry." Simone paused, considered. "But it's good to hear your voice."

"Why don't you come over for dinner Monday? Evan will be away, so we'll have a chance to really talk like we used to."

Before Meghan's marriage the previous year, they'd spent most weekends together. Simone wondered what it would be like to see Meghan again.

"It would mean a lot to me," Meghan said.

"I'd like that. What time?"

They arranged to meet Monday at six o'clock.

"By the way," Meghan said, "Kathleen called. She said you were at the store with somebody who looked like a derelict. What gives?"

Simone lowered her voice. "She's from the hospital. I'm just helping her out."

"Are you sure that's healthy?"

"It's just for today. I'm going to have my monthly lunch with Dad tomorrow."

"You need to focus on taking care of yourself. You know how you tend to get wrapped up in other people's problems. Be careful who you hang out with, that's all. Don't give Kathleen any more doubts."

Torn between anger that Kathleen would judge her based on how Satch looked, and fear over the very same thing, Simone didn't respond.

They exchanged farewells and hung up. When Simone emerged from the bathroom, Satch had changed into her makeshift "swimsuit." Battered face, bulges, uneven red cut-offs and a yellow tank top, she was quite a sight. Simone thought it safer not to comment. She went back to the bathroom and changed into her suit then wrapped a thigh-cloaking towel around her waist.

They headed for the pool. The temperature hovered near an exceptional eighty, the first hot day that spring, and the pool was already crowded. Or rather, the chairs around the pool were crowded. A dozen people sprawled on lounge chairs facing the sun. She pulled out the last two chairs, sensing the conversations around them cease, all eyes brazenly or covertly assessing Satch. Simone was grateful she didn't really know any of these people.

Suddenly Satch ran past, screaming. She cannonballed into the water; it splashed high. The other people exchanged glances of surprise or disapproval, which irritated Simone, maybe because she knew if she and Meghan were observing, they might well do the same thing. To hell with it, she decided. To hell with all of it. Getting up, she dropped her towel and also cannonballed into the water, something she hadn't done in years. She landed on her back. It stung. She quickly righted herself, thrust up with her arms while she exhaled, and sank beneath the surface to conceal her scars.

Satch swam underwater the length of the pool, turned around still underwater, and swam back. Simone began doing the crawl, her favorite stroke, maybe because it took energy and concentration, relieving her mind from its perpetual clamor. Satch kept swimming underwater; she'd come up for air every two laps and immediately go back under. As Simone swam laps, she watched Satch's dark form glide across the bottom of the pool.

After thirty-five minutes of nonstop lapping, Simone pulled herself out of the pool to collapse on a lounge chair. She spread a striped towel over her thighs. A mild breeze had sprung up, raising goose bumps as it whispered across her wet skin, but the sun soon warmed her. She put a white towel over her face and closed her eyes.

In another few minutes Satch collapsed on the chair next to Simone's. "Doing okay?" Simone asked without removing the towel. Satch grunted, which Simone took to mean yes.

"You swim real good," Satch said.

Satch's voice seemed to float around her, disembodied. Simone found that comforting. "Thanks," she said. "You can really stay underwater long."

"Always sink," Satch said, "but I love water. Figure if I'm gonna sink to the bottom, might as well swim there."

Satch's voice lacked its normal edge and Simone wondered if water soothed Satch, too, or if not seeing her made her sound different. "Do you mind sitting out here for a bit?" Simone asked.

"Fine," Satch said. "Got to work on my tan."

Simone smiled and relaxed, drifting off, sleeping until she was awakened by drops of water that plopped on her neck and slid down her collarbone. She lifted the corner of the white towel from her eyes. The other towel had fallen off. A dripping Satch towered above her, her gaze riveted on Simone's exposed thighs. Simone wondered how they looked to her. Satch turned her eyes to Simone's; Simone picked the towel off the ground and spread it over her thighs.

"You do that your own self?" Satch asked.

Simone didn't respond.

"Why?"

Simone's body pumped the adrenaline that comes when you see a car swerving into your lane. It was a question she couldn't begin to answer, not really, not to Satch and not to herself. She dropped the other towel across her face and shut her eyes. Tight.

Satch snatched the towel that covered Simone's legs and raised her voice. "You go around the hospital acting like you all fine, but you go home and play butcher on yourself?"

Simone glanced around. Every other person at the pool was watching them. She couldn't stay here. She stood, wrapped the second towel around her waist and started toward her apartment.

"Why you do that?"

"Why do you let yourself be a punching bag?"

"'Least I don't do it to my own self. That's sick."

No one made even a pretense of reading.

"You let someone else do it to you. That's sicker. I have control over what happens to me. You don't. Not if you stay with Thomas. So don't tell me how fucked up I am. You take care of your own damned problems. I'll take care of mine."

"Yeah. You doing a real good job of that."

"I'm going back to the apartment."

"I'm gonna swim."

"Fine. Just ring the bell when you're finished." She turned her back to Satch and the titillated sunbathers and strode away.

"Oughta start talking about this shit in groups," Satch called after her.

Face flaming, Simone hurried for the sanctuary of her apartment. Images of razor blades jammed her mind; she wasn't sure whether she wanted to cut herself or Satch. But she knew better. If she cut herself, some way, some how, Satch would discover it, her dark suspicious eyes evading Simone's defenses like heat-seeking missiles, locking in on a truth she would broadcast to everyone at Oakhill, Jun included.

Desperate to calm herself, Simone heated a cup of hot milk in a pan. Then she spooned in Vosges cocoa mix and watched the chocolate flakes melt. She wished Satch would melt away, too.

TWELVE

As she opened the door to Satch, Simone girded herself for a withering blast or glare.

"I look like a big-ass raisin," Satch said.

Wrinkled from being so long in the water, Satch's skin did have a raisinish quality. More importantly, she hadn't continued their argument.

"Do you want to shower?" Simone asked.

"Yeah."

"Help yourself to my stuff."

Satch raised an eyebrow, but all she said was "thanks." She started toward the bathroom.

Simone cleared her throat. Satch turned to face her. "About my thighs. I don't want—"

"They your business. Just like my bruises is mine. Ain't gonna talk about your business. You don't talk about mine."

"Agreed."

Satch went to shower.

That was easier than she'd anticipated, Simone thought. The last thing she wanted was to have Satch ranting about her many cuts at Oakhill, especially in front of Jun.

After her shower, Satch lay down on the sofa and was soon snoring softly. Simone looked down at Satch's bruised and swollen face; her wounds registered for the first time in several hours. She was amazed at how fast she'd come to take Satch's injuries for granted, and she wondered if Satch did the same thing, if she stayed with Thomas because after a short while her injuries just didn't register.

That night after they finished the pizza they'd ordered—Simone ate two slices to Satch's six—they watched a thriller Satch had heard was good. Simone fixed popcorn. They sat together on the sofa, cramming it in.

The set changed from a police station to a park, where a woman walked alone at night. Simone's heartbeat quickened. *Relax*, she told herself. *It isn't real.* Footsteps sounded behind the woman on the screen. She ran. A man behind her tackled her. She fell on dead leaves. *This didn't happen to you.* The man held a knife to her throat. *Spence hadn't done that. This was a movie. Just a movie.* The man raped the woman.

Simone jumped off the sofa, spilling the popcorn, ran into the bathroom, and heaved mozzarella cheese, tomato sauce, popcorn, and garlic. Once. Twice.

A knock. "You okay?"

"Yeah." Simone splashed water on her face then gargled with mouthwash. *It was a movie.* Grabbing the sink, she focused on the feel of the cold porcelain. Eventually she returned to the living room where Satch had cleaned up the popcorn and turned off the television.

"Wanna talk about it?" Satch said.

"I just ate something that disagreed with me." Did her words sound as constricted as her throat felt?

"The movie pissed me off. Piss you off?"

"It's just a movie."

"You ain't answered my question."

Simone fluffed her pillow. "Anger is a destructive emotion. I don't believe in it."

"Ain't something you believe in like Santa Claus. Anger just something you feel."

"No way. I've seen what happens when people let their anger go. They do all kinds of stupid things. I believe in communication. People don't communicate well when they're angry."

"Shit." Satch sucked in her lips. "Just 'cause you angry don't mean you got to throw no chair through no window."

"You going to turn the movie back on?"

"That your idea of communication?"

"Sorry. I guess I'm tired."

Satch yawned; Simone could swear it was faked. "Me too. Tired from all that swimming. Let's sleep."

Relieved, Simone changed into her sweats, Satch into a T-shirt and shorts, and together they made up the bed. As they lay back to back, Simone smelled the mixture of peach lotion and chlorine that lingered on their skin despite their showers. Satch soon snored. Simone counted to a hundred, counted back to one, did it again, but her mind kept tumbling from thoughts of the movie to thoughts of cutting to images of Spence. She gave up, opened her eyes, and kept them open staring into darkness.

The phone rang at six. She leapt from bed to answer. When Satch groaned and pulled a pillow over her head, Simone took the phone into the bathroom.

"Hi, doll."

She was eager to see her father, though she hadn't resolved what to do about Satch.

"I can't get together for lunch today," he said.

"What's wrong?" She sat on the closed toilet lid.

"Everything is right. You know how I've been telling you about Claire?"

"Yeah. I know you like her."

"It's more than that, doll, much much more. I'm head over heels in love with her!"

"But you've only known her three weeks."

"That doesn't matter. When I'm around her—well, zing go the strings of my heart. She's beautiful and funny and intelligent and sexy and sweet like an angel. I get goose bumps just thinking about her! I feel like violins are playing a symphony inside me."

"How old did you say she was?" she asked, imagining someone twenty, which was about six years older than her father sounded.

"She's my age, but when we're together we both feel young."

She could believe that. Simone realized she'd torn off a strip of toilet paper and was shredding it in her lap. She dumped the pieces in the trash. "I'm happy for you," she said. She had to admit that over the years she'd proclaimed to Meghan her own love for various men in less time than her father had taken. Maybe it was genetic.

"Anyway," he said, "I promised Claire I'd take her to the flea market today. You'll have to come up soon to meet her. It's about time you had a mother."

Simone's head jerked back. She'd had a mother, a mother she'd loved fiercely. "I'm a little old for that."

"You're never too old for a mother. I've got to go. I'm cooking her breakfast."

The image of her father cooking stunned her more than anything so far. The only time he entered the kitchen was on his way outdoors. She wondered whether he was going to serve peanut butter sandwiches or fast food chicken.

It was as if he were reading her mind. "I'm making waffles."

"Waffles? You're kidding. You know how to make waffles?"

"Well, you know. The frozen kind. I need to set the table. Love you. *Au revoir.*"

He hung up. Simone remained seated on the toilet staring at the phone, astonished, though she told herself she shouldn't be. Her father had dated lots of women since he retired, and her mother had been dead twenty-four years, so there was no reason he shouldn't date and fall in love. He was a good-looking, successful older man at an age when the available women far outnumbered the men; it was a seller's market.

Had he been excited about her mother when they were dating? What had happened to the love between them? Her mother's eyes—illuminated with joy when she was painting or strolling at the ocean or sometimes when she was playing with a young Simone—smoldered with fury when her husband came home from work. Satch's eyes were like that, at least when they watched Simone at Oakhill. She wondered if she and Satch had moved beyond that, or if Satch would retreat into hostility once they were back at the hospital. She wondered why her mother had stayed with a man she didn't love.

She stood up to shake off her loneliness and turned on the shower, hoping Satch would wake up soon.

When she emerged from the bathroom, Satch was up, stretching.

"You look like shit," Satch said.

"And you think you look good?"

"Just did my make-up for my next movie. *Zombies from Oakhell.*"

"Oh? Who's going to play you? Oprah?"

"Naw. Eddie Murphy."

Simone smiled. "That's one movie I've got to see."

"You taking me back today?"

Was there reluctance in Satch's voice, or did she only want to hear it? "My father canceled. He's entertaining his new love."

"Let's go surprise 'em."

For an instant Simone pictured herself and Satch showing up at her father's door unannounced. She had to admit, the prospect had its appeal. But she couldn't.

"Naw, don't look like you wanna do that. What you got in mind?"

A strenuous hike might help her sleep. Besides, nature had always comforted her. When she was little, her father had delighted in revealing to her nature's many marvels. "I'd like to go hiking in Redwood Park."

"Girl, you is crazy. A park ain't nothing but dirt, bugs, and snakes."

"How much hiking have you done?"

"Only hiking I do is down the hallway to my apartment."

"See? Parks have streams, beautiful trees, and trails that soothe your soul."

"My soul just fine."

"Satch." She could hear how plaintive her voice sounded. "Please."

Satch must have heard it, too. "Damn. Guess I owe you one. But when we come back, we gonna swim."

"Fine."

"Shit. Musta lost my mind."

They hiked up a steep slope, Satch huffing. Simone welcomed the silence, broken only by the squawking of an occasional jay.

"Where the music?" Satch said.

"Think of the wind in the trees as music."

"Ain't no bass. Nobody singing. All this quiet making my head hurt."

Simone couldn't tell if Satch was joking. She hoped Satch would experience even a piece of her own awe when they reached the grove of redwood trees, so massive, so tall. Sunlight gleamed off the leaves of the poison oak that edged the path. Pointing it out to Satch to avoid, Simone walked into sticky strands of a web that clung to her cheeks. A spider hovered inches from her face. She quickly stepped back, wiped the residue from her cheeks, and regretted that she'd damaged the spider's design. "Look at this web." She pointed to a spot where it was intact, a series of ripples. "How can something so small know how to weave something so intricate?"

"Web just made to kill something. Kinda like the electric chair."

Bemused, Simone said, "Humor me? Go under it?"

Satch ducked beneath the web. "Thomas not gonna believe this. Man hates spiders. Stomps 'em when he can."

Appalled more by Satch's casual reference to her abuser than by Thomas's unsurprising cruelty, Simone cast a last look at the web before scooting under it.

As they hiked on she took long, quick strides, confident that exercise would further clear her mind. She deliberately tromped on the caps of eucalyptus nuts, enjoyed the crunch of them underfoot.

Ahead rose the redwood trees she wanted to share with Satch. Sunlight dimpled the grove. She inhaled the smell, a woody fragrance that might be coming from the undergrowth as much as the trees. Trees that were so straight. So tall.

I'm going to rape you.

Cold clotted her chest.

Tell me you like it!

Beneath redwoods. How had she forgotten?

Satch moved in front, blocking Simone, facing her. "What's wrong?"

The interruption jarred Simone back to the present. "Nothing."

"Uh-huh."

"I don't want to talk about it." She wanted the safety of her car, and she went around Satch, fleeing back to it, walking right through the spider web, sundering it.

The parking lot was full. A white BMW convertible practically kissed Simone's Echo. The driver had parked too close. She opened her door, resting it lightly on the BMW's.

"What the hell do you think you're doing?" came a loud voice. The man striding toward her was short and angry, unlike Spence, who had bought her white roses and taken her to an elegant dinner, had brushed her cheek and told her she was lovable. Who had raped her.

Normally she'd have reassured the approaching man, but she felt she'd splintered internally. Slivers jabbed her insides. She drenched her voice in sarcasm. "I seem to be getting in my car, now don't I?"

He slammed her door shut. "No way," he said. "You aren't scratching my door."

"Maybe you shouldn't have parked so close." She stepped toward him. Stubble made his face look prickly.

"Get in the passenger side," he barked.

She quivered with the desire to swing, imagined her arm to be as straight and sturdy as a redwood branch. She curled her fingers. "Fuck you!"

Satch jerked Simone's arm. She pulled Simone back from the man, to the passenger side of the car. Simone struggled to get free. She wanted to swing at his sneering face at least once. He could beat her. He could kill her. She didn't care, so long as she landed one good punch.

The man leaned against the driver's side of her car. Satch shoved Simone in the passenger side.

"Back out, motherfucker," Satch yelled at the man, "or you gonna piss me off."

The man spat at the Echo. Simone watched his saliva slide down her windshield. She began trembling. She wanted to cry.

He got in his car, backed out of the space, and spun up rocks as he peeled out.

Satch got in the driver's side. "You be saying you got no anger. What was that? That anger and stupidity is what that is. That man coulda killed you. No telling what a man like that's gonna do. Why you let him mess with you?"

Simone hugged herself. She smelled her own sweat, couldn't tell if it came from rage or fear. Her voice was gone. Everything inside her had been erased, everything except every detail of that one night with Spence.

"What's happening?"

"I just… I thought… I can't."

"Sure you can. We ain't going nowhere 'til you tell me what's wrong. We can sleep here if you want, though I expect lions and hyenas and shit be hunting around here at night."

Simone wondered if it would help to talk, to admit to Satch what she hadn't even admitted to herself. "It was a big deal," she whispered.

"What?"

"What Spence—when he—when I was raped."

"What happened?"

"Promise you won't tell Jun."

"Ain't telling nobody your business."

Simone wasn't sure she wanted to tell Satch about Spence—wasn't sure she wanted to tell anyone—but something compelled her to start. "At dinner, he said he could love me. I wanted to believe him. And he said he wanted kids, too." A bitter laugh tore from her throat. "He suggested we go stargazing. I was so stupid. I never even questioned if it was safe."

"That ain't stupid. Man good at bullshit."

"He drove to a redwood grove on a dirt road. There were so many trees." She remembered thinking that the few visible stars dotted the interwoven branches like Christmas lights. "He turned the motor off and said he was going to rape me." Simone felt like she'd felt that night when he said it, like her lungs had collapsed.

Satch didn't say anything, just sat watching Simone, waiting.

"It's weird," Simone said. "The first thing I thought was how the redwoods were so straight and tall. That's fucked. I mean, the man says he's going to rape me and I start thinking about the goddamned trees."

Satch's dark eyes appeared neutral. "Sound like you in shock."

"I guess so. I told him he couldn't, that he couldn't touch me, but I wasn't loud and strong like you'd be. I remember thinking even the crickets in the woods sounded louder."

"Musta been real scared."

"Yeah." Sunlight streamed in the window of Simone's Echo, so different from the clammy air that licked her that night.

"Go on," Satch said.

"He opened the glove box. There was a big knife inside, sheathed, like a hunting knife. He said my only choice was with or without violence."

"Like rape ain't violent?"

"He didn't use the knife," Simone said.

"Yeah he did. Showing it was using it."

She pictured his goatee that drew his chin to a point, his lips so straight they could have been drawn on with a ruler, his suede jacket, his hollow eyes watching her through the smoke that drifted up from the cigarette he lit. "He told me to take my clothes off or he'd rip them off. I was afraid he might burn me with his cigarette. So I did."

He'd ordered her to climb into the back seat of his Bronco. Naked, she'd scrunched into the corner and crossed her arms over her breasts. "For some reason I started thinking about how my breasts were too big. He said I had great tits." She colored with the shame she felt then and the shame she felt now. "The air was cold. It was January. It had rained earlier that day, so it was damp too, and I was really scared. I was shivering. He told me to relax, that he wasn't going to hurt me."

Satch blew air dismissively.

"He put on a condom. Then he got on top of me." His body was bulky, like Satch's, it struck her now, an eerie similarity.

"Go on."

"He pulled me flat on the seat. The doors were open, and my head hung over the edge of the seat. He shoved his tongue in my mouth. I gagged. I thought I was going to vomit." She'd smelled the restaurant soap on his hands and the sweet, nauseating odor of his cologne. "Then he sucked my nipples. Hard. I was so scared. He told me to tell him I liked it, but I kept picturing him biting them off, my blood spurting."

"You say it?"

"Not at first. He repeated it, louder. I was afraid if I made him mad he'd cut my throat." She'd done as he wanted. Simone couldn't bring herself to look at Satch, who must be contemptuous of her cowardice. She'd capitulated without a fight. Satch would fight, she was sure of it.

"Well?"

"I said I liked it, but I didn't. Oh god, I was so scared." Simone bent over and clenched her shoulders. She wanted to scream and she wanted to cry and she wanted to just disappear. That's what she'd wanted then, too, to melt into the night even if it meant forever.

"Don't stop 'til you done," Satch said.

Simone risked a glance. Satch sat arms crossed, silent, her face impassive. Her neutrality gave Simone courage. "He thrust into me. I was terrified, so I was real dry and tight. It hurt so bad. He was tearing my insides. My head kept banging against the edge of the seat. He just rammed into me. It felt like he was ripping fire through me." Her mind had seemed to float away. She'd noticed a tear in the car liner, and she'd wondered what had caused it. "He kept thrusting. Then he demanded again that I say I like it. It hurt a thousand times worse than anything I'd ever felt, worse than when my appendix ruptured. But I gave in. I said yes." She swallowed a sob. If only she'd refused, if only she'd fought him. She might be dead, but at least she wouldn't be a coward.

Satch's face betrayed no judgment.

"He just stopped." Simone's voice cracked, her throat as parched as her insides had been that night. "He didn't come. He said he couldn't enjoy it if I didn't."

"Man a trip," Satch said.

"I was shivering with the cold and fear. I wondered if he was going to kill me. He told me to get dressed, and then he started the motor and turned on the heater and pointed all the vents at me. I was shaking so hard I couldn't button my blouse, so he did. He told me again to relax, that he wasn't going to hurt me."

"Fuck that shit! Man making me mad. Make you mad?"

Simone put her hand to her head to hold in her shame. "No. I was just terrified." How on earth was she going to confess the rest of that night to the one woman she was convinced would have fought Spence even if he'd wielded his knife?

"Why you say it weren't no big deal?" Satch said. "Sound like a big deal."

Satch was right. It had been a huge deal. So why had she convinced herself it wasn't?

Satch shook her head, whether to emphasize Spence's brutality or Simone's cowardice, Simone wasn't sure. She licked her cracked lips. She wished she had water. Enough to drink. Enough to drown in.

"Go on," Satch said.

"He drove back to the highway. When I saw lights from houses, that's when I thought maybe I was going to survive." She'd listened to the whisper of the tires on the asphalt and taken her first deep breath since the nightmare began.

"What he do then?"

Simone's throat felt so constricted she could barely speak. "Apologized."

"Say what?"

"He said that I was beautiful and that he'd thought I wanted it, that he'd thought he saw desire in my eyes at dinner. He promised he'd never do it again."

"Again? What he mean?"

Simone covered her own eyes, shielding her humiliation.

"Don't be stopping now."

"He said he wanted a family as much as I did and that I'd be a great wife and mother. When he got to my house he gave me a card with his phone number. He told me I was lovable and that he wanted to take care of me. He asked me to forgive him. To give him another chance." Simone's voice trembled; she stopped.

"Man really messed with your mind," Satch said.

The sun shone in Simone's eyes, and she let herself feel it burning into her, but it couldn't begin to dispel her shadows.

"You call the man?" Satch asked.

It was too late for silence. Simone wished she'd never begun to confess her sins. "Not right away. But I wanted a family so bad. I thought we could meet in public, drive separate cars. So I called. He didn't answer. I left a message. He didn't call back. A couple days later I called again. His number had been disconnected. I guess it was all one big con. He wanted to rape me and see if I'd crawl back. And I did." If she'd had Spence's knife, she would have used it on herself.

Satch let out a soft whistle. "That man one sick motherfucker."

"I should never have called him back."

"Ain't like you done nothing wrong or you bad. Sound like you was just real lonely." Satch looked away and ran her fingers over her lips like she was pondering something. "I ain't never left Thomas. Not for real."

"Why?" Simone compared the two, the man who raped her, the man who beat Satch.

"He a good man. Love me. Man got a bad temper sometimes, but he real easy most the time. Just gotta forgive him. But Spence, that man sound like he crazy. What Evelyn call that kind of rapist?" Satch asked.

"Smooth talkers, I think."

"Man smooth all right. But rape, that ain't smooth."

"Remember, you promised not to tell Jun."

"You oughta."

If she told Jun about how she'd groveled, Simone was sure he would lose any respect for her he might have.

"That why you went nuts with that man just now?" Satch said.

"I guess so. I felt like it was happening all over again." She still did. Felt like Spence was assaulting her, threatening her with violence. How had she convinced herself she wanted to see him again?

"Man today coulda had a gun," Satch said. "Need to talk about this shit at Oakhill before you get yourself killed."

"I thought you said therapy was just folks blabbing."

"Don't pay attention to half what I say. Sometimes I just be blabbing, too."

By the time they got back to the condominium, Simone craved her blades. When Satch said she wanted to swim, Simone told her to go ahead, that she'd be out after she made a couple of calls. As soon as Satch left, Simone went to the bathroom where she'd stashed her razor blades amid the spare towels. Satch could say what she would, Simone knew the truth. Spence had raped her, brutally raped her. Not only had she surrendered without fighting, she'd come crawling back.

Cut, coward.

She had to keep the truth out of her eyes so Satch wouldn't detect it. A single cut would satisfy her. The blue box—a friend she'd postponed seeing for too long—felt good in her hand. She fingered the sharp plastic edges. Simone extracted a blade, holding it by the ends. She stared at the mirror. At her own ugliness. Where should she cut? The blade beamed in the light. Her thighs were already marked. She thought of Marvin and looked at the reflection of her white stomach. Perfect. It wouldn't be visible beneath her swimsuit. This was a private, personal penitence.

She pressed the blade until it pierced her skin. Blood seeped out. It hurt, far more than her thighs or face had.

Cut, coward. Wimp. Cut, bitch.

She pressed down and dragged the blade for almost two inches, blood oozing. As she focused on the raw, biting pain, the rage and terror that had overwhelmed her so much of the past few hours eased away.

She washed the blade in the sink, put it and the small blue box back between towels, and waited for the bleeding to stop.

"I got to pee," Satch said at the locked door.

"I'll be right out."

She had violated her contract, but she would be careful not to let it show, not to tip off Satch or Jun or anyone else. This wasn't about them. She wiped away the blood and pulled on her swimsuit. This was about demonstrating her bravery. And she had.

Thirteen

Fog had settled above the gaping hole of the Caldecott Tunnel Monday morning, and as her car approached it, Simone felt like she was driving into oblivion. The idea both tempted and terrified her. If only the fog would come into the hospital with her, maybe she could get through the day without betraying her secrets. She hadn't slept well, felt strange. "Remember you promised not to tell about the rape."

"Naw, that's your business. And don't you be saying nothing about Thomas."

"I won't. But you should."

"Gonna play the radio. Being in this car with you's like being in a coffin when you ain't dead." Satch searched through the stations until she found rap music, which she played at a volume so loud the car seemed ready to shatter under the force of the hammering beat.

When Simone walked through the gate at Oakhill after picking up Viola, she felt like her skin was suddenly stripped off. Satch and Viola stayed outside to talk with the others. Simone went in, past scattered hellos, past the tables, the coffee, and took refuge in one of the small group rooms, where she turned off the light switch and sat in comparative darkness, feet drawn up, arms encircling her knees, numb and hiding. She was hiding.

The light flicked on. "Simone?" It was Jun.

She covered her face. "Please turn it off."

He did then walked over and extended her a cup of coffee.

"No thanks."

Jun sat as far from her as he could get. Maybe he was worried she had something contagious. Maybe she did. "What's wrong?" he said.

"Nothing." She hugged her knees tighter. "Satch stayed with me. We shared a bed. I didn't sleep well."

"Did something happen to upset you?"

She shook her head but didn't look at him.

"Are you angry with me about something?"

Simone almost gawked, wondering how Jun could possibly think that. "No. Never."

"It's okay to be angry. What matters isn't how you feel. It's how you act that counts."

How wrong he was, how very wrong. She had to guard against her emotions or she would end up dead. "I'm just tired."

"I believe it. It takes a lot of energy to put up walls as high as yours. Tell me what happened. I can't help if you won't trust me."

"Sometimes it just hurts too much."

"What hurts?"

Tears welled in her eyes. She was thankful for the darkness. Dropping her hand down to the pocket where she'd brought a safety pin, she drove it into her leg to dissolve her tears.

"Everything hurts," she said. "It's like I'm at the bottom of a dark hole and I'm falling down deeper and deeper and the air's getting thinner. And sometimes I want to just stop fighting and plunge all the way down."

Jun didn't comment right away, and when he did, his voice was gentle. "Do you feel that way now?"

"I don't know."

"Something must have happened over the weekend."

"No."

"Something triggered this."

She couldn't tell him because she was too ashamed, not of cutting but of the events that had prompted it.

"I care about you, Simone."

"Yeah, right." *I could love you,* Spence had told her. Men said what you wanted to hear. She'd always believed them. Not any more. "You care about all your clients. I'm nothing special."

Jun leaned toward her. "Oh yes you are. Believe me."

"Everybody's special."

"That's bullshit! You have no idea how rare you are. And I do care about you. A lot."

"Therapists are just hired guns."

"What?" His voice sounded like an explosion, half way between laughter and anger.

"If I disappear, you'll find another patient to coordinate."

"Of course I'd keep seeing clients." He sounded angry now, his voice trying to batter down her defenses. "But that wouldn't make me care about you any less."

Simone pricked herself harder with the pin to keep the tears deep inside. "People go away. Love goes with them. It isn't safe to care about someone."

"It isn't safe not to. Did you cut yourself this weekend?"

She was too tired to lie. "Yes."

"Why?"

"It was no big deal. Just a superficial cut."

"Any cutting is a big deal!"

His voice scalded her. She'd made him angry. He'd probably say he didn't want to be her treatment coordinator any more—if they even let her stay. She wondered if she wanted them to show leniency or just to go ahead and kick her out.

He flipped on the lights and left.

All eyes in the small group room watched Satch, who drooped in her chair. Satch hadn't called the group. During business meeting, Muslimah had scheduled it. Simone had always thought Satch looked invincible at Oakhill. She wanted to do something to give Satch back her strength, but she didn't know how.

"Don't want no group," Satch said, her voice both mournful and angry, a combination saxophone and trumpet.

The room was filled with members.

"I know," Muslimah said, her hair braided and beaded, her dress long and flowing, Oakhill's own royalty. "It's time we discussed your bruises."

Satch kept her eyes on her hands.

"Satch," Simone said, hoping to nudge her, to make it easier. "People can see anyway."

"Don't you be telling my business!" Satch said.

Simone looked away.

"This isn't about Simone unless she's the one hitting you," Muslimah said.

"Simone's right," Viola said.

"We ain't blind, girl," Regina said.

"Thomas hit me sometimes." Satch's voice was gruff.

"Tell us about it," Muslimah said.

"Ain't much to tell." Satch lowered her chin to her chest. "He just hit me."

"Why he do it?" Regina asked.

"Say I was flirting with his friend. I didn't. Hit me anyway. I hit him back. Made the man mad, so he start hitting me harder. Say he gonna teach me to be a good woman. That's all."

Satch had done nothing to set Thomas off? Having experienced Satch's sarcasm firsthand, Simone had assumed Satch had at least made a wisecrack, done something that triggered Thomas's wrath. "Why would you stay with a man who beats you?" she asked.

Satch raised her chin like she was prepared to defy skeptics. "He my man. Loves me. And makes sweet love. Good looking. When I'm out with Thomas, people looking at him 'cause he's so sexy, and they be looking at me thinking I must be one sexy woman. Make me feel good."

"It took a lot of courage for you to admit that," Muslimah said, her hands clasped together almost as if she were cheering on a boxer. "A lot of courage."

"Thomas never hurt me bad. Never put me in no hospital. And he treats me real good after."

"Does he give you flowers?" Muslimah asked.

"Yeah."

"Buy you presents? Treat you to dinners?"

"He always be real sorry." Satch nodded as if to say yes, that's right, he did all those things, that's why she stayed with him.

"That's the pattern of abusers," Muslimah said. "They beat you, then say they're sorry and treat you like a queen. They swear they'll be perfect. They try. They fail. Then they take their feelings of failure out on you. And Satch, there's always a next time, no matter what he promises."

Eyes back on the floor, Satch didn't speak or even glance at Muslimah.

If Simone had gone out with Spence again, if he had answered the phone, there would have been a next time, too; she suddenly knew that. But what if the rapes were occasional, if they'd married and had children, would she have left him? Or would she, like Satch, for whatever reason, have stayed around?

"I don't understand," Muslimah said. "I'm not telling you anything you don't know. Why do you keep allowing yourself to be victimized?"

"Love the man. When he look in my eyes, I be feeling all soft. And he's real nice to kids. Treats his mama good. Maybe I'm bad. Maybe he's right." Satch's eyes had the look of a frightened child.

"No way!" Simone said. "Nobody deserves to be beaten. You certainly don't! You aren't bad. Thomas is. You must know that."

Satch shrugged, not a shrug of indifference but one of confusion.

"Think about it," Muslimah said. "And use drama group to investigate why you stay with Thomas. In the meantime, you should give yourself credit for your courage in speaking up. It's a courage I guarantee you Thomas doesn't have."

When Satch's group ended, Muslimah rose and touched Satch's shoulder in encouragement and tribute. Viola took Satch's hand. Simone resolved that when it was time for her group, she'd be as brave as Satch. Silence wouldn't heal her.

At Jun's signal, Willy closed the door. It seemed to Simone that there was a limited amount of oxygen in the small room, that so many people would use it up, that she and everyone else would suffocate.

She sat up and straightened her shoulders. "I don't know where to begin," she said.

"You need to tell people about your habit," Jun said.

"Damn," Regina said. "You do drugs?"

"No. I cut sometimes." The wound on her stomach felt raw.

"Say what?" Regina's face wrinkled in confusion.

"You mean yourself?" Viola asked. "On purpose?"

"Sometimes. Just superficially."

"Can't imagine you doing that." Viola's normal odd smile had mutated into an open-mouthed look of horror. "You always seem so strong."

"Why you do it?" Regina said.

"I don't know. It makes me feel good."

"Good?" Regina looked mystified, which Simone thought odd. It all seemed so clear. "How can it feel good?"

"It just does."

"Sound like you talking about somebody else," Satch said.

"I agree," Jun said. "It's like you're discussing your best friend's second cousin's grandmother."

Simone didn't respond.

"You're always asking about us." Viola looked so caring, Simone felt herself start to tear up. "You give a lot to us. Let us give to you."

"Viola right," Regina said.

"Yeah," Marvin said. "You always taking care of me. Don't need to."

"Maybe you hide behind our problems to avoid your own," Viola said.

Simone caught her breath. Was Viola right?

"How come you going around asking everybody else how they doing but you don't tell us nothing about your own problems?" Satch sat so close to Simone their knees nearly touched.

"I'm afraid."

"Of what?" Jun asked.

"I'm afraid if I don't ask, people won't like me."

"You crazy," Satch said.

"Why wouldn't we like you?" Viola asked. "You're real good to everybody."

"You make me laugh," Regina said.

"People are more comfortable with you when you can also show you're vulnerable," Jun said.

"Yeah," Satch said. "When you real."

Simone clawed her neck. She didn't want to be real. Her "real" self had to stay hidden. Other than Satch they didn't know the truth. If they did, they would be contemptuous.

"What you need from us?" Regina asked. "How we help?"

Simone couldn't get it out. She tried, but the word sunk deep inside while people waited silently, watching. She ached to say "forgiveness." But it strangled on itself. What she needed was to hear them say that it was okay, what she didn't say, didn't do, didn't let herself feel the days after the night she was raped. But she couldn't get out the words to tell them about the rape and her own cowardice, the words to tell them what she needed, because what if she told them, if she asked them to say it was okay, and they didn't because it wasn't?

"How come you ain't talking?" Satch said.

Simone jabbed her leg with her safety pin to reinforce her walls. "I appreciate everyone's caring."

"Sound like some damned Hallmark card," Satch said. "You cut this weekend?"

How had Satch guessed?

"Now that's fucked up," Satch said. "I'm right there and you cutting yourself? That piss me off. Piss me off real bad. How you like it if I let Thomas come in and hit on me when you there?"

"I wouldn't."

"Uh-huh. Fuck you!"

"Satch," Jun said, "I know you're angry, and you have good reason to be. But I want to be sure Simone understands. Are you angry with her because you don't like her and don't care what she does, or because you do care?"

Simone clenched her jaw so tight she almost bit her chin.

"Used to be, I hate Simone," Satch said. "Pissed now 'cause she helped me. Seen her good side. Woman made me laugh. Now she sitting here saying she didn't never ask me for help. That's fucked up."

"Simone," Jun said. "I want you to look up and make eye contact with everyone in this room."

She closed her eyes. Didn't dare breathe. If she held her breath long enough, maybe she could disappear.

"Please."

She slowly lifted her gaze. Every eye, every brown eye, looked full of caring—and pain. Could what she did to herself really have that much impact on other people? She must be imagining it. She really must have lost her mind.

"What made you cut?" Jun asked.

Simone fixed her eyes on her hands. "I remembered when I was raped."

"Tell us about it."

She did, confessing the events of that night. But she stopped short of her calls afterwards.

"There's something you leaving out," Satch said.

She jabbed her pin into her leg. "A few days later, I called him. Twice. The first day I got his machine. Then his phone was disconnected. The rape—he just wanted me to come crawling. And I did." She pushed the pin deeper.

"But Simone," Regina said, "he raped you. Why you do that?"

"What you did was sick!" Yvonne crinkled her nose like she was smelling something spoiled.

"What you know about it?" Satch challenged. "Only problem you got is heart attacks that ain't real."

"How dare you!" Yvonne's fingers fidgeted with her collar button.

"Stop!" Jun said sharply. "Simone needs our support."

Simone stared at a corner of the ceiling and tried to imagine herself as a spider above it all, but she was too aware of her body throbbing with humiliation, too aware of astounded eyes, too aware she was sitting in a chair and that she had just confessed her craven desperation, a desperation she should never have confided to anyone, not even Satch. Maybe Satch hadn't judged her, but everyone else surely was judging her. Their verdict was clearly *guilty.*

"There were reasons why you called him back," Jun said. "Do you know what those reasons were?"

"He said he could love me." Even to Simone her voice sounded young. "All the men I've dated, I've loved them, but they haven't loved me back. Not really. I only thought they did."

"That's what I want," Regina said. "Man to love me."

"But you have to love yourself," Jun said, "so you can pick men who will love you, too. You deserve that."

She deserved no such thing. She'd done something heinous, though she didn't know what it was. She must have committed some terrible crime because why else hadn't anyone loved her? If only she knew what it was she'd done. If only she understood why she had called Spence for another date. If she couldn't begin to sort that out, she wouldn't be safe, not from the Spences of the world. Not from herself.

"I think there's more you need to say to your rapist, or maybe to yourself," Jun said. "I suggest you use drama sessions to explore your feelings about all this."

Lonnie barged into the room for his group. "Hate my mama, the ho. Gonna kill myself."

"You need to come with me," Jun said to Simone.

He guided her to Evelyn's office. Would Evelyn throw her out? She'd broken her contract; there must be punishments just like there were consequences for students who violated classroom rules. She half wished Evelyn would evict her and half prayed she wouldn't.

At Jun's knock Evelyn opened the door. Her green silk blouse made her eyes vivid.

"Simone cut herself."

Evelyn gestured them in. A small fountain rested on her desk, water bubbling up from beneath sand-colored stones.

"Show us where you cut," Evelyn said.

"I don't see why that's necessary." She didn't want to expose herself to Jun. "You broke your contract," Evelyn said. "If you can't do as I ask now, I don't see how we can help you. And in that case, we'd have to ask you to leave."

Reddening, Simone raised her shirt just enough to reveal the red line she'd cut. Jun winced. Simone told herself that was how she should feel. She didn't.

"That's enough." Evelyn's face revealed no emotion.

Simone adjusted her clothes.

"Are you trying to kill yourself?" Evelyn asked.

"No," Simone said quickly. She wasn't.

"That's where you're heading."

"I'm not. I can control it." If she chose to kill herself, Simone thought, it would be just that: a choice. A conscious choice.

"Do you really believe that?" Evelyn said.

"I didn't cut near an artery. It isn't dangerous."

Evelyn waved her hand dismissively. "Any cutting is dangerous. If you can't control your self-destructive impulses, you need to be in the hospital."

"I thought that's where I was," Simone joked and glanced at Jun to see if he appreciated her humor, but he wasn't smiling and neither was Evelyn.

"Inpatient," Evelyn said.

"I don't need that. I didn't cut myself *badly.*"

"Can you guarantee us that you will not cut yourself tonight?" Evelyn asked.

Simone's throat constricted so she could barely utter a "yes."

"You need to understand," Evelyn said, pointing her finger at Simone as if to pin her. "We can't work with you if you keep cutting. It's like an alcoholic. Treatment when she's drunk is pointless."

Evelyn was calling her a drunk; the very word made Simone recoil.

"If you keep cutting, we'll kick you out. Do you understand?"

"Yes."

"If you feel like cutting yourself at night, any night, call," Jun said, handing her a card.

In that brief moment before she read the embossed print, Simone thought Jun was handing her his number, his personal number. Her heart fluttered. Then she read the words CRISIS HOTLINE, embossed in bold black letters. She blushed.

"I can't give you my home number," Jun said, unsettling her.

"I don't *want* your number," she said.

He pulled back, and she felt bad for snapping at him, felt certain he'd never want her now. When they said she could go it seemed like someone else's feet took her to the kitchen, where several members immediately surrounded her.

"They kick you out?" Viola asked.

"No." Simone forced a smile.

"Good. Woulda told 'em I be quitting too," Regina said.

"Well, you're going to have to put up with my ugly white face for a while longer."

Satch shook her head in mock disgust.

"You ain't ugly," Regina said. "You want ugly, look here." She pointed to herself.

"I don't see ugly. I see a really big heart."

"Damn, girl, you blind." Regina put her hand to her mouth, but she couldn't hide her smile.

In drama that afternoon Jun dumped out a bag of various colored swatches of fabric and asked everyone to pick out one and talk to it, to say whatever came up. The fabric could be a particular person or just a good listener.

Regina chose a piece of brown velvet and pressed it to her cheek. "I want a man," she said. "Want a man to hold me. Ain't never had that. Only man I ever knowed was my stepdaddy."

With each word, Regina's voice got smaller, younger, and it seemed to Simone that she got smaller, too, that Regina wasn't a fat woman but a little one encased in an enormous prison.

"Ain't none of y'all never gonna love me. Know I'm fat and ugly. But I'm so lonely. Don't care if you fat and ugly too. Just want you to love me."

Regina sat beside Simone. How different they were, Simone thought. How very much alike.

Viola picked orange rayon and talked to Aisha, her daughter, about how much she missed her; her words were spattered with tears. Marvin, eyes on his bears more than the purple fabric he'd chosen, told his grandmother that he was sorry for all the trouble he'd caused. Willy addressed a scarlet material that represented his girlfriend, repeating again and again that she was "fine."

"Satch?" Jun said.

Satch selected a swatch of shiny gold rayon. "Hi, baby," she said. "You know I love you."

Simone could barely hear her.

"Thing is..." Satch began. "Please don't hit me no more."

Simone wanted to shake her; Satch should be shouting, not using a voice that sounded as fragile as a bee's wings. "But Satch—"

Jun held up his hand. "Drama's different from small groups. It's important to give people the opportunity to express something they're feeling without having to worry about others' reactions. You can ask for feedback, but you don't have to. Satch, why don't you continue."

"Don't got nothing more to say."

"You sure?"

"Yeah."

"Okay. Simone?"

She selected a piece of camouflage fabric, determined to show Satch how it was done. "I was just wondering if you had any idea what you did to me when you raped me," she said, standing and staring down at the material. "I mean, I imagine you enjoyed it, but I didn't. I really didn't. I told myself it was no big deal, I don't know why, but it was. It was a huge deal." She was proud of her level, reasoning tone. She was sure Satch and Jun and everyone else would be impressed.

"I have to tell you," she continued, "the whole thing with the roses and saying you could love me and all, that was really brilliant. But do you have any idea how demeaned I feel now? I started cutting myself after that. Not that you'd care. You'd probably be glad. But I feel sorry for you. You are one pathetic excuse for a man." There; that was how it was done.

"Anything else?" Jun said.

"I think that pretty much says it all."

"Shit," Satch said, "sound like you talking about pancakes."

"You don't have to shout to express yourself," Simone said.

"Do you want to discuss this?" Jun asked.

She felt finished. "No."

"Okay. Rick?"

Rick didn't say a word. He stood, rising to his full six-foot-three inch frame, selected a black piece of fabric with silver moons and gold stars, and stomped on it, kicking it around the room, then wadded it up and threw it against the wall again and again.

"Very powerful," Jun said when Rick sat. "You made your feelings quite clear. Do you want to talk about what caused your anger?"

"It doesn't matter now," Rick said. "It happened a

long time ago." He put his hand to his neck as if to pet his snakes.

"Talking about it might help," Jun said.

"Talking only makes it worse."

Something in Rick's anger, in his walls, sounded a chord in Simone. "If you ever do want to talk, I'd be happy to listen."

He scrunched the fabric in his hands.

When drama ended, Simone approached Satch. "I'm sorry I didn't tell you instead of cutting this weekend. Do you want to stay with me tonight?"

"Don't got nowhere else to go."

After closing comments, a new member began talking fast to Jun. Simone walked on outside with Satch into the blare of the afternoon sun. A tall man stepped toward them carrying a bouquet of lavender roses: Thomas. He handed the flowers to Satch.

"Hi, baby," he said. "I've been missing you."

The sun went behind a cloud. Simone hoped Satch would ram those flowers into his fucking face!

But she didn't. Satch just stood there staring at him, at the flowers. Viola grabbed Satch's arm and tried to lead her toward the car, but Satch pulled away.

"Let's go, Satch," Simone urged.

"I'm sorry, baby." Thomas got down on one knee and took Satch's hand. "I don't know what got into me. I didn't mean to hurt you."

Satch just kept standing there.

"This is bullshit!" Simone shouted. "He's going to do it again!"

He kept his eyes on Satch, pleading. "I can't live without you, baby. I'm never gonna lift a finger against you again."

"How can you believe this crap?" Simone asked. "He's said it before. I know he has, just like Muslimah said."

"Come on home with me, baby. Forgive me. You know I love you."

"He's got a great way of showing it," Simone said.

Thomas kept looking at Satch.

Satch kept staring at Thomas. Simone dug a compact from her purse and thrust the mirror at Satch so she could see the remnants of Thomas's love on her face. "Look at his love."

Satch knocked Simone's hand away. The compact sailed out of it and thunked against the concrete. Simone retrieved it; the mirror had shattered. Thomas pulled Satch to him. They kissed. A carload of passing strangers honked and whooped. When Thomas released her, Satch turned to Simone with a sheepish smile, mumbled thanks, told Viola they'd give her a ride, and allowed herself to be led away, Viola walking silently beside her.

"You can't make Satch leave Thomas." Jun moved in front of her.

"She deserves so much better."

"So do you."

Simone closed the compact. She didn't want to see her mutilated image in the fractured glass. It was too tempting.

"You need to affirm your contract. And mean it. Promise me you'll be safe tonight."

Simone glanced into his soft eyes and remembered Meghan and the dinner they were to share that evening. With Evan out of town, she could stay with Meghan if need be. Just the idea filled Simone with relief. "I'm visiting a friend. I'll be fine." She would tell Meghan about the rape and Meghan would help her understand why she'd told everyone—especially herself—it was no big deal.

Simone picked up her pace to her green Echo, which was parked in front of a stop sign. She smiled at the thought of its perfect symbolism: from now on she would stop hiding, especially from herself.

FOURTEEN

Meghan flung open the door to her Tudor-style house before Simone could knock. "It's so good to see you!" She grabbed Simone's hand, pulled her inside and embraced her tightly. "I've really missed you!"

What had possessed Simone to think she wanted to discard the one person in her life who knew her, really knew her, the one person with whom she'd shared so much? "I've missed you, too," she said.

Hands on Simone's shoulders, Meghan surveyed her. Simone was surprised to see that her friend was developing a small paunch.

"You look a little thin," Meghan said.

Her face struck Simone as fuller than she remembered. Meghan's customary red scarf and matching earrings set off her blonde hair.

"Are you eating enough?" Meghan asked.

"I'm fine. How are you?" Exuberant is how Meghan looked, Simone thought, an exuberance that couldn't be explained just by their reconciliation.

"I'm pregnant!" Meghan exulted.

The news froze Simone. Meghan was pregnant, while she in all likelihood never would be. She chided herself for her jealousy. This wasn't about her. She needed to be happy for her friend. "That's great! How far along are you?"

"Four months. I didn't want to say anything before the end of the first trimester, didn't want to jinx my baby. And then you... Come on."

Meghan led her down the hall scented with cinnamon potpourri to a pink nursery that could practically contain Simone's whole home. "It's a girl. I'm so excited!"

Simone had long fantasized introducing a daughter to oranges sucked through peppermint sticks and anemones that closed on touch. Now Meghan—five years younger, married—would live out Simone's dreams.

"Look at these." Opening a closet big enough for Simone to sleep in, Meghan took out a host of baby outfits: cotton, pastel, soft, adorable.

"They're really cute," Simone said. "You've got a lot already."

"I'm just getting started. I wanted to be sure of the gender. I'm thrilled it's a girl. The next one can be a boy."

A white bear on top of a dresser made Simone think of Marvin.

"Aren't these the most precious things you've ever seen?" Meghan set a pair of tiny blue tennis shoes into the palm of Simone's hand, shoes so light Simone could blow them away. She pictured a foot little enough to fit. They made her chest tight.

"Yikes. Dinner." Meghan hurried to the spacious kitchen, the counters tiled in various earth tones.

The aroma of curry tantalized Simone, and her mouth watered. Her hunger surprised her. Now that she was here, seeing Meghan so absorbed in her pregnancy, she couldn't imagine bringing up her rape.

Meghan served a stir-fry dish of curried chicken, onions, raisins, and snow peas. They sat down at the kitchen table in a nook with a bay window overlooking a sparkling pool. Thanks to Evan's high salary, Meghan was living in the house Satch had expected Simone to have. She could just hear Satch drawing out the vowels: *Woman got her own swimming pool. Got a closet big enough for a party. Shit.* Simone took a bite. The food made her tongue sizzle and she gulped milk.

"Oh no," Meghan said. "Too hot?"

"It's delicious," Simone said. Wary of burning her throat, she consumed each bite of stir-fry with milk, though she would probably float her insides with this dinner.

After she'd detailed two ultrasounds, Evan's enthusiasm, their plans for the nursery and her decision to take a leave from teaching to be with their daughter, Meghan paused in mid-bite. "So what's new with you?"

"Nothing really."

"Are you sure you're eating enough?"

"I'm fine."

"Are you...hurting yourself?"

"No. I stopped." She had really; Sunday had been an aberration.

"Good. How was your weekend with that woman from the hospital?"

"Satch. Fine."

Meghan sipped her milk. "What are the other patients like?"

"They're"—uneasy with her friend's tone, Simone searched for the right word—"troubled."

"Well, I'm sure you can help them."

Simone remembered her group that morning, all those eyes reflecting her own pain, their insights about her. "It's not like that."

"Like what?"

She realized that Meghan was as unaware of her underlying assumptions as Simone had been after her first visit to Oakhill, when she was convinced she had nothing in common with the other members. "They help me, too."

"Good," Meghan said, but she didn't look as if she believed it.

Simone forced herself to eat more of the stir-fry. The curry tasted hotter with every bite. "May I?" She held up her empty glass of milk.

"Since when did you have to ask?"

Simone refilled her glass.

"Seeing you with that woman made Kathleen wonder if you were getting worse, but I told her you're a rescuer, which you are, and that you were just helping the woman out. But I hope you're not going to hang out with her. It's lucky none of the parents from school saw you. You know what this community is like."

Simone took a long swig of milk. She didn't want to do anything to increase Kathleen's doubts—or Meghan's, for that matter. Her job had been much of her life for fifteen years and she wanted it back. But Satch had needed her help. What was she supposed to do, just leave Satch at Thomas's mercy? Of course, given that Satch had gone off with him again that afternoon, she wasn't sure what the point of helping her had been.

"I've been thinking about this a lot." Meghan fiddled with one earring. "What made you start hurting yourself?"

Relieved her friend had broached the subject, Simone wished she'd confided in Meghan three months ago when she first started cutting. "I was raped."

"Oh my god, Simone! I'm so sorry!" Meghan reached across the table and took Simone's hand. "When?"

"January."

"And you never told me?"

"I was ashamed."

"Why?" Meghan gently squeezed Simone's hand. "Rape isn't the woman's fault."

"I just..."

"Who did it?" Meghan's eyes brimmed with caring.

"Spence."

"Spence?"

"The man I met through Match.com."

Meghan looked like she was trying to remember something. "The one I warned you about?"

Meghan had advised her to drive to a public place to meet him, not get in the car with a complete stranger, but his emails and phone calls had disarmed her. She wished she could convey Spence's appeal so that Meghan could understand. So that she could. "He was tender and witty. And he was a good listener, unlike most of the men I've dated. He seemed like a wonderful man."

"Have the police caught him?"

Simone averted her eyes.

"You did go to the police?"

The chicken was darkened by the spices; her cheeks burned like they, too, were coated with curry.

Meghan released her hand. "Why not?"

"I... It's complicated." How could she explain to Meghan what she didn't understand herself?

"What's complicated about rape?"

Simone looked out the window at the pool, its surface unmarred by ripple or leaf. No matter what she said, Meghan was not going to understand.

"I don't get it." Meghan's face reflected her confusion. "Why didn't you report him? He may be raping someone else while we sit here."

She hadn't even thought of that. What a fool she'd been! She had to resist the impulse to seize the knife beside her plate and cut.

"We can go to the police tonight. I'll go with you. Maybe they can track him down through his emails."

"It's too late."

"What do you mean?"

"I called him back."

Rape, officer? The bitch wanted another date.

"After—?" Meghan put her hand protectively on top of her stomach

Shame engulfed her. "He apologized. I believed him."

"Are you saying you were willing to go out with him again?"

"His phone was disconnected."

Meghan leaned back in her chair, eyebrows arched, appalled.

"I just want someone to love me," Simone said.

Meghan didn't say anything else for a long time. Neither of them did. Despite the abundance of food still on her plate, Simone no longer felt hungry. She kept stabbing pieces of chicken with her fork.

"It's still rape," Meghan finally said. "But maybe the best thing you can do now is to forget about it, to move past it. You can't change it."

Trying to forget about her pain was like using a dry-board eraser on permanent ink. It didn't even smear her memories, let alone wipe them away.

"It doesn't do any good to dwell on the bad things in life," Meghan went on. "My miscarriages devastated me—"

"Wait a minute. Miscarriages?" Simone's fork clanked against the plate. "You never told me you'd miscarried."

Meghan folded her arms over her stomach. "Well I did, twice, but if I'd dwelled on them I never would have gotten pregnant again."

"My god, Meghan. How could you keep that from me?"

"The same way you didn't mention your rape."

Her urge to cut overwhelming, Simone stood.

"What are you doing?"

"I have to go."

"But I made you brownies. Your favorite."

"Good-bye."

Meghan stood. "I'm sorry if I… I only want what's best for you."

"I know." Simone started toward the door.

"Call me," Meghan said as Simone stepped outside. "We can go shopping for baby toys. Retail therapy might be just what you need."

Keeping her back to Meghan, Simone waved and got in her car. She turned on the ignition and pressed the accelerator, driving down the street carefully, slowly. Her mind raced. Meghan had hidden two miscarriages. She had hidden her rape. What kind of friendship did they have? And was Spence even now raping someone else? By not going to the police, she'd left him free to prey.

She turned into the parking lot of a convenience store, didn't want to wait until she got home to cut. Inside, she searched odorless aisles—products covered in cellophane, like Meghan's world. Toward the back of the store came the prepared foods section with its stink of cheap coffee, nachos with fake cheese, and greasy doughnuts. Satch liked doughnuts.

Searching the ends of aisles, Simone found the blades on the third row back among health aids, which seemed an odd place for razor blades to be stocked because she couldn't imagine how shaving improved your health. She picked up the only remaining box of single-edged blades, a small blue box, just what she needed. She closed her fingers around it, felt the hard ridged plastic.

Jun would see this as a betrayal, but if Satch could betray everyone who cared about her, so could she. But Jun would be able to tell and maybe Satch would, too. Evelyn would kick her out. Cutting would revert to a daily routine. Or worse. She set the box back on the shelf and rushed from the store.

In her car she debated her options. If she went home, the lure of cutting—the means to do it whispering to her from her linen closet—might seduce her. It wasn't safe. She turned on the motor and started driving without knowing where she was going. She drove through the small community of Talaveras and on to the rolling hills that bordered it.

A sliver moon rose—so thin, so lovely—and as she studied it, she remembered a distant night. She'd been maybe seven or eight. Her parents were going out, and she sneaked out of the house and hurried to their brown Mercury parked in front. Heaven was supposed to be a happy place, she'd thought, and she wasn't happy on earth so why not go ahead and get to heaven? In the street she positioned her small body up against one of the tires. She lay in the dark waiting for her parents to come out and start the car, for the car to crush her. The minutes dragged by. Rocks from the road bit into her. She smelled the newly mown grass her father had cut that afternoon. Her mother had caught her masturbating a few days before and told her she would go to hell if she kept it up. If she died, she suddenly realized, she might go to hell rather than heaven. Scared, she got out from under the car, convinced she'd have to repent first so she didn't end up in hell.

Simone tightened her hold on the wheel and tried to remember what had made her so miserable. What she remembered was her mother baking her brownies and her father teaching her to ride a bike. Whatever had prompted her to think of suicide that night eluded her. It must have been a fleeting impulse because she didn't remember any similar moments. She wished she understood what had sent her in front of her parents' car and why she hadn't gone to the police and how she'd convinced herself her rape had been no big deal—wondered, too, what other lies she believed. She drove on through the darkness, the headlights of oncoming cars glaring off her dirt-smeared windshield.

Fifteen

"I was wondering whether most children at some point consider suicide. You know, I think I'll ask Santa for a bike. I think I'll kill myself." Simone glanced around at the other members in the dimly lit room. Nobody smiled.

"Why do you ask?" Jun said.

His peace earring made her feel safe. "When I was about seven, I laid down in front of my parents' car, hoping they'd run over me."

"Why you do that?" Satch asked.

"I don't know." Someone in the room smelled of talcum powder, and she thought with regret of Meghan and Meghan's baby.

"What happened?" Regina said, bunching up the fabric of her orange muumuu.

"I changed my mind."

"Seven?" Viola said. "You were just a baby."

The tenderness in Viola's voice made Simone yearn to be held. "Did any of you think about suicide when were you were little?"

"Naw," Satch said. "Murder maybe."

"Wasn't your mama good to you?" Marvin asked.

"She was. I had a great mother. All my friends envied me."

"How about your daddy?" Regina said.

"He was wonderful, too. He treated me like a princess."

Satch looked exasperated. "So why you try to kill yourself?"

She turned her palms up to emphasize her uncertainty. "Damned if I know. I don't even know if I did. Maybe I just thought I remembered it. Can you make up memories?" She looked at Jun.

"Yes. You can bury them, too."

"How do you know which is which?'

"It's tricky. My guess is there's an emotional truth to the memory, whether it's factual or not."

"An emotional truth?"

"That you felt a lot of despair as a child, at least at some point."

Despair isn't what she recalled. She wished she hadn't brought this up, because it made her uneasy.

"I hate my mama!" screamed Lonnie from the adjoining room. "I'm gonna kill myself!"

She wondered if he'd tried. Lonnie seemed like someone who would use too flimsy a rope or stick his head in an *electric* range.

"What's coming up for you?" Jun said.

She didn't want to think about suicide any more, so she told them about Meghan's pregnancy and concealed miscarriages, Meghan's horror at her failure to report her rape, her invitation to retail therapy.

"Sound like you need new friends." Satch shook out her broad shoulders as if she was readying herself for a fight.

"She's been my best friend for the past fifteen years."

"Don't mean you gotta be friends for fifteen more."

"She just wants me to be happy."

Satch rolled her eyes. "You happy last night when you was with her?"

"It was my own fault. I should've called the police. What if he rapes someone else?"

"Ain't your fault. You ain't raping nobody. Sound like she don't understand being lonely."

If Satch knew Meghan had advised Simone not to be seen with her, Satch would be even more hostile to Meghan.

"She said you needed retail therapy?" Viola said.

"She was just trying to cheer me up. She thought I should go shopping with her. That's what friends do for each other."

"Uh-huh."

"Maybe Meghan wasn't totally sensitive, but she's just excited about her baby."

"She as sensitive as a hamburger," Satch said, her voice flat and certain as if she were stating something indisputable, like that the sun was shining. "'Sides, she ain't told you about no miscarriage. You ain't told her about no rape. Don't sound like friends."

"Did you consider hurting yourself?" Jun asked.

"Yes, but I didn't."

"You might want to think about your friendship," he said. "At least wait to see her again until you're more stable."

Simone's head hurt. She hadn't slept well, hadn't gone home until past midnight. She glanced at her watch, relieved to see it was time for someone else's group, and decided she'd think about all this later. She wished she'd worn a jacket. She wanted to zip herself up to keep her thoughts—and her memories—from spilling out.

After a volleyball game that ended in a tie, Simone wandered over to Regina and Viola's table. Satch joined them, perspiration glistening on her forehead. She wiped it off with her sleeve.

The sun shone down unusually strong for early May. Simone thought she could hear her sweat sizzle.

"I wanna be with a man tonight," Regina said. "Don't wanna be alone. But that ain't never gonna happen."

"Never know," Satch said. "Lotta men like big women."

"And big hearts," Simone said.

"Only time I don't feel big is when I'm dancing. No man gonna end up in my bed, but I dance real good. Always somebody wants to dance with me when I'm getting down. What you say? Wanna go dancing?"

"I can't," Viola said. "I got to watch my babies."

"I don't dance," Simone said.

"What you scared of?" Satch said.

Surprised Satch could tell it was a question of fear, Simone said, "Looking ridiculous, I guess."

"Girl, *not* dancing's ridiculous."

"Not necessarily. I make Frankenstein's monster look like Fred Astaire."

"Music make you feel good." Regina crossed her arms in certainty.

"You right," Satch said. "Thomas got tonight off. Man dance just as sweet as he play his sax."

"Gonna make an announcement at closing," Regina said. "Smooth Jackie's. Downtown. Gotta go tell Marvin." Regina left.

"You coming?" Satch said.

Simone started to shake her head no.

"Can't just hang around dreaming about—what you say you call him? Tweety Bird?"

Was she that that obvious?

"Man's a therapist. Probably think blabbing be foreplay. When you in bed, fixing to make love, want your man to be sweet talking, like"—Satch dropped her voice— "'oh baby, you feel good.' Jun be, 'What's coming up for you today?'"

If they were in bed together, Simone thought, she'd hope Jun would be the one with something coming up.

"Tell you what," Satch said. "You and me gonna do a little shopping when we leave here. Get you some of that retail therapy. If you gonna go dancing, you need something new. Know what I'm saying? I know just the place. We gonna look hot tonight."

Dim lights barely lit a small, gloomy shop. Clothes racks were crammed together, many items on them stuffed in the wrong size categories. Pants and blouses littered the threadbare carpet. The store smelled like someone had spilled cheap perfume. It was a long way from what Meghan had in mind.

Simone shoved clothes away from a slate blue blouse so she could get a good look at it. The blue was a great color for her eyes, but it was a small. Too tight.

"That look good," Satch said, joining her, a purple outfit slung over her arm.

"Too small."

"No it ain't. Problem is you wear clothes two of you could fit in. Try it on. Go real good with your eyes."

"No thanks."

Satch curled her lip in disgust. "Girl, you don't got no idea how to dress."

"Did you find anything?"

"Yeah. Ain't gonna try on nothing I don't gotta push my way into. You oughta do the same."

"I'll just wear something I already own." She couldn't afford to buy anything anyway, though the prices were a lot less than Macy's.

"Here." Satch took a red Spandex jumpsuit off the rack and thrust it at Simone. "Try this on. Look real good with your hair and the body you got. Come on."

Simone followed her to the single fitting room. She'd let Satch go first. When it was her turn, she'd pretend to try on the jumpsuit. Spandex? She'd sooner wear an umbrella.

"How many do you have?" said a young clerk with multiple body rings: clusters on each ear, one through a nostril, one through an eyebrow, one through her lip, a stud through her tongue.

How did the girl ever get past a metal detector? "You can go first," Simone told Satch.

"Naw. We gonna share."

"Share?"

"Come on."

The dressing room would barely fit a small poodle. She hung back.

"Come on, girl," Satch said again.

The lone clothes hook already held a full load of someone else's rejects. Satch draped them over the curtain pole and put the clothes she'd selected on the hook. She glanced toward the main room. "Girl oughta wear rings on her fingers, not her face. Look like she hate herself."

"Shh," Simone said, finger over her lips. "She might hear you."

"Naw. She ain't close. White folks worry too much." Satch unzipped her pants. "What you waiting for?"

Simone turned her back to Satch, pressed as far from her as possible, kept her eyes averted, wondered if she did worry too much, if she was too inhibited, and took off her pants and blouse. Their bodies occasionally bumped. In the classroom she wasn't inhibited. During her unit on describing sensory details, she tap danced on her desk, challenging her students to describe the sound.

"Your scars fading," Satch said.

She glanced at her thighs. Satch was right. It had been a while since she cut them. Many of the lines had disappeared, while the most recent were only faint. She found herself hoping that all her scars would fade away.

"Here." Satch handed her the red Spandex jumpsuit. Simone felt like she was struggling into a wetsuit.

"*Your mother's fat,*" her father had told her. Simone tried to recall how old she'd been. Twelve? Thirteen? She'd noticed her mother's weight gain over the preceding years, from what must have been a size ten to a sixteen, and had promised herself never to gain that kind of weight.

When she had the outfit on, she and Satch stood side by side in front of the small mirror. Satch zipped up purple pants and a blouse that fit her so tight they emphasized every wrinkle, fold, and bump of her body.

"Purple's a good color for you," Simone said.

Satch ran her hand over her purple velour clothes. "Thomas gonna love this. When we getting down to it, man grab me and hold me and I know I'm looking good, and I be feeling fine. Tight clothes show a man what he's got to look forward to. Way you dress in them big clothes don't show a man nothing. When you got it, show it, and girl, you got it."

Facing the mirror, Simone tried to see herself as Satch did. Since Spence she'd dressed to hide her breasts. The jumpsuit hid nothing. To the contrary. Her breasts bulged while her waist, her best feature, was small. Naked her thighs seemed fat, but the Spandex tightened them, made her bottom half slimmer. She owned nothing remotely similar to this outfit.

"You looking good."

Simone ran her hands over her waist and down her slender-ized hips. If it were someone else's reflection she would undoubtedly agree. Maybe Satch was right.

"Gonna get it?"

She studied her image, trying to determine what she was seeing, what she was really seeing, imagined Jun and then Michael glimpsing her in this outfit, looking at her with desire.

Satch looked back in the mirror, put her hands on her hips, tilted her head and smiled. "Uh-huh. My man gonna love this."

As she entered Smooth Jackie's, Simone pulled at the clinging Spandex, just as she saw Satch and Thomas dancing to a blues song. His hands were all over Satch's butt, pulling her so close she was the flap to his envelope. Eyes closed, arms around her abuser, dressed in her new purple outfit, Satch looked the picture of bliss. It was almost enough to make Simone scream.

Jackie's large rectangular dance floor was flanked on three sides by tables. The walls were a surprising pastiche of Greek classic murals, while the club reeked of alcohol, perfume, and sweat. A deejay wearing sunglasses and an A's cap sat atop a red-carpeted stage. The music changed to rap. The dancers, most in their twenties and thirties, wore a wide range of clothes, many in vibrant colors like flamingo pink.

"Hi, Simone!" Marvin danced with one of his teddy bears. He waved, beaming, whirled off the dance floor, and waltzed Katrina amid the tables. Several people cast disparaging glances his way. A stocky man lurched up and bumped into Marvin, sending both of them sprawling to the floor.

Simone hastened to the collision. "Crazy motherfucker," the stocky man said as he got to his feet, brushing himself off.

Simone moved between the man and Marvin. "Sounds like you have some self-esteem issues," she said. "I know a good therapist."

The man turned away, muttering.

Marvin remained on all fours, groping with his hands in the darkened room, searching for Katrina. Simone saw the bear, helped Marvin rise, then dusted off Katrina and returned her to Marvin's arms.

He scurried to a table, hiding his face in his arms. Simone sat beside him. "Is Katrina okay?" she asked.

Marvin nodded.

"You two dance divinely."

He raised his head and gave a brief smile, the corners of his lips flitting up and retracting back like the flaring of a match.

The deejay announced a short cigarette break and invited smokers to join him outside. Regina danced over to the table, moving as smoothly as a slinky toy, followed by the dreadlocked Willy.

"All right," Regina called as she saw Simone, giving her a high five, revealing the dark circles of sweat on the underarms of her brightly flowered shirt. She sat down and took a big drink of Coke.

The others greeted her. Willy offered Katrina a sip of his Budweiser.

"She don't drink," Marvin said.

"No, but she sure do dance," Willy told him. Marvin gave a shy smile.

Satch and Thomas walked up holding hands and grinning at each other like teenagers in love. Thomas wore all black—tight black leather pants, a tight black T-shirt. The earring in his left ear, a black-and-white yin-yang symbol, surprised and then irritated Simone. She liked the earring, and didn't want anything to blur the clarity of her hatred for him.

"How you doing?" Thomas said to her, smiling as he nonchalantly sipped the Johnny Walker Red a tired-looking waitress served him.

"Fine."

"You looking good." Thomas smiled like he was paying her a sincere compliment, his eyes lingering on her breasts.

"You fixing to dance?" Satch said.

"She gonna dance the next one," Regina said. "Right?"

"I don't dance. I trip."

"Got to dance," Marvin said. "It's a dance club."

"He's right," Thomas said. "Doesn't matter how you dance. You just got to grab on to the music and move."

Satch massaged Thomas's neck while he spoke, her eyes darting from him to Simone and back to him.

Simone smelled his whiskey and remembered other men, former lovers, drinking whiskey, remembered nights spent barhopping though she drank only Coke, nights when she'd had to help lovers up stairs because they were too drunk to walk. Alcoholics. Many of the men she'd dated were alcoholics. She suddenly knew that, and was overwhelmed by her willful blindness, hiding from the truth even as drunken lovers vomited in the toilet. She wondered if that was at least partly why she wasn't married, because she'd ended up with so many alcoholics who couldn't commit to anything beyond the next drink. If she had a year back for every man she'd dated who drank excessively, she'd be an egg in her mother's womb.

She fast forwarded through her two years with Michael, scanning for scenes of inebriation. She recalled only one, though he usually smoked a joint before sitting down to write. That was different; it didn't incapacitate him, just made the creative juices flow, or so he'd claimed. She wondered if he still smoked pot, and if he'd changed his mind about calling her.

Thomas had finished off a couple whiskeys by the time the deejay came back and put on a rap song.

"Dance with Thomas," Satch said, pushing Simone out of her seat and toward him.

Thomas danced in front of her to the pulsing of the song, pantomiming slow-motion punches. Some of the men around them danced with their fists up; most held their hands flat, fingers separated and punctuating the beat.

Her body felt stiff, awkward. Thomas grabbed her around the waist and clasped her to him, her breasts against his chest. He moved her around the floor, their close embrace at odds with the music and the other dancers. She remained rigid, but had to admit that on a very simple level, it felt good to be held by a man.

The song stopped. Thomas's muscles slackened. She tried to get loose. A new song boomed from the speakers, and Thomas pulled her to him again. She pushed against his chest to free herself. He held her tighter.

"Let me go," she said. Her voice was drowned out by the music.

Simone put her hands on Thomas's arms and shoved. He lifted her feet from the floor.

"Oh baby, you feel good," he crooned.

The music finally ended and Thomas released her. She felt like someone was coiling her insides. Without a word or a final glance, Thomas strolled back toward the others. Simone wanted to run from the room. She hadn't done anything wrong, not really, but she felt a smothering sense of guilt.

She walked slowly back to the table where Satch sipped a beer. Still standing, Thomas put his arms around Satch, who tried to pull away.

"You want that white woman, she yours," Satch hissed.

Simone stopped.

Thomas laughed. "I was just messing with you, woman. No way I want that skinny white bitch. Come on. I need my woman. Give me something to hold on to."

Thomas pulled Satch to her feet.

Simone was in their path. "I didn't..." she began.

Satch and Thomas walked around her toward the dance floor, hand in hand, as if she didn't exist, already moving to the beat.

Reeling, Simone sat back down at the table, trying to understand what had happened. Regina and Marvin watched her.

"I didn't..." She hadn't come on to Thomas, but she felt as guilty as if she had. If only she hadn't worn the Spandex.

"This ain't about you."

"Why does she stay with him?"

"Don't know," Regina said, "but the man ain't your business. Go on home. By tomorrow, she ain't gonna care."

The music seemed even more discordant to her and she wanted to cry.

"Baby-sit Katrina tonight?" Marvin asked, holding the bear out to her. "She's lonesome for female company."

Simone buried her face in the bear's fur, using it to stop her tears.

Sixteen

When Simone walked through the gate at Oakhill the next morning, dressed in her most oversized shirt, the sun blinded her. Sitting at a table with Viola, Satch raised her voice, no doubt for Simone's benefit. "Gotta keep your eyes on white women. They steal your man if you let 'em. Guess white men got little dicks. That's why they want ours."

"That's right, girl," someone said.

Simone hoped to make Satch realize the truth. "You pushed him at me."

"Don't hear nothing but the sun shining," Satch said.

"I tried to get away."

"That sun mighty loud."

Gut coiled, Simone handed Katrina to Marvin and went on in. For general meeting she waited until Satch was seated, then took a chair as far from her as she could. Evelyn announced that Jun wouldn't be in. Disappointed, Simone kept her eyes on the floor.

Regina came to the group Simone had reluctantly called with Evelyn. She needed to talk about the dance. Willy came, too, as did Viola, Marvin, and, surprisingly, Rick. To her relief, Satch did not. The bright light in the small room bounced off beige walls; it seemed like a set-up for interrogation, not therapy, whatever that was. Folks blabbing, as Satch would say.

Simone's gut knotted. For the hundredth time she regretted going dancing.

"What's going on for you today?"

Evelyn's eyes seemed as piercing as the lights. Simone told her about her experiences at the dance club, how she hadn't wanted to keep dancing with Thomas, and how much she regretted making Satch angry.

"You seem to run a lot on guilt," Evelyn said.

"Only when I'm guilty."

"What exactly were you guilty of?"

"Enjoying Thomas at first. Betraying Satch."

"Betrayal is a harsh word." Evelyn's thin lips were taut, like wire. "And it involves intent. Did you intend to enjoy dancing with Thomas?"

She hadn't intended anything. And she'd only briefly enjoyed his arms around her. "No."

"Tell me," Evelyn said, "were you angry with anyone last night?"

"Of course. Thomas."

"Who else?"

She replayed the events in her mind. True, she'd have liked to dump a tall beer over the man who'd insulted Marvin, but she didn't want to embarrass Marvin by bringing it up. "Nobody."

"Come on, Simone. There's not one other person you're mad at?" Evelyn thrust her head forward as if to batter down Simone's defenses.

"Maybe the oil-company CEOs."

"Stop it!" Evelyn's voice cut sharp. "Stop trying to make jokes. Who else are you angry with?"

"You tell me. Obviously you can read minds."

"Satch."

"That's ridiculous. She was right. I should never have danced with Thomas."

"Satch push Thomas at you," Regina said. "Wasn't like you stole the man."

Regina was right, but the one clear image Simone had was of Satch's scowling face.

"You seem to be consistently unwilling to confront Satch," Evelyn said, settling back in her chair like she was preparing for a prolonged stay. "Why is that?"

"Because it just makes her angry. I want to help Satch, not piss her off."

"And you see it as your job to help her?"

"I like Satch. Of course I want to help her."

"But why should fixing her be up to you?"

"I'm not trying to fix her. Like I said, I just want to help her."

Evelyn smiled that superior smile, almost a smirk, that made Simone want to slap her. "For an English teacher, you seem to like to hide behind semantics."

Simone leaned further back in her chair. "I hide wherever I can."

"So I've noticed." Evelyn's eyes swept over Simone. "There's something we can't let go any longer. The staff has expressed concern about your weight."

Simone wondered if "the staff" meant Jun, if he thought she was skinny.

"Just how well are you eating?"

She put her hand to her belt, feeling her waistband beneath her shirt where Evelyn couldn't see. Her pants were loose, very loose. She smiled.

"Why are you smiling?"

"Because I like being thin."

"There's nothing wrong with thin. But you go way beyond that. You're approaching malnourished. Tell us what you eat on an average day."

She struggled to recall a typical menu. "A half-cup of cereal for breakfast. A small carton of yogurt for lunch. Sometimes for dinner I eat half an English muffin and a serving of vegetables. Sometimes I just eat a couple cartons of yogurt." Even to her, it sounded meager.

"Damn," Regina said. "I oughta be on your diet."

"That's less than half of what you need just to maintain your weight," Evelyn said, her face grim. "You're fading before our eyes. It's almost as if you're trying to disappear."

You don't eat enough to keep a bird alive, Simone's mother used to say. *One of these days you're going to dry up and blow away.* She'd always swelled up at those words, pleased to have her mother's attention.

"So what?" This time she made eye contact with Evelyn.

"You've replaced cutting with starving," Evelyn said. "And you might not even be aware of it. If you keep losing weight, we'll hospitalize you for forced feeding."

"You're joking."

"I couldn't be more serious." Evelyn's lips were set in a line that underscored her words.

"What about Alev? She weighs much less than I do."

"Alev has been hospitalized."

Stunned, Simone realized that she hadn't seen Alev for several days. Her mind struggled to take in Evelyn's words. Hospitalized? She wasn't anywhere near as thin as Alev. She looked into Evelyn's cold green eyes. She needed Jun, his tenderness, his caring. Even if he had to deliver the same message, he'd do it gently, not like a drill sergeant. She wouldn't call another group with Evelyn even if it meant she never opened her mouth at Oakhill again.

"What's going on for you?" Evelyn asked.

Simone was too furious to speak.

"If you're angry with me, say so. You have every right to be mad."

"I don't need you to read me my rights!"

Evelyn smiled. "It's good to hear you get mad at the right person for a change. Our time's up." Evelyn left to go to some duty or other, and Simone stood, anxious to get outside.

Satch blocked the door, her red pants and green shirt like a malfunctioning traffic signal: Stop. Go. Stop.

"Don't you go nowhere," she ordered, standing there in the doorway, her body forming a barricade too massive to detour around. "I got something to say to you."

Simone studied Satch's crimson toenails.

Muslimah came in. Everybody who had been at Simone's group stayed and a few others jammed in, no doubt smelling blood. Shedding her own blood didn't bother Simone. Losing Satch's friendship did.

"Don't want you flirting with Thomas," Satch said. "He's *my* man."

Satch's anger made Simone shrink back. "I didn't flirt. You told me to dance with him." Though her words sounded strong, her voice was little more than a whisper.

Satch studied her through narrowed eyes. "Didn't try much to get away."

"I'm sorry, Satch. He pinned me. I didn't know what to do. You're living with a man who flirts with other women and beats you." She had to convince Satch to leave Thomas. "Maybe you could live with your aunt."

"Don't need advice from somebody who carve on herself." The mole that crowned Satch's upper lip formed a nearly perfect circle.

"But you can do something! You can move away from Thomas. I can't exactly move away from myself."

"Thomas my man. You butt out."

"Simone doesn't hit you," Viola said, startling Satch. "Thomas is who you ought to get mad at, not Simone."

"Thomas ain't here," Satch said to Viola then turned to Simone. "Don't be telling me how to live my life."

"Lunch," someone called from the hallway.

In the kitchen, Viola took the seat next to her. "Satch'll get over it."

Simone hadn't removed the lid on her yogurt, didn't intend to. Fuck lunch.

"You gonna eat that yogurt or choke it to death?" Viola asked.

She offered it to Viola.

"No thanks. I don't eat dairy foods. But you need to eat. Evelyn's right. You're too skinny."

If she took one bite, she was sure she'd vomit. "I'll eat later," she said. After volleyball, after she'd enjoyed the physical release of hitting the ball.

From outside the portable came the sound of a series of small explosions; Viola jerked.

"It's fireworks, I think," Simone said.

Tears began streaming down Viola's cheeks. She gently patted her hands against her face.

"You're safe here," Simone said. "Go ahead and cry." She took one of Viola's hands in hers.

Satch left her seat at the next table and came over to them. "How you doing, girlfriend?" she said to Viola. She didn't even look at Simone.

Simone wondered if she'd ever seen anything as healthy as Viola's tears. She wished she could shed her own, but something inside blocked her tears whenever she felt herself start to cry.

Simone and Satch held on to Viola's hands until Viola straightened, rubbing her eyes. Simone handed her a clean napkin.

"You're getting better, girl," Satch said. "I'm real proud of you."

Viola gave a wan smile. "Thanks," she said to Satch, then turned to Simone. "Thanks a lot."

That afternoon Simone affirmed her contract with Evelyn and headed toward her car, wishing she had somewhere to go and someone to go with.

"You okay?"

Rick was talking to her. Surprised, she said a simple "yes."

"Want to get something to eat?" His dark eyes made brief contact before darting away.

Though she desperately didn't want to be alone, she wasn't sure she wanted to be with Rick, either. He was a big man. The snakes tattooed on his neck underscored a sense of menace.

"We can go to a coffee shop," he said. "You didn't eat lunch. Evelyn said you need to eat more."

Surprised he'd paid attention, she looked at him closely, at his six-foot-plus frame, his rough cheeks that were somewhere between tanned and sunburned. "Okay. I'll take my own car." If he became abusive, she could leave.

They drove separately. As they walked in, the aromas of bacon and hamburger grease scratched her nose. It had been so long since she'd fixed more than yogurt and vegetables. Crumbs of food dotted the floor.

"It's not the Ritz," Rick said.

"It's fine."

They slid into an orange vinyl booth. Colored chalk filled glasses at every table, and colorful children's drawings decorated the walls. She wondered if Viola's children had ever been to this diner, and if so, which pictures they'd drawn.

Rick grabbed two menus. The one he gave her was so sticky with grease, she could practically just eat it. She studied the offerings: bacon and eggs, sausage, hamburgers, hash browns. Nothing appealed to her. "Think I'll just have a glass of orange juice."

"That's not eating. It's drinking. Have some oatmeal or something."

"Do you think I look skinny?"

"I think you look like a prisoner of war."

His eyes pinned her, and she couldn't look away though she urgently wanted to. "I'm just small boned."

"Right."

"Look, those snakes make you look intimidating, but that doesn't mean you go around beating up people."

Rick's face remained impassive. His gray-flecked hair fell over his eyes. "I like to fight, and you are skinny."

She didn't need to hear this crap. She picked up her purse to leave just as a waitress arrived, her pen poised above her order book. *"Cindy, Trainee. Have a nice day,"* her nametag read. Her face was pinched with worry. "Hi!" She greeted them cheerily, like best friends at a school dance. "What can I get for you?"

"BLT and Coke," Rick said.

She scribbled Rick's order and turned to Simone. Much as Simone wanted to, she couldn't just walk out on her. Something in the waitress's eyes resembled the fluttering of a trapped bird. She reminded Simone of students she'd had, and she longed to be back in front of her classroom. She consoled herself with the thought that it was less than a month until she was to see Kathleen about teaching summer school. "I'd like oatmeal and a small orange juice, please."

"Be back in a jiffy," Cindy said.

Rick was silent. Simone glanced around at the other customers. Three children drew animal pictures on the wall with the concentration of Rembrandt while their mother shredded a straw wrapper. Two men wore protective hard-hats. She hoped it wasn't because pieces of the ceiling kept dropping.

She squirmed. The lengthening silence discomforted her. Excusing herself, she went to the dimly-lit bathroom, where graffiti about sex and gangs had been scrawled on dingy walls. She leaned toward a large, chipped mirror and studied her face. Shadows under her eyes were from too little sleep, not too little food. Her brown hair didn't shine like it used to, but that was because scattered gray hairs dulled it. She asked herself if she was skinny, if she was too skinny.

The truth faced her. Evelyn and Rick and maybe Jun were right. She was thin, though not like Alev. Her arms weren't skeletal, but her face was gaunt, her skin slightly stretched. She had to eat more, beginning by putting a ton of whole milk on her oatmeal. For dinner she'd make something caloric, mashed potatoes maybe, with butter and milk and garlic. She would eat more not so much from concern as from desire: she wanted to attract men, not repel them.

Rick was pinching his red-and-white striped straw in alternating squares when she returned to their booth and drained her orange juice without pause.

Cindy set a plate of sausage and eggs in front of Simone, a platter of pancakes in front of Rick.

"These aren't ours," Simone said.

"They aren't?"

"We had oatmeal and a BLT."

"You did?" Reddening, Cindy flipped through her order pad.

"I didn't order this," a woman in the next booth said accusingly, staring at a bowl of oatmeal. Her young son began crying loudly. "That's my eggs and my son's pancakes."

A craggy-faced young man approached. He wore a baggy suit; red sauce stained his white shirt. "What seems to be the problem?"

"Your waitress messed up our orders," the woman said, her son howling.

"Again, Cindy?"

"I'm sorry, Mr. West."

"You must not want this job."

"It's no big deal." Simone passed the sausage and eggs to the woman while Rick gave the pancakes to her son.

Cindy started to set the oatmeal in front of Simone, but she was so nervous she turned it over, spilling the thick oatmeal on the plastic tablecloth. A few hot drops plopped into Simone's lap.

"That's it," the manager said. "You're fired."

Cindy's eyes filled with tears; she fled to the back.

"She's young," Simone said, spooning the oatmeal off her shirt. "Give her a chance to learn."

"She isn't a good waitress."

"You scared her, that's all." Dabbing her napkin into her water glass, she smeared the splotch on her pants.

"I think I know how to run my restaurant."

"But do you know how to be kind?"

"I'll send the busboy to clean up the oatmeal." He turned his back.

She stood. "What's wrong with you? She's just a kid. Give her another chance." She looked around the restaurant at the other customers, most of whom were watching. "Right?"

No one spoke.

"You're disturbing the other diners," the manager said. "I'm going to have to ask you to leave."

"Gladly." She threw three dollars on the table. "For the orange juice."

Rick seemed amused as he slid out from the booth.

"What an asshole!" she said when they stepped outside. "Cindy will be better off working elsewhere."

Rick just smiled.

"What?"

"You defend other people a lot better than you defend yourself."

"What are you talking about?"

"When Satch went after you today, you didn't say hardly anything. Yet you stood up for a waitress you didn't know like she was your sister."

"She didn't do anything to get fired." Maybe she did defend others easier than she defended herself, but wasn't it a good thing to care about other people?

"Did you do anything to make Satch mad? Really?" He rubbed his neck, wrinkling his snakes.

"Satch thought I did. That's what counts."

"Is it?"

"Look, I'm sorry about your sandwich, but I'm going to head home."

"Suit yourself." He turned and walked toward his van.

A green-and-white AC Transit bus rumbled to a stop near them, spewing smoke that reeked of diesel, which made her think the bus was farting.

She walked in the door of her home with a bag of groceries intent on preparing herself a snack, but the flashing light on her message machine diverted her. She pressed the play button.

"Hi, it's Michael."

Her heart thumped.

"I'll be there next Friday, May thirteenth. How about meeting at Laceys at seven? My treat. I'll let you make the reservation."

Simone wished Michael had left his number, and was slightly annoyed he just assumed she'd show up. Still, she felt like her brain was playing cymbals, her toes the xylophone, her heart the timpani, that her whole body had become a veritable orchestra performing the finale of the *1812 Overture*.

Giddy, Simone fixed herself a huge bowl of oatmeal with blueberries, almonds, and honey. Not wanting to risk looking gaunt to Michael, she added a cup of yogurt and began to eat.

Seventeen

Thursday and Friday, Satch ignored Simone, refusing to respond to her greetings. Simone spent a lonely weekend brightened only by Thai food and the prospect of seeing Michael in less than a week.

On Monday she went to Oakhill hopeful Satch would have gotten over her anger. She said a determinedly cheerful hello, but Satch just walked right by her, making Simone feel invisible. Tears filled her eyes. She wanted a friendship with Satch even more than she wanted a date with Jun.

At volleyball the next day Lonnie served by using two arms like a baseball bat, walloping the ball over the trailer roof, bellowing and laughing. While Rick went to retrieve the ball, Jun banished Lonnie from playing for a week. Lonnie went into the main trailer talking rapidly to himself. The game resumed; Simone did her best to focus on the ball rather than Satch. She had just picked up the ball to serve when she heard a loud shout. She looked up to see Lonnie. Naked. His penis was erect, baton-like, a weapon. He raised both fists and gyrated his hips.

Then Jun was shoving Lonnie back toward the trailer door, but Lonnie slipped away from him. Rick tackled him, bringing Lonnie down hard on the asphalt.

Simone turned away, gripping the chain-link fence, picturing Spence looming over her, naked, his penis engorged, his eyes moist, remembered his grasping fingers, his tongue gagging her, the smell of his thick cologne. She stuck her finger down her throat and vomited to clean herself of the filth he planted inside her. Bent over, she tasted bile and half-digested cheese. When she'd finished heaving, she squeezed the fence with trembling fingers until the wire bit into them.

Strong arms encircled her. "I got you."

Satch's arms. Simone rested her cheek against the hot metal of the fence.

"You safe."

Gradually Simone stopped trembling. She released the fence.

"You okay?" Satch said, letting go of her.

"Yeah. Thanks."

Tears threatened. Simone wiped her rough linen sleeve across her eyes.

"Crying a good thing," Satch said.

Simone shook her head. They stood together watching Evelyn spread a blanket over Lonnie, who struggled to free himself as Rick and Jun kept him pinned on the ground. Two paramedics hustled through the gate. One injected something into Lonnie's arm. When he ceased struggling, they lifted him onto a stretcher and carried him away.

"Man crazy when he don't take his meds," Satch said.

"Yeah. Satch, I'm sorry—"

Satch held up her hand. "Don't matter."

"I didn't—"

"Yeah. I know."

Jun walked up to them. "Are you all right?"

"Yeah," Simone said. With Satch's help, she was more than all right.

Satch stayed near Simone through the rest of the day at Oakhill, even walking out the door with her. "Wanna go to Lake Merritt?" Satch asked on the sidewalk outside the hospital. "Say nature make you feel good. Lake Merritt's got birds and shit, but there's buildings, too. About as close to nature as I get."

Simone gladly agreed. They drove separately to the lake, which was beautiful if you ignored the trash on the fringes of the water. Brown splotched the bordering green lawn; the sky was blue. She enjoyed the sun's touch and watched the cormorants and ducks that flocked to the water.

They walked along the lake on a paved path crowded by hikers, joggers, and geese, dodging the frequent dark green streaks of goose droppings.

"I haven't seen this much shit since the last Presidential race," Simone said.

Satch grinned. "Know what you mean."

The passersby were a mix of races and nationalities, a far cry from the typical Talaveras crowd. Two women went by gesticulating wildly and jabbering in a language Simone couldn't identify. She wondered if she would like living in Oakland.

A toddler half-ran, half-stumbled after several geese, which waddled away. A teenager on roller blades skated toward them, blue hair spiked, his black leather vest and bracelet studded with spikes, too. Maybe he was silently crying out to be seen; maybe he was expressing his defiance of an indifferent universe.

"Um-um," Satch said when he'd passed. "What's his mama thinking?"

"Maybe his father has custody," Simone said.

Satch's face assumed a removed expression, like she was seeing something that wasn't there.

"What?" Simone asked.

Satch pulled at the collar of her red shirt. "Thinking about my daddy."

"Is he still alive?"

"Naw. He die when I was five."

"I'm sorry."

Satch's shoulders hunched, like she was troubled. They walked in silence.

"You okay?" Simone said finally.

"Yeah. Reckon I just figured something out."

"What?"

They had to move off the path to avoid a group of rambunctious children in yellow T-shirts that identified them as members of Happy Tyke Preschool.

"Daddy didn't have no college degree. Worked two nasty jobs. Janitor. Seven-Eleven clerk. One boss a white woman like you. Blue eyes. But she blonde. A real bitch. Mama say woman wanted my daddy to fuck her, but he wouldn't. Made him work twelve days without no day off. Daddy got to feeling bad. She wouldn't let him go home. He had a heart attack. Felt like she killed him. Like she took my daddy away."

"I'm so sorry, Satch," Simone said.

"Weren't you. But when you was dancing with Thomas, seemed like you was wanting to fuck my man."

Simone started to say that she'd had no intention of stealing Thomas, but she realized Satch knew that. "That must have felt awful," she said.

"You didn't do nothing. So how come you didn't tell me to stop messing with you?"

"I don't know."

"Shoulda got angry," Satch said.

"You were angry enough for both of us." Simone tried a smile.

"Naw. Got to have your own anger. Got to stand up for your own self."

Simone wondered why she hadn't gotten angry. Thinking back on it, anger would have been a healthier emotion than guilt.

Satch stopped walking and faced Simone. "If it happen again, you tell me I'm fucked. Okay?"

"Okay." Simone wondered if she could.

A man strode toward them, swinging his arms like he was wielding ski poles. Satch watched the man, amused. "Think we oughta tell him it ain't snowing?"

"Only if he tries to snowplow." Simone remembered how happy she'd been skiing with Michael. A thrill went through her. "I've got a big date Friday."

"Who the man?"

"Michael, the guy I basically lived with for two years."

Satch scanned her eyes over Simone. "Looking all happy. You excited, huh?"

"Yeah. I guess I still half love him."

Satch gave her a suggestive smile. "Top half or bottom?"

"Both."

"Sound like more than half."

"Maybe so."

"Make sure the man treat you good."

"I will." Her foot landed in goose droppings; Simone slid but recovered, then wiped her shoe off on the grass.

"Naw. Got to mean it."

"I do." She glanced at the sole of her shoe. It looked reasonably clean. "Come to think of it, I'd rather say those words to Michael."

"Thought you in love with Tweety Bird."

"I don't even know if Jun's single. But Michael is. Wish me luck."

"Wear the red jumpsuit. Won't need no luck."

Several snowy egrets landed in a massive birch growing on an island in the lake. Egrets had such elegance in their lines, such grace in their landing. From a distance they looked to Simone like crystalline clumps of snow. "I love egrets," she said. "How about you?"

"They too skinny," Satch said. "I like geese. They fat, and they waddle around looking silly, but they still fly. Don't care if it be raining or snowing or the sun be shining. They real strong. Fly real far."

"So can you," Simone said, wanting to infuse Satch with the hope she felt at that moment.

"Shoot, it probably be hunting season."

"No way," Simone said. "You're an endangered species. Off limits."

Satch snorted. "Girl, you one crazy white woman."

"Yeah, but you're here with me, so what does that make you?"

"I don't even wanna know," Satch said. "Don't even be wanting to know."

EIGHTEEN

Simone raised her leg above the bubbles in her bath and slid her razor along it, pleased that it held no temptation for her. She carefully shaved off stubble. Then she lathered her washcloth and ran it over her body, lingering on her privates, stroking them until she was aroused. She was tempted to satisfy herself but didn't; she wanted to emit an air of arousal to Michael. Sex had been one of the highlights of their relationship. She wouldn't sleep with him that night; she didn't want to be easy, and she still had a few visible lines he might question. But she hoped to leave him wanting more. Much more.

She rinsed and stood. Gently she dried off, the plush towel soft against her skin, psyching herself to feel sensuous. Then she applied the expensive apricot-scented lotion she'd bought that afternoon to make her skin feel silky.

She hung up the towel and emerged, naked, from the bathroom. Searching through her closet, she rejected a blue rayon blouse he'd liked, considering it too obvious an attempt to please him.

She reached for the red Spandex.

Michael beamed when he saw her. "Simone," he said, embracing her. Then he held her shoulders as his eyes took her in, took all of her in, and seemed to like what he saw. "You look great!"

"You too." She noted the new, closely cropped beard that covered his square jaw, the stylish white shirt and pleated tan slacks that flattered his trim body, the tousled hair that looked like he disdained combs and mirrors, giving him a knowingly modest air. The "old" Michael wore his hair short, his clothes loose, his face shaven. She had to admit that the new look made him even more sexy.

"I've already got us a table." He led her to a seat by the window; it looked out on a garden of flowers, a riotous mixture of purple and pink. She'd eaten at Laceys only rarely because it was pricey, but she liked the flowers, light and space. The fact that Michael had chosen so expensive a restaurant—and offered to pay for it—boded well. They'd always gone Dutch. Always.

Two menus rested on the table. A waiter materialized to ask if they'd like a drink.

"We'll take a bottle of the Merlot." Michael glanced at Simone. "You do still drink Merlot?"

"Yes, but just a glass."

"A bottle, please," he repeated to the waiter, who left. "That's what I like about you." He closed the menu. "You're a cheap date. In L.A. it seems like everyone can consume an entire bottle and still pass a sobriety test. Dating's expensive."

She'd expected him to be dating, but her spirits plummeted. She tried not to show it. "So tell me about your writing."

Michael brushed back the hair that fell over his eyes. She was surprised to note that his hair seemed to be thinning. "Well, I optioned the Oakland film noir to an independent producer who's trying to get financing, and I've had a lot of interest in the teen revenge fantasy."

"It sounds like you're on the brink of making it."

He threw his hands in the air in frustration. "It's hard to tell. Nobody in the business wants to say the word 'no.' If they pass on a project that hits big, they lose their jobs, so even if they're not interested they hesitate to say that. You never know quite where you stand."

She wanted to take his hand, but she wasn't sure where she stood, either. "You'll make it. Your writing's too good not to."

"You helped give me the confidence to make the move, you know."

Simone marveled at the irony: her support had encouraged him to move away from her. She should have told him he had the talent of an inkblot. "So what do you think of L.A.?"

"It's extravagant. They waste water and gas big time. And it's obsessed. Delivery boys carry their screenplays with them in case they get to deliver to 'Somebody.' Dry cleaners display photographs of stars praising their starch. The whole town's intoxicated." He looked bemused. "Of course I've never seen so many beautiful people. Even the meter maids are drop-dead gorgeous. But how are you?"

"Super!" she said.

The waiter returned and poured Michael a taste of the Merlot, which he swirled before sampling. "Excellent, thanks." Filling their glasses, the waiter asked if they were ready to order. "We'll wait a while," Michael said.

Simone hoped her stomach wouldn't rumble. She wished she'd snacked, had forgotten how long he liked to linger before eating.

"Do you have plans for the summer?" he asked.

Her heart leapt. Was he suggesting they do something together? "I haven't gotten that far. How about you?"

He gave a rueful smile. "I'd like to find the Fountain of Youth."

"You look like you already discovered it." She gave herself a minus ten on the repartee scale.

"I should have moved to L.A. twenty years ago." He spread his fingers and looked at them as if he found them ugly. "Most people I've pitched to seemed about half my age. I keep expecting the guys to suggest we pick up a six-pack and some 'babes' and hit the beach."

Though he kept his tone light, Michael had an injured look that made Simone want to hug him. "You may be forty, but at heart you're still childlike."

"Are you saying I'm immature?"

"I prefer to think of it as youthful."

"To you, maybe. To the kids I pitch to I'm practically doddering."

"Michael!"

A gray-haired man in fashionable suit clapped Michael's shoulder. He was accompanied by a leggy woman in a skirt more the length of underpants.

"Hey, Alex," Michael said, standing and shaking hands.

Alex put his arm around the woman with him. "Michael, this is my girlfriend, Lauren."

Simone wasn't sure whether to stand or remain seated. Alex and Lauren looked at her, waiting for Michael to introduce her; she was eager to hear what term he would use.

He didn't even glance at her. "How's the law practice?" he said, his eyes trained on Alex.

Alex looked away from Simone back to him. "A pain in the ass."

Lauren smiled sympathetically at Simone before snuggling closer to Alex.

If Simone's cheeks flushed any hotter, they would ignite her eyebrows. Even the tips of her ears burned.

"What's new in the movie business?" Alex said.

Michael launched into a repeat description of L.A.'s obsessions. Seated, Simone suspected she could stand and strip and Michael would still ignore her.

"Have you met any movie stars?" Lauren asked.

Michael named movie stars he'd met through AA. "I'm not an alcoholic, but AA's a great place to make connections."

Satch would tell her to be pissed, not humiliated. She couldn't understand why Michael hadn't introduced her. True, he'd once spoken of avoiding marriage as not wanting any woman to "get her claws" into him, but was the mere pronunciation of her name a claw? She decided to experiment and coughed as if she were on the verge of choking. Alex and Lauren looked at her. Michael didn't. He just kept talking. If he couldn't even be bothered to say her name, their relationship had no future. *Got to stand up for your own self.*

"Hi, I'm Simone," she said, rising. She firmly shook Lauren's hand, then Alex's. "I'm Michael's ex-lover. And ex-friend." She grabbed her purse.

"Simone, where are you going?" Michael said. The expression in his eyes was the embarrassed confusion of the little boy who'd been caught playing with himself.

Alex and Lauren stepped back out of the way.

She felt white inside. "I've decided I don't want to dirty my claws by getting them into you, Michael. Have a nice life." She turned from him and without a backward glance strode from the room.

By the time she got home, her righteous adrenalin had subsided. She stripped off the Spandex jumpsuit and crammed it in the back of her closet.

Nineteen

Depleted from yet another night of too little sleep, weighed down by the sense of glumness that had plagued her in the week since her aborted date with Michael, Simone sat at one of Oakhill's concrete tables and propped her head on her arm, her limbs like wet bread. A slight breeze blew goose bumps over her. She'd expected it to be sunny—the forecast had been for clear skies—but the gray of the fog mirrored her insides.

Someone set a cup of coffee on the table beside her; it smelled like it had been brewed about the time she cut her first tooth.

"How are you?" Jun sat down across from her. Shoulders round beneath his red Goofy T-shirt, a yellow pencil resting above his ear, he looked jaunty.

"Okay." He was her only prospect, an attractive man she still faintly hoped might want to date when she—hopefully—went back to the classroom in four weeks. She forced herself to sit up and tried to smile, but her lips felt too tired to curve. The coffee tasted like charred mushrooms.

"So what are your plans for this weekend?" he asked.

"I'm going to my father's tomorrow."

Unwrapping peppermint Lifesavers, he gave her one and popped one in his mouth. The sweet taste of the candy tempered the bitter coffee.

He didn't have a cup. "Did you stop drinking this stuff?" she said, trying to make herself sound teasing rather than tired.

"Yep. I swore off caffeine."

"You're kidding."

"It wasn't hard."

She took a sip. "I see what you mean."

"You look beat."

His voice was so warm, so sympathetic it almost made her cry. "Yeah," was all she trusted herself to say.

He stood, positioning himself behind her, and she wondered what he was doing.

"You look like you could use a massage."

His hands cupped her shoulders, jolting her. He pressed his fingers firmly into the muscles of her shoulders, which arched to meet his touch. Maybe, she thought, her fantasies about their dating weren't just wishful thinking.

On the street a car idled, music throbbing. Jun seemed to pick up the beat, his thumbs pressing into her with the thumping of the bass, kneading her. She melted beneath his touch. He leaned closer, massaging her neck. She smelled peppermint.

The gate clanked open. Her stomach thudded. She stiffened. Straightened her shoulders.

"Relax," he said. "You're getting more tense."

She forced her shoulders down, but footsteps approached.

"I'm having a heart attack!"

Simone jerked forward, away from his hands. "Stop!"

Jun released her. Yvonne went on in the trailer. Simone covered her face with her hands. She felt an overwhelming sense of guilt.

"What's going on?" Jun sat back down across from her.

Face still hidden, she voiced her bafflement. "I don't know."

"Simone?"

She glanced up.

"What's coming up for you?"

"I don't know!"

"Did I press too hard?"

"No!" She said the word with a vehemence that mystified her. "It's just... It felt"—she tightened her hold on the coffee cup—"wrong."

"Why?"

"It just did." His face was furrowed in doubt, and she looked down at the coffee, a black substance she wished could shield her from his questions and her own.

"I'm sorry I upset you. Tell me what's going through your mind."

"I'm just confused."

"Jun," came a voice from behind them. "I need you."

It was Evelyn. Jun signaled he'd be right there. "Try to figure out more about how you reacted. It's important."

"Okay." He left. Trembling, she grabbed the cup so hard it spilled. Tepid liquid coated her hands. She just sat and felt her wet hands and watched the coffee drip off the edge of the table.

Marvin materialized on the bench where Jun had been. "What's wrong, Simone?" he asked in a worried voice.

Shaking, Simone took Kleenex from her purse and wiped off the table. "I'm just having a bad morning."

"I get those sometimes."

She wiped her hands with fresh Kleenex.

"Look! They're acrobats!" Marvin tossed the bears up one by one, juggling them, his face lit in a goofy smile.

"Cool," she said.

Confused about her reaction to Jun's massage, certain he must feel distanced by her inexplicable rejection of him, Simone didn't request a group, attended those led by Muslimah and Evelyn, and passed over the vacant seat beside Jun at lunch to be the first person to sit at the table furthest from him.

"How come you didn't call no group?" Satch said, sitting across from her.

"Didn't feel like it."

"Sound like a heroin addict saying she don't need no fix."

"You're calling me a therapy addict?"

"A Tweety Bird addict. Why you blushing? Know I'm right."

Jun was talking to Yvonne, whose hand was over her heart, her eyes shut. He looked so sweet, so appealing. Viola took the seat across from Simone, blocking her view of him.

"Nobody noticed," Viola said, looking from Simone to Satch with reproof.

"Noticed what?" Simone asked.

"What I'm wearing."

Only then did Simone register that for the first time since she'd come to Oakhill, Viola wasn't wearing black. Her pants and shirt were a soft gray. "Wow."

"Damn, girl, you looking good," Satch said.

"Satch is right," Simone said. "What prompted the change?"

"Woman got herself a date." Satch nudged Viola with her elbow.

"Really?" Simone said. "Terrific!"

Viola gave what Simone judged to be a dazzled smile.

"With the Christmas man." Satch winked at Simone.

"Huh?" Simone said.

"Yule his name, Viola his game."

"He's from church," Viola said.

If Viola looked any happier, Simone thought, they would put her on meds.

"We're just going to dinner."

"Make sure that dinner last a long time." Satch drew out the word *long* and took from her bag a piece of chocolate cake, which she broke into pieces and passed around.

"Did you make it?" Simone said, taking a chunk.

"Yeah. It was Thomas's birthday. Man loves chocolate."

Though Satch's continued attraction to the man who beat her almost took away her appetite, Simone reminded herself that Thomas was Satch's business. She put a bite of cake in her mouth. The rich taste was as close to orgasmic as she figured she was likely to get for the foreseeable future. "Delicious." Memories of the chocolate chunk brownies her mother used to make flooded her, one batch in particular.

Her mother had made a game of preparing the batter, declaring they were fixing Brownies Royale for the king and queen of France. Delighted, Simone stirred the batter, watching the lumps dissolve, tantalized by the smell of chocolate. When the mix was in the oven, she and her mother ran fingers around the bowl, linked arms Roman style, and licked the chocolate off.

Her father came in, inviting her to go to the hardware store with him. He promised to buy her a plant, said he was lonely for company. When Simone asked if it was okay, her mother said, "That's up to you." When she asked if they could have brownies and milk on her return, her mother simply said, "We'll see."

She didn't know whether to go, but her father took her hand and led her away. She would have had to pull away from him to stay with her mother. He promised they'd be right back, but at the store he took forever, talking to the clerk about squirrel-proofing bird feeders.

On their delayed return, she dashed from the car, cradling her new plant and a new paintbrush she'd chosen for her mother, and pulled open the door. A tendril of smoke drifted out. The smoke alarm clanged. The smell of burnt chocolate stopped her.

Her father rushed to the kitchen. Slowly she followed him, clutching her plant. Smoke seeped out of the oven door. He flipped off the controls, grabbed a hot pad, and took out the blackened Brownies Royale. She thought how disappointed the king and queen would be.

"Something wrong?"

Satch's question brought Simone's thoughts back to Oakhill. "No. I just spaced out."

"Need to eat your lunch." Satch pointed to Simone's unwrapped avocado-and-cheese sandwich.

"Yes, Mom."

"Shit," Satch said.

On the way home from Oakhill, Simone thought about Saturday's upcoming lunch with her father and decided to fix him the special red-hot chili he loved. It was time to be honest with him—finally. He'd always understood her, the one person in whom she'd been able to confide, even as a teenager, the person she went to when she was hurt by others or bewildered by her own behavior. There was so much she wanted to ask him. Why she'd lain in front of her parents' car. Why she'd blinded herself to the flaws of every man she dated. Why she'd ever conceived of cutting. It was time to risk hurting him in order to heal herself.

Twenty

"Simone, this is Claire, the love of my life."

Her father's arm clasped a woman with hair dyed an unnatural shade of red, a woman who wasn't supposed to be there. This was to have been Simone's day to explore with him the many questions that had arisen for her recently.

"I'm so glad to meet you!" Claire said.

Claire's accent fairly dripped of hominy and grits. Her red lipstick looked like it had been slathered on with a putty knife, her foundation applied with a roller.

"Your father has told me *so* much about you. I just know we're going to be great friends!"

Her father's age, Claire wore a yellow skirt with ruffled blouse and high heels.

"I fixed a little lunch for us," she said. "I hope you like fried chicken."

"I love it."

"Claire's the best cook I've ever met," said her father, linking his arm through Claire's and turning their backs to Simone to head for the kitchen.

Simone lingered behind, holding the bowl of her father's favorite chili she'd gotten up early to fix. He seemed truly smitten. He'd introduced her to few of his dates, and never had he looked gaga over one like he did now.

She ran her hand over the back of the leather sofa, so different from the old upholstered one on which every Saturday night the two of them had sat eating popcorn and watching monster movies. He'd always seemed to know when the monster would appear. She'd thought him the smartest man in the world, too young to realize that it wasn't superior intelligence that enabled him to foretell monsters' sudden appearances—but the clunky music. Still, he'd always had insight into her. What was she supposed to do with her questions? Maybe Claire would leave after lunch, giving them the afternoon together to talk, but that seemed about as likely as national health insurance. She joined them in the kitchen.

"What did you bring?" Claire took the lid off the bowl and sniffed. "Chili. Smells good!"

"Claire's made a big lunch," her father said.

"I wish you'd told me she was cooking." Wished he'd told her they wouldn't be alone.

"I wanted to surprise you." He put his arms around Claire and kissed her on the cheek. He looked and sounded so sappy, if Simone were diabetic she'd be lunging for insulin.

"Did you know your father was such a romantic?" Claire asked.

Simone couldn't recall even a single kiss between her parents. "Not really."

Claire shook off her father's arms and reached out for the chili. "Thanks for cooking. We can have this as a side dish, okay?"

"Sure."

A pan of fried chicken sizzled on the stove beside pots of black-eyed peas and mashed potatoes. Judging by the smell, Claire was a firm believer in the liberal use of garlic. Saliva formed in Simone's mouth. She was hungry.

"What can I do?" she asked.

"You just relax," Claire said. "You must be tired from the drive. We'll wait on you. That can't have happened often in your father's kitchen." She winked.

Simone's father put his hands on Claire's shoulders from behind. "A woman's place is in the kitchen," he said. "A man's place is just passing through."

"Kind of like gas," Claire said, provoking a laugh from Simone and him.

She helped Claire set lunch on the table—so, amazingly, did her father. Had he helped her mother in the days before he married her, or before Simone was old enough to remember?

When her father pulled the chair next to him from the table, in his usual gentleman's routine, she automatically moved to sit in it, as she had at every meal they'd shared.

He touched her shoulder. "Sit at the end of the table. This chair's for Claire."

She didn't know whether she paled or blushed. Claire quickly seated herself at the end. "Don't be ridiculous, John. Simone, you sit next to your father." Claire heaped mashed potatoes on Simone's plate as if the mechanics of eating might overcome the awkwardness of Simone's still standing by the empty chair. "Lunch is getting cold."

Simone sat without looking at her father. The urge to cry swept over her, and she dug her nails into her palms under the table to prevent tears.

Claire questioned her about teaching, and Simone asked about Claire's life—a Georgian, widowed, two grown children living in the Bay Area.

Her father rose to refill Claire's wine glass, running his hand over Claire's neck and shoulders as he did so. He used to do that to Simone at times, making her feel loved and important. She half wished he'd do it now, but of course he didn't.

Simone excused herself to go to the bathroom. When she opened the door, she remembered the bowl of seashells that used to sit on the back of the toilet. Her father had admired the colors and patterns, but it was her mother who had collected most of the shells. She recalled once when she was small searching for an undamaged sand dollar. She'd seen several she'd thought were intact, but her mother's artist's eyes saw flaws. When her mother found a perfect sand dollar, she'd grabbed Simone under her arms and swung her in circles. Why had that day stuck in her mind?

She pulled the door closed, feeling strangely forlorn to be doing so. She'd never closed the door all the way in her parents' house; leaving it open was a symbol of closeness. Her father had always felt free to enter the bathroom. He'd come in without knocking when she was brushing her teeth, when she was dressing, even when she was bathing. Indeed, he almost always came in when she was bathing because he knew how much she prided herself on her unblemished skin, and of course she couldn't reach her own back. He would kneel by her side, soap up the washcloth, then run it over her back, pressing just right, in circular motions, his fingers guiding the cloth, sliding it from her shoulders down to her waist. When he was done, he would cup his hands and drip water down her back, warm water, rinsing her.

You're the only woman I've ever met who understands me, he'd told her repeatedly.

This chair's for Claire, he'd told her now.

Her stomach cramped. She'd told Jun that though her parents didn't always get along, she'd enjoyed a happy childhood.

Now she questioned whether that was true or whether her whole life had been a fantasy, a lie. It occurred to her that her father's back washing might well be connected to her reaction to Jun's massage. Her head spun. She reached out her hand to steady herself against the sink. But she'd always enjoyed her father's touch, she was sure she had.

A knock. "Are you okay?" Claire said.

"Fine."

"I hope you've got room for dessert."

She couldn't imagine sitting back down at that table with her father. "I'll be right out."

Claire's heels tapped against the hardwood floor as she walked away. Simone scrubbed her hands roughly, repeatedly. Did Regina feel this sullied? Splashing water on her face, she reassembled her mask.

When she returned to the table, a plate of perfectly baked brownies rested in front of her. She took her old seat beside her father, the seat that no longer felt like hers.

"Your father said brownies are your favorite dessert."

She couldn't decide what surprised her more—that Claire had fixed brownies, or that her father remembered they were her favorite.

"Your father told me how much your students love you," Claire said. "He's very proud of you."

"Isn't she special?" her father said.

From the expression on his face, Simone knew he wasn't referring to her.

By the time she got home, Simone felt herself fragmenting into jumbled pieces of a puzzle. She didn't know how to put the pieces back together or what picture they formed. She recalled the night her freshman year of high school when she excitedly told her father a boy had asked her to be his girlfriend. It was her first real crush, and she'd expected her father to share her glee. Instead, he'd turned and walked out of the room without comment.

"You can't expect him to be happy," her mother had said.

And now he didn't even want her to sit by him?

Jerking open a kitchen drawer, she seized a long, sharp knife and ran her fingers lightly along the blade edge. If she started cutting again, there was no telling when—or if—she would stop, but she had to do something to discharge the frenzy that had seized her. She strode into the main room, where she lifted the knife over her head and brought it down, slashing her begonias, slashing her spider plants, slashing her ferns, slashing her jade plants, slashing her philodendrons, slashing her orchids, until every single blossom and leaf of every single plant was no wider than a shoestring.

Twenty-One

On Monday, Simone didn't get called on in time to request a group but was almost relieved.

In volleyball, she scrambled around the court that glistened in the hot sun, lunging for every possible shot as she and Satch played against Jun and Rick. Serving, Rick tossed the ball high and slammed his hand against the white leather. The ball barely cleared the net. A few weeks earlier, Simone had been impotent before Rick's serves, but this time she triumphantly hit the ball up for Satch, who set it high. Simone spiked it into a corner out of reach.

"Yes!" she shouted, thrusting her fist in the air.

Satch slapped her high-five. "You snort coke?"

"Why?"

"Playing like you high."

"I'm high on life."

"Shit."

Though they lost, Simone felt revved.

"You've gotten good," Rick said to her after the game, shaggy hair falling over his eyes. "You almost beat us."

She thanked him and bounded up the stairs for drama. To her dismay Jun started them off with the falling circle. Like Rick, she had yet to let herself fall. Marvin volunteered to be first. Glasses still taped, arms hugging his bears, he fell easily, giggling, forward-backward-sideways, over and over until Jun bid him stop.

"Closer." Regina's barely audible voice sounded as if a pile of leaves muffled it. Again she tilted more than fell, but she participated.

Rick passed. Satch, silent, toppled in every direction, heavy but limber. Viola flopped like a doll without stuffing, her smile full and exuberant. Willy was equally uninhibited.

"Your turn," Jun said to Simone.

Her feet felt moored to the floor.

"Try."

She stepped into the circle. Black bars on the outside of the windows striped the shades. She smelled her own sweat. Closing her eyes, she hoped the darkness would embolden her.

"You can do it," Jun prompted.

She plunged backward. Hands braced her fall. Fingers touched her back. She sprang from the center, broke between Regina and Marvin, and held herself apart, hunched over.

Jun joined her. "What came up for you?"

"I just... The fingers. I can't stand the touch."

"Why?"

"It felt like Spence touching me. When he raped me."

"I think you have more to express to him."

"But I told him how I felt with the fabric."

"Yes. You told him calmly, like you were giving directions to the theater. But you haven't really expressed your emotions. I think it might help you to do that."

Maybe he was right. Certainly she'd like to be able to enjoy falling. "Okay. What do I do?"

Jun pulled out a huge blue pillow and a soft padded bat from a props bag, positioned the pillow on a chair and handed her the bat. "There are lots of ways of expressing yourself."

She ran her fingers over the black plastic handle, ridged for gripping. The padded part, a vivid red, was about two feet long and several inches in diameter.

"The pillow's Spence. Let him know how you feel."

Silly. She felt silly. Jun's Daffy Duck shirt didn't make it any easier to take this whole thing seriously.

"Go ahead."

The sooner she started, the sooner she could stop. She swung the bat. The pillow barely moved.

"That's how you feel?" Jun said.

She tried again.

"Shit," Satch said. "You ain't telling him nothing."

She swung again.

"That all you got to say to that man?" Satch taunted.

Jun stood behind the chair. "Harder, Simone. Let him know how you feel. He can't hurt you now."

She swung, hard. Swung again, harder. The pillow sagged.

"Now you getting it," Satch said. "Come on."

She smashed the bat into the pillow. "Fuck you!" Hit it again. "You fucking bastard!" And then she exploded in a frenzy of destruction, of release, of power, bashing that pillow, bashing Spence, and it wasn't the pillow sagging, it was Spence crumbling to his knees, his hands up in a futile effort to ward off her blows, Spence crawling, Spence groveling, Spence pleading. She kept swinging. "Fuck you fuck you fuck you AND STAY OUT OF MY FUCKING BATHROOM!"

She gasped. The pillow toppled from the chair. She flung the bat. Her hands shook.

"Take hands and sit in a circle," Jun said.

Satch took one of Simone's hands, Viola the other. She focused on their touch, trying to anchor herself.

"Who were you talking to?" Jun said.

"Spence."

"And?"

"My father," she whispered.

"Tell us about it," he said.

"He used to come into the room when I was bathing." She had to force words from her constricted throat. "It didn't matter how old I was. Five. Thirteen. Sixteen." Her baths were usually at the end of the day. Her father's face would be darkened by whiskers he wouldn't shave off until morning. "As I got older I'd cover my privates with the washrag. I guess I felt violated, but I never told him to stop. He'd take the washrag to wash my back." His eyes always gleamed. "Sometimes I smelled whiskey on his breath." Her face got hot. "Part of me loved the warm water trickling down my back, and part wanted to slide beneath the water, out of reach. 'Sit up, gorgeous,' he'd say." She leaned into her knees. "He'd run the washrag over my back. He has long fingers. I could feel them press into me. I felt special, but as I got older I felt dirty, too." Ashamed, Simone couldn't bring herself to look at the other members. "When he was done, he'd wrap me in a towel and dry me off. 'You're beautiful, doll,' he'd tell me. 'Wish I'd married a girl like you.'"

No one spoke. She asked herself why in all those years she hadn't closed the bathroom door.

"He touch you *there?*" Regina's features scrunched in an expression of horror.

"No! Never!"

"His words touched you," Jun said. "That was damage enough."

"Man sick," Satch said.

"Satch is right," Viola said. "Your daddy shouldn't ever have talked to you like that."

"Say it felt kinda good?" Marvin said.

"Sometimes. But bad, too." Her face blazed.

"Why you didn't tell the man to stop?" Satch said. "Or lock the damned door?"

Simone cringed. Telling her father to stop—shutting and locking the bathroom door—seemed like what any young woman would do. Why hadn't she? "I don't know."

"You know, your relationship with your father meant you never learned how to set normal boundaries," Jun said, his face tender. "No wonder you forgave Spence."

Simone massaged her temples, not because they hurt but because her brain felt too full.

"How your mama feel about your daddy messing with you?" Satch asked.

"He didn't mess with me. He just washed my back."

"Uh-huh. Like I said, how your mama feel about it?"

Had her mother witnessed their transgressions? Heard her father's words? She couldn't remember. "I don't know." She felt like a siren, spinning, flinging off bolts of red. She wanted her razor blades to cut through all the confusion and get her old life back, the life she'd thought she had. She hugged her knees tighter. The hospital would close in half an hour. The blades awaited her.

"Do you want to talk more?" Jun said.

"No." Her head hurt. "It's someone else's turn for a skit."

"We have time. You've dealt with a lot today. How do you feel?"

Like cutting. "Fine."

"Look like shit," Satch said.

"I want to caution you," Jun said. "All of you. Sometimes when you do a skit that reveals family secrets, there's a backlash. It can make you feel you have to punish yourself. Simone, you need to take special care tonight. Get your mind off all this. See friends."

She glanced up; he studied her with worried eyes.

"Can you confirm your contract not to cut?"

She didn't want to lie.

Before she could decide how to answer, Satch spoke. "Don't got to worry. Gonna be with Simone tonight. Gonna make sure she don't cut nothing, not even a fart."

Simone's mind circled on itself. No, she didn't want Satch with her, preventing her from carrying out her desire to use a razor blade. But yes, she did. She desperately did.

Jun studied her. "Simone?"

"Don't need to ask her," Satch said. "Woman ain't got no choice."

"Okay," she told Jun. "I'll be okay."

His shoulders lowered as he visibly relaxed.

"See? Just like I told you."

TWENTY-TWO

"Eel eggs? Raw octopus? Seaweed?" Satch looked disgusted by the menu posted on the outside of Nobuko's Sushi in Talaveras Plaza. "Girl, you think I'm gonna eat that shit, you crazy."

Simone peered wistfully into the small restaurant where closely packed customers sat moving with small gestures. Her stomach rumbled. Though it was only six o'clock, she was famished. After she picked up her vitamins, she hoped to persuade Satch to eat an early dinner, though it would obviously not be sushi. The heat was seeping out of the day as they strode toward the drugstore, past boutiques with store names painted in delicate script on windows, spindly trees adorned with white lights as if it were Christmas, gaslights on lean poles.

"Ain't no black folks around," Satch said.

"Your being here doubles Talaveras's black population."

"For real?"

"Close."

"Huh." She stopped in front of Anna's Active Wear. "They sell swimsuits?"

"Yes, but—"

Satch shoved open the door. Classical piano played from an unseen stereo. A bouquet of lilies overpowered the small store with its cloying fragrance. By the flowers stood a saleswoman, her navy blue suit so perfectly creased Simone decided the woman probably dry-cleaned her underwear.

"Good evening, ladies." The woman glanced at Simone in her oversized shirt, at Satch in red blouse and purple pants, her glance ping ponging between them before settling on Simone. "May I help you?"

"She past help," Satch said. "Got any swimsuits?"

"Right back here." The woman's clipped manner of speaking made even her words seem creased. She held up a skimpy black bikini. "This is a popular item."

"Shoot," Satch said, "Seen bigger dog collars. How much?"

"A hundred-and-sixty."

"Dollars?"

"It's a MariLee." The woman paused as if they should recognize the name. "She's a top designer."

"Who design the bottom?"

"Pardon me?"

"Say she a top designer. Who design the bottom?"

That was like something her mother might say, Simone thought. Her mother liked to clown around: tell waiters that Simone and her friends were the world champion miniature golf team, put a pillow under her coat in public on Girl Scout outings and feign being in labor.

"Got anything around twenty?" Satch asked.

"No. There are plenty of other stores for the economy-minded."

"We've got to be going." Simone addressed the woman. "The warden's expecting her back."

Satch grinned. "The governor, he gonna pardon me." She held up two fingers touching. "We tight."

"The governor wouldn't pardon his own wife if DNA evidence, a videotape, and eight eyewitnesses proved her innocence," Simone said.

The sales woman didn't smile. "Do come back, ladies."

"Don't think she mean that," Satch said outside.

"I think you're right." Simone laughed.

"Woman got her nose so high in the air, she lucky ain't no birds nesting in it."

"Yeah. I'm surprised she doesn't need oxygen."

The two women grinned at each other and began walking toward the cleaners.

"What I'm gonna swim in?"

"The same outfit as last time?"

"Kinda big." Satch spread her arms wide as if to suggest just how big the outfit was.

"We'll swim in the dark."

"Sound good. Don't need no suits."

"Skinny dipping's against the rules."

"If breathing against the rules, you probably stop."

That wasn't how Simone saw herself. "Do I really seem that compliant?" Hadn't she painted her classroom despite district policy that specified only the maintenance crew could paint rooms?

"Sometimes."

What was it about swimming nude that discomforted her? Associations with her father and her own nudity? With Spence? "Fine. I'll swim naked."

"Don't have to."

"As a wise woman once told me, don't gotta do nothing but die some day."

Satch chuckled. "Sound like that woman be real smart."

"Damn."

Simone tried to see the sprawling Talaveras High School through Satch's eyes: bordered by a clean creek and green lawns, surrounded by flowering beds of daffodils and tulips, freshly painted white with yellow trim. No bullet holes. No broken windows. No graffiti. No metal detectors. Satch had requested a tour of Talaveras. Though she must have registered the huge size of many of the houses and the high cost of the (mostly foreign) cars, she hadn't reacted except with a laugh when Simone pointed out Meghan's five-bedroom Tudor. Until now.

"Where your classroom?"

As she led Satch down a hallway adorned with display cases of student art, past a computer lab with forty new computers, Simone could almost hear the bell clang, could almost see the bustle of students changing rooms, opening and shutting lockers, flirting, laughing, calling greetings. She stopped at her room, the last one in the wing.

Satch peered in the small window in the door while Simone pictured the bright airy room, the windows that looked out on lawn and creek, the new carpet. When Satch moved aside, Simone looked. The desks were in rows, not the horseshoe formation she used. Her posters about the importance of kindness and the dangers of perfectionism had been replaced with grammar rules. Dizzy, she backed away.

"What?"

"It's just—they took down my posters."

"You ain't here."

"But I'm coming back. Soon." She was doing so much better. She had to return—before she was permanently replaced.

"Got any black students?"

It took her a moment to register Satch's question. "One."

"Shit."

"It's not my fault."

"Ain't said it was. Oakland need good teachers."

"I know."

"Naw. You surviving Oakhell. Oakland need good teachers like you."

Satch's compliment made her smile broadly. "Thanks."

"Mean it. Oughta teach in Oakland."

It was something she'd considered when she first applied to teach fifteen years before, but Talaveras had made her the best offer. She wondered what students—let alone their parents and her colleagues—knew about the reasons for her prolonged absence, and what they speculated. Would she be comfortable returning? "How much violence is there in the Oakland schools?"

Satch scowled. "Most the students fine, long as you firm and friendly. They wanna learn. Want teachers who care about 'em. Violence mostly between the kids. But if you wanting to be all safe, stay here." She turned away and started back up the hall, the strident screeching of a jay punctuating her steps.

Satch's anger was so much like Simone's early days at Oakhill. She'd thought they'd worked through that. She caught up to Satch and put her hand on Satch's shoulder. Satch stopped, turned. "I wasn't safe from myself. And I'll think about Oakland."

"Good. I'm hungry. When we gonna eat?"

"I thought you'd never ask."

Satch stood in the doorway of Simone's condominium, eyes wide, surveying the wreckage of the plants Simone had slashed the night before, the leaves rent, shredded bits of browning blossoms littering the floor.

"You cut these plants up or they committing suicide?"

"I got a little crazy."

"When you do this shit?"

"When I got home from my father's."

"Don't be going back real soon."

"Don't worry. I don't plan to." Her father wouldn't even notice if she didn't visit. He had her replacement.

Satch plopped down on the couch while Simone vacuumed, then they served themselves from Chinese take-out, attempting to eat with chopsticks. Satch scissored an egg roll and tried repeatedly to get it to her mouth, but each time she got close the egg roll plopped to the plate. Finally she raised a chopstick up and brought it down hard, skewering the egg roll into submission.

Simone assayed broccoli and noodles, which kept slithering away. "Why'd you come tonight?" she said.

"So's I could eat with sticks. You wishing I wasn't here?"

"Not at all. I'm glad you're here. I was just curious."

"Come 'cause you helped me."

"You didn't have to."

"Don't gotta do nothing but die some day. There another reason." Satch didn't look at Simone as she said this, just added a lot of salt to the cashew chicken. "Thomas ain't never come home last night."

"You aren't worried about him?"

"Naw. He do that sometimes. Figured it my turn. Let him wonder." Satch dumped soy sauce on the cashew chicken.

"Oh." Simone wanted Satch at her place for her own sake, not because of Thomas.

"Coulda gone to my aunt's," Satch said, "but I figured you needed some looking after."

Simone smiled.

"What?"

"I'm just really glad you came."

Satch added still more salt.

"Keep that up," Simone said, "and cows will use you for a salt lick."

"Hmm. Got any silverware? These things"—she held up her chopsticks—"must be why so many folks in the world be starving."

Simone set out silverware for both of them. With fork in hand, she took her first satisfying bite. The more she ate, the hungrier she felt.

"Won't Thomas, you know, get mad or anything?"

"Probably."

"Do you ever *want* him to hit you?"

"That's a damned fool question."

"Is it? I mean, he's going to be pissed about your coming here, right? Doesn't that mean that maybe you do want him to hit you? I used to hit myself. I slapped my face until it got red. So maybe it's like that only you get somebody else to do it for you."

Was she making Satch angry? She glanced at her as Satch wiped a crumb from her own lip.

"Damn, girl, you sure know how to ruin a good dinner."

"Sorry."

"You practicing for your therapist license?" Satch licked her fingers. "Now it my turn to ask a question."

"Fire away."

"You glad you come to Oakhill?"

"Definitely. Why do you ask?"

"I'm just remembering that look on your pale white face the first day, your eyes all big and your little self all scared. Guess you ain't been around a lotta black folks, huh?"

Simone chewed slowly, hoping the motion would make her cheeks less flushed. "I think it was more because of anger. Yours especially. I'm not comfortable with it. And then so many people seemed so depressed. And uneducated."

"And black?"

"I'd like to think not."

Satch's eyebrows raised to underscore her skepticism. Was Satch right? She didn't want to believe that. But she recalled her reaction that first day. Her fear. "Maybe that did scare me."

"I never liked many white people. Think I be scared, too. But you and Rick different. Even Evelyn. Jun, he only half white, but I like him. Oakhill made me see lotta things different."

"Me, too," Simone said. "Me, too." She took another bite and thought about their conversation, about her own admission. And Satch's. Though she felt close to Satch now, she recalled Satch's earlier anger. Did racial or economic differences render their friendship forever fragile? The thought made her want to cry.

Satch sat back, hand on her stomach. "All this eating and talking wearing me down."

Simone glanced at the clock. It was nine-thirty. "Do you want to go to bed?"

"No way. Want to swim."

Simone turned off the pool light. They eased their way into inky black water that reflected the stars' sparkle. Satch tossed her cut-offs and halter top on the side. Naked, she treaded water facing Simone, who looked away, at the stars.

"Oughta take off that suit. Feel real good."

"In a minute." The air was cool, the pool heated; mist rose from the water like clouds drifting back to the sky.

Satch dove under and swam along the bottom as she had before, nearly invisible.

The pool stank of chlorine, a smell that made Simone's nose close. She asked herself why she was so resistant to taking off her suit. She'd always enjoyed skinny dipping—like when she backpacked to isolated mountain lakes—and certainly the odds of anyone coming close enough to see her nudity were small, the odds they would care even smaller. Telling herself to stop being a prude, she slid the straps off her shoulders, peeled the suit off and set it on the side in easy reach. Just in case. She swam a few strokes into the center of the pool and stopped. Water lapped at her like flames. She swam back to the side.

Laughter sounded from the walkway. Positioning her arms in front of her breasts, she huddled in the water. The laughter stopped at the apartment nearest the pool. Someone opened a door.

Her mother had watched. She knew that suddenly, knew it for sure. From the hallway. Watched her husband wash his daughter's back. Heard him say *Wish I'd married a girl like you.* Simone sank down in the water until she was fully immersed, blocking the thought of her mother's tears. For years she'd caused her mother anguish because she wouldn't shut—let alone lock—the bathroom door. She needed air, but she stayed under, pushing against the water above her until her lungs screamed. She surfaced.

Satch appeared beside her. "How come you ain't swimming?"

She shoved off from the side, stretched, and kicked, kicked hard, harder than she ever remembered. She wanted to slap her father. Forget her intention not to see him. Tomorrow after Oakhill she would make him confess.

When they finally got out of the pool, she insisted Satch take the first shower. She had other priorities. As soon as Satch closed the bathroom door, she seized the phone.

Her father didn't answer until the fifth ring. "Hello?"

"I need to see you. Tomorrow night. Alone."

"Do you know what time it is?"

Surprised, she glanced at the clock: 10:35. He went to bed early. "It's important."

"I'm taking Claire to Tahoe tomorrow morning. We won't be back until Sunday."

She caught her breath, hadn't considered the possibility he might be gone.

"What's this all about?"

If she brought it up on the phone, he'd find some way to deny it all. "I'll explain Sunday. What time will you be home?'

"Around four. Claire has a meeting Sunday night."

"Good. I want it to be just the two of us."

"Are you all right?"

"Fine. I'll see you Sunday at five o'clock." She hung up before he could question her further. Though part of her wanted to get in the car and drive to Sacramento right then, perhaps it was better to wait a few days. She'd have time at the hospital to plan what to say, to practice confronting him. Yes, it was partly her fault for not shutting the door. But she'd been a child. It was her father who bore primary responsibility for her mother's misery. She needed to hear him admit the truth.

Two hours into the night she was still wide awake, silently rehearsing the impending confrontation.

"You ain't sleeping, huh?"

"I thought you were."

"Naw. Just wishing I was."

Simone sat up in bed. Light from the lamp outside knifed through the slim gap between blinds and window frame, stabbing her eyes. She moved slightly and settled into darkness. "What were you thinking about?" Simone asked.

Satch sat up too. They stayed that way for a while without talking. Only the occasional humming of the refrigerator motor broke the stillness.

"I was thinking about my mama."

Simone's stomach tightened. Mama. Mother. Mommy. "What was she like?"

"A bitch. Beat me all the time. Hit me. Kicked me. Busted my jaw. My collarbone. My ribs. She be taking me to different doctors saying I tripped."

"God, Satch, how awful for you. I'm so sorry."

"Run away when I was thirteen. Heard the bitch died. Got high to celebrate."

Her own problems seemed trivial in comparison. "You should talk about her at Oakhill."

"Uh-huh. Like you talk about your mama?"

"She was fun. She had her down days, sure, but she was nothing like your mother." That was certainly true. Satch's mother was a perpetrator; hers was a victim.

"My daddy didn't act like I was his wife."

"Nobody beat me. You had it a lot harder."

"'Least I knew who the enemy was."

Satch's body blended into the darkness. "What do you mean?" Simone asked.

"Hated my mama. Hit back when I could. Blamed her. Now I get angry at other people, like when you come walking into Oakhill. But you blame your own self. So that's who you hurt."

"But you chose someone to punish you. How different are we, really?"

"Girl, we both fucked up."

"Girl, you right."

Satch yawned. "Getting sleepy. You?"

"Yeah."

They stretched out on their sides. Simone kept thinking about what she would say to her father. Satch's soft snores broke the stillness. Simone told herself to relax and began counting backward from a hundred. Just as she began to feel sleepy, the refrigerator make a loud, gasping sound. She lost her place and started over.

TWENTY-THREE

The next morning the sun danced off the hood of her small green Toyota, creating dazzling sparkles that made it seem like the whole world was laughing. Simone grinned to herself.

"How you be so damned happy so damned early?" Satch grumbled.

She broke into the song she used to greet her students. "Oh What a Beautiful Morning," from the musical *Oklahoma*.

"Stop!"

"You don't like sunshine?"

"Don't like nothing this early in the morning 'cept maybe music that sound like I feel." Satch switched on the radio, tuned in rap music and turned up the volume so that the whole car vibrated. "Now that," she shouted over a song as they drove along, "is morning music."

Though initially the loudness bothered Simone, she got caught up in the pulsating beat and enjoyed the spectacle they must have presented among the zooming BMWs and Mercedes—an average-seeming white woman in a somewhat homely Toyota with an orange-clad black woman passenger, listening to blaring rap music. She began moving to the beat, swaying, shaking her shoulders, dipping her head, Satch joining in, the two of them dancing in their seats.

A passing car flipped up a rock that hit the windshield, causing a tiny fracture.

By the time they picked up Viola and came through the Oakhill gate, a thin layer of clouds like smeared chalk muted the sky. Simone marveled again at how different the climate often was on the other side of the tunnel.

Satch and Viola went in the trailer as Marvin came out, his bears poking out of his jacket pockets. Though Big Ma and Big Pa looked impassive, the stitching of Katrina's mouth made it seem she was smiling.

"Hi," Simone said.

"Shh." Fingers to his lips, Marvin pointed to the bears and whispered. "They still sleeping."

Their yellow glass eyes were wide open; Simone smiled.

Jun stood before her, the scent of lemon hovering about his hair. "You get through the evening okay?"

"Yeah. Satch helped."

"Good. Will you walk with me?"

"Sure."

He led her along the tall chain-link fence toward the back of the hospital yard, his pink shoelaces tied in bows on his blue sneakers.

"I want to apologize for the massage."

"There's no need to apologize. You were just trying to make me feel better."

The lines around his eyes bunched. "After drama yesterday, I realized I'd crossed a line I shouldn't have."

"You didn't know about my father." She remembered being simultaneously delighted and discomforted by Jun's touch… until someone came through the gate: a witness just like her mother had been. "It was my whole family dynamic." She felt the rush that sometimes came with important realizations and was convinced she could bound right over the fence.

"I think so."

"Jesus!" Her dynamic with her father must have colored all her relationships with men. Was it possible that without his warped behavior she might have been attracted to healthy men, that she might now be a mother? She quivered.

"It's okay to be angry with me," Jun said.

"I'm not angry with you. I'm angry with my father. I'm going to see him Sunday and make him admit he was wrong to treat me like his wife."

"I don't think that's such a good idea."

"Sure it is." She stopped, squinted through the fence at the scraggly weeds in the yard of one of the houses bordering the hospital. The fence so clearly marked the hospital's boundaries. She vowed to start being definite about her own. "Thanks."

"For what?"

"For admitting you were wrong. We all make mistakes. I just hope my father takes responsibility." Jun could help her practice drawing boundaries, but she'd be leaving Oakhill soon. Tender green leaves on a bush in the yard next door held out hope for a vibrant summer. "Can I ask you something?"

"Sure."

"I'll be leaving here in less than a month." She wondered if she were being presumptuous. If he weren't wearing his peace earring she might not have continued. "When I leave, can we get together sometime? Like for coffee?"

His eyes seemed to linger on a patch of splintered pavement. "I'd love to, but I can't. We're not allowed to see patients or former patients outside of the hospital. It gets...too confusing."

She listened to a vacuum cleaner devouring dirt from the house next door.

"I'm sorry," he said.

"I can't believe that when I leave, I'll never see you again." How was that right, that someone who had been so important in her life would have to disappear from it as if he, too, had died in a car wreck?

"I'll miss you," he said.

"Really?"

"Really. I'm new at this, and sometimes with you I think I've crossed a lot of boundaries."

"Meeting time," Regina called from the porch.

"I wish…" he began, but he didn't finish.

A crow cawed overhead, drilling loneliness into her heart.

"Are you okay?" he asked.

She would not let this derail her. Maybe Jun would be out of her life, but she wasn't as swept away by him as she'd been a few weeks ago, and she had Satch's friendship. Plus, she had a mission. "I'm fine. I guess we better go in."

The morning check-in seemed interminable, a long litany of misery from which she deviated by saying she felt happy and determined. Most of the other two dozen members slouched in their seats and reported varying degrees of depression. Viola, who expressed joy at finding love, seemed like a bright yellow spot in a very drab room.

When check-in ended, Evelyn stood. "I have to make a very difficult announcement." Unsmiling, she walked to the front. Evelyn's glance around the room seemed to take in each member. "As you may know, federal, state and area governments have recently slashed funds for health-care services. Oakhill receives its principal funding from government spending. The bottom line is, we're being forced to close. I—"

Several gasps stopped her.

"I know this is hard. We have a month to process."

"I'm having a heart attack!" Yvonne said.

Someone sobbed. Jun and Muslimah joined Evelyn at the front of the room.

"Stay calm, people," Muslimah said.

"Shoulda warned us," Satch said, her face pinched in anger.

"I'm sorry," Evelyn said. "We had no idea Oakhill was in danger. There was no preliminary discussion. Apparently it was a last-minute decision."

Simone realized she'd been holding herself rigid. Close? Yes, she was planning to leave if she could teach summer school, but she wanted her departure to be her choice. And she couldn't begin to imagine what some of the more fragile souls would do without the hospital.

"Where we gonna go?" Marvin asked.

"Unfortunately, there's no other group program like Oakhill left," Evelyn said. "But we'll do everything we can to help each of you prepare for this unfortunate reality, including helping line up private therapists for those who don't have one."

Simone's mind flared at the injustice. Many of these people depended on Oakhill to stay safe, to say nothing about getting better. And what about all those people in the future, who would have no place to go?

"Shit," Satch said.

"There must be something we can do," Simone said.

"Call small groups." Evelyn raised her hands like she was about to say a blessing. "Work through as much as you can in the next month."

"How about a protest march?" Simone said. "Or a sit-in."

Satch snorted.

"In this political climate, I seriously doubt it would be effective." Evelyn shrugged as if in apology.

"We can't just do nothing," Simone said.

"Working on your issues is doing a lot. And I'd be happy to discuss this further in a small group. To that end I'd like to move on to scheduling those groups so we can have time for everyone who wants one."

"I'm gonna kill myself!" Lonnie said.

Simone wondered how many others felt the same.

Huddled in the sofa chair in the corner of a small group room, Marvin hunched over, silent, his eyes on his bears, his face nearly buried in their fur.

"Katrina scared," he said finally, his voice like leaves trembling.

"I understand," Jun said. "It's scary news. But she has Big Ma and Big Pa. And she's got you. She's not alone."

"She real sick. Big Ma and Big Pa can't help her. Needs a doctor, but the hospital's closed. There ain't nobody to help."

"You can, Marvin," Jun said. "Hug her. Let her know you're there for her."

"What if the voices start talking to her again? Who gonna help her then?"

Simone wanted to take Marvin in her arms and hold him, just hold him.

"She can be inpatient if she needs to be," Jun said. "Like she was before."

"She don't want to go back there."

Jun talked in a gentle voice. "I understand that. And maybe she won't need to. But if she does, she can get help. It's important she remember that."

"They don't let me stay more than a few days. What I'm gonna do then? Don't want to be back on the street no more." Marvin moved his head from side to side to side.

"You can call me to talk to if you're lonely," Simone said. "I'll give you my number. You can call any time."

"Me, too," Satch said.

"And me," Viola said. "Maybe you could bring Katrina to play with my kids. They love bears."

"See, Marvin?" Jun leaned toward him as if to imbue him with hope. "People really like you. You aren't alone. Can you remember that?"

What Marvin needed was a place to be seen as well as heard, Simone thought. A place to be held. What he needed was Oakhill.

That need was echoed by other members whose groups she attended, especially Regina's plaintive "Folks here don't care if I'm fat."

"Some rich folks spending two hundred dollars for a damned swimsuit," Satch said in her group, her face set in the anger Simone associated with her early days at the hospital. "Ain't right to close Oakhill."

"I agree," Muslimah said, the beads in her hair clacking softly as she moved her head.

"Make me mad. Feel like I'm getting beat again."

"By Thomas?"

"Uh-huh."

Muslimah spoke slowly as if to emphasize her words. "What I hear you saying is that you're a victim. It's true you can't do anything about the hospital closing. But you don't have to take Thomas's beatings."

"Don't just take 'em." Satch made fists. "I be fighting back."

"But you're still living with him," Muslimah said.

Satch's scowl deepened, but Muslimah had opened the door. "Leave Thomas," Simone said. "Now, while you still have the hospital for support."

The silence swelled. Simone feared she'd made Satch mad.

"Maybe you right."

Simone wanted to cheer, but Satch seemed strangely fragile, slumped in her chair, her unguarded expression fearful. Fearful? Satch?

"Might leave Thomas. Left my mama."

"Tell us about her," Muslimah said.

"Bitch used to kick me in the stomach. Punch me in the face. Break my bones. When I was little, I'd be wailing. But then I got older. Decided I wasn't never gonna cry again. No matter what she did, couldn't make me cry no more."

"I'm glad to hear you talk about her," Muslimah said, "and I encourage you to explore that more. But remember that you have choices now you didn't have when you were a child."

"Left my mama when I was thirteen. Ain't ready to leave Oakhill." Satch's chin jutted out, defiant, but she crossed her arms around her body as if to hold herself together.

"You can make it, Satch," Muslimah said, her palms tilted prayer-like toward Satch. "You're one strong woman. It takes courage to survive an abusive parent. Believe in yourself. It will be a struggle, but you can do it. I know you can."

Muslimah's words seemed to inflate Satch, who straightened up in her chair, giving Simone hope Satch might really leave Thomas.

Jun's slots had been taken; she'd scheduled her group with Evelyn, who entered the room and glanced around like a captain rallying the troops.

"I want to do something," Simone said. "Are they holding hearings? I could testify. I'm used to public speaking."

"I know you want to help, but the budget hearings are over. And they didn't discuss Oakhill's closure before voting for it."

Evelyn wore a muted, rose-colored blouse, and Simone wondered if she'd selected it in the hope it would soothe. If so, it wasn't working. "It makes me so angry!" Simone brought one fist against the other. "The poor are invisible."

"That's sadly true," Evelyn said, "but you need to focus on taking care of yourself."

"I intend to." She'd moved to the edge of her seat and felt as if she were plunging off a high dive. "Sunday I'm going to my father's, and I'm going to confront him about how he messed me up."

"I heard about drama yesterday. Congratulations for getting in touch with some difficult feelings."

Evelyn's praise pleased her. "I wish today were Sunday. I can't wait to tell off the son of a bitch!"

"Your reaction is certainly understandable, but you aren't giving yourself space to have your feelings about this very important realization."

"That's not true. I'm angry. You've pushed me to be in touch with my anger, and I am. That's new for me."

Evelyn flashed a smile that seemed to Simone to pat her back. "It is new, and I congratulate you, but you must let your other feelings come up, too."

"What other feelings?"

"I have no idea, but I expect there are some."

"I'm angry. Period."

"What do you expect to get from confronting him?"

"Satisfaction. Closure." She looked at the other members, who seemed to be half-listening, caught up in a fear she wouldn't let paralyze her.

"And what if he denies it all?"

"He can't. I won't let him."

Evelyn gave a half-smile; she looked tired, her short gray hair limp. Simone realized how bad Evelyn must feel about the hospital's closing.

"It sounds like he's been in denial for years," Evelyn said. "Unlike you, he's not in therapy. Why would he suddenly be able to acknowledge what he did?"

Simone ran her fingers over her lips. She hadn't considered the possibility he might not admit his guilt.

"It sounds as if you're so focused on confronting him, you're expecting a fairy-tale outcome, following which you'll live happily ever after. You need to take time to prepare for talking to him."

"But there's so little time left!" Tears pricked her eyes.

"We're going to help you find a therapist. Discuss it with her. Tell me, how did you feel when your father came in the bathroom?"

"I don't know." She thought back to her feelings the previous night in the pool, to her feelings in drama. "Happy. Guilty. Scared."

"Good, but right now those are just words. You need to let yourself feel them again, really feel them."

Some feelings didn't make you strong. Sadness and fear, for example. Sadness made you silent and fear paralyzed you, like the proverbial deer caught in the headlights. "How does being sad and scared make you strong?" she asked.

"If you let yourself have your feelings beforehand, the odds are you won't be retraumatized when you do see him."

"You don't understand. My mother heard him say he should be married to me. That was wrong. I have to make him admit it. I'm going to see him Sunday."

"I urge you to wait."

Simone turned to Satch for support, but her friend's eyes were glazed; Satch was lost in her own thoughts.

The rest of the day Simone fluctuated between anger, determination, and puzzlement. During the final meeting, member after member expressed fear about the hospital's closing. She felt sorry so many people were so distressed. Satch glowered, arms crossed like a raised drawbridge.

"Come back to my place," Simone said as they exited into a warm afternoon sun, Satch so close they bumped coming out the door. "Skinny dipping will make you feel better. Hell, I may never swim in a suit again."

She didn't even see Thomas until he'd grabbed Satch's arm and thrown her back into the fence.

"Where were you last night?" he screamed, gripping both of Satch's shoulders, pulling her from the fence and shoving her back against it.

"Stop it!" Simone jerked Thomas's wrist and tried to pull him away from Satch. "She was with me."

Thomas shoved her aside. "You better learn to stay out of my business."

"This ain't none of your business, Simone," Satch said as Thomas took her arm and shook her.

"Who were you with?"

"Simone," Satch said.

Enraged, Simone felt adrenaline spurt through her. "Let her go, asshole!"

He ignored her.

"Let her go!" Simone grasped his arm, yanked him around and swung at his leering face. Her fist crunched into his nose. Blood seeped from it. Thomas put his hands to it, saw the blood on his fingers, and his nostrils flared. His hand went back, and Simone steeled herself for his blow, but Satch grabbed his arm and pulled. He whirled back to Satch and slapped his hand across her mouth.

"No!" Simone kicked him in the back of his knee. He yelped, turning toward her. She swung at him again; this time he dodged the blow and cocked his fist. She made no effort to duck but found herself jerked back out of Thomas's reach. Jun, Evelyn, and Rick quickly encircled him, pinning Thomas against the fence.

"Racist motherfuckers! Let go!" he bellowed, struggling vainly for release, blood still trickling from his nose.

Simone feared that the black residents of this street might come out, see three nonblacks pinning a black man, and turn to violence of their own. She scanned the street but saw only one older man across the way, and he was shaking his head as if in disgust.

Muslimah hurried to their group. "The police are on the way."

Simone tried to offer Satch a tissue to wipe the blood from her lip, but she angrily shoved Simone's hand away.

When the police pulled up, Evelyn, Rick, and Jun released Thomas. There were two policemen, one hulking, one thin and acned. "What's going on?" the big one asked.

Evelyn introduced herself as the director of Oakhill and explained that Thomas had assaulted one of her patients, indicating Satch.

"What do you mean?" Thomas bellowed and pointed at Simone. "She hit me. She swung first!"

"That's because you were hurting Satch, asshole!"

"Let me get this straight," the policeman said. "You," he pointed to Simone, "hit him?"

"Yes, but only because he grabbed Satch and threw her against the fence. And he hit her, just like he's hit her before. Lots of times!"

"You lie, bitch!" Thomas said.

"You want to press charges?" the policeman asked Satch.

"Yes she does!" Simone said.

"Let's let her speak for herself," the cop said.

Satch wiped the blood from her lip with the back of her hand and stared at the red drops against her brown skin.

"What's it gonna be?" the cop repeated. "Want us to run this guy in?"

"Satch, show yourself your courage," Muslimah said, but Satch silenced her by holding up her hand.

Satch looked at Thomas for a long moment.

Simone's heart raced.

"He's just like your mother," Muslimah said. "You stood up to her. You can stand up to him."

"Come on, Satch," Simone said. "Stand up to him."

"Press charges," Evelyn urged.

"Do it," Jun said.

Satch looked from Evelyn to Muslimah, but Simone didn't think Satch saw anybody. Not really.

"No charges," Satch said finally, and she seemed to collapse down, to give in to despair.

Simone's heart plunged into her stomach. Muslimah, Evelyn, and Jun simultaneously frowned.

"Satch," Muslimah said.

"Please," Simone said.

Satch hesitated again. Looked at Thomas. He looked right back. "No charges." She averted her eyes from them and walked off down the street.

"Stay with me tonight," Simone called after her, but Satch just walked away without turning around.

"Now, do *you* want to press charges?" the policeman asked Thomas.

Thomas straightened himself up. "Naw," he said with a cocky grin that enraged Simone even further.

"Don't you touch her again, you bastard!"

"Officer, you gonna let this bitch threaten me?" Thomas said in a mocking tone.

She stepped toward Thomas, but Jun took her arm, restraining her. Thomas winked at her. "I know how to make that woman feel all good inside. That's something you can't ever do." He sauntered off after Satch, who was walking ahead of him, her eyes on the sidewalk.

Muslimah frowned.

Simone saw with a start that Jun was watching her.

"Go ahead," he said. "Let it out."

She brusquely wiped her eyes.

"You can't let this throw you off," Evelyn said. "Satch has to make her own choices. Just like you do."

"Uh-huh." She turned to leave, but Evelyn put a strong, restraining hand on her arm.

"Are you sure you can stay safe tonight?" Evelyn said.

Rage filled her. Rage at Thomas, at Muslimah, at Evelyn, at Jun. Rage at her father. "You should have done something about Thomas!"

"Like what?" Evelyn thrust her hands down in a signal of her own frustration.

"I don't know!"

"I don't either," Evelyn said. "But the question at the moment is, can you keep from cutting tonight?"

"You don't need to worry about it. It's *my* problem."

"You're wrong, Simone. It's ours too," Jun said. "We care about you."

"What about Satch?"

"Of course we care about Satch." Evelyn sounded angry. "But the only question you have to answer is whether you can guarantee us you'll be safe tonight."

She listened but, surprisingly, heard no maniac's voice urging her to harm herself. "Yes, okay." Thomas and Satch. Her father. Her betrayal of her mother. The hospital closing. What could possibly keep the cutting voice from overwhelming a simple pledge?

After the staff went back inside, Rick still loomed beside her, so big he blocked the sun. "How about a walk?" he said.

Walking around this neighborhood seemed too threatening to her. Too many pieces of shattered glass. Too many temptations.

"You know Lake Temescal?" he asked.

Surprised, she looked at him directly. He poised lightly on his feet, seemed ready to back away if she gave him cause. "No. I live in Contra Costa."

"Then it's on your way home."

She wasn't sure she wanted to go with him, but she wasn't ready to go home, to be alone, and she felt grateful for his help in restraining Thomas.

"Okay," she said. "I'll follow you."

He led the way, driving his rusting old Volkswagen van with care, stopping at yellow lights so they didn't get separated. Though she hated to admit it, she'd enjoyed smashing her fist into Thomas's nose. If only it would convince Satch to leave him, she'd happily clobber Thomas every day. Still revved, Simone replayed the assault in her mind. What made her begin to come down from her adrenaline rush was the memory of the defeat in Satch's eyes.

Twenty-Four

Walking out of the parking lot at Temescal Lake, Simone and Rick crossed a bridge over a trickling creek. Grand willows draped down toward green grass, shadows and light mixing in painterly patterns. Red-winged blackbirds sang from cattails that lined a portion of the lake. Geese honked, ducks quacked, and children shouted in the distance. The vise that had inhibited her lungs loosened as she inhaled the fragrances of dried cattails and newly mown grass.

"It's beautiful," she said.

"There's a swimming section at the other end. But it's a little cold still."

They walked around the lake once, tension easing further. In the swimming section, little children waded in the water, filling the air with their laughter.

They circled back to where they'd entered and perched on a large rock overlooking the water. Simone pressed her hands against the craggy rock. "Do you come here a lot?"

"Spent the night a few times. Just my sleeping bag. Never got caught."

"You're not afraid?"

"Nope."

"I would be."

Two ducks swam near them, quacking loudly, like old ladies complaining. She smiled.

"You weren't afraid today," he said.

"No. I was too pissed."

The late afternoon sun caressed them, and she leaned back against the rock. Rick remained seated upright. Studying his profile, she realized with surprise that he had a masculine, sensual quality. His hair was thick and wavy, the edges close to white. His gray eyes reminded her of feathers. Despite the snakes coiled around his neck, she felt safe with him, this man who had once told her that all you had to do to get a woman to love you was to laugh in her face.

"You were great today," he said.

She sat up. "I feel bad."

"That you hit Thomas?"

"That I enjoyed it so much."

"Sometimes hitting people feels good."

Rick kept his eyes on the lake. She felt a nauseating thud in her gut. "It shouldn't."

"Not defenseless people. Assholes like Thomas."

"You *like* fighting?"

"Why not?"

She leaned away from him. A red-winged blackbird called, its song both piercing and peaceful. "There's better ways to express anger than hitting people."

"Think you could have stopped Thomas with words?"

It seemed like he'd spat out *words*. "That's the exception," she said.

"World's full of exceptions."

"We might have to fight sometimes, but I don't think we should enjoy it."

His shoulders seemed to let down a little. "Maybe not."

"What makes you so angry you like it?"

He didn't answer her for a while, and when he spoke he sounded casual. "My mom used to hire me out for men to fuck."

"Oh god, Rick, I'm so sorry." An egret glided to a landing on the shore near them, so smooth, so silent. It seemed like egrets went through life quietly, while humans so often screamed and wailed. "How old were you?"

"Started when I was six. Lasted 'til she got shot in a drug deal. I was eleven."

"What about your father?"

Rick shrugged. "He was a junkie. He'd just sit there using and saying it was wrong. Never really tried to stop her."

"No wonder you…" So much about him suddenly made sense to her. "Who raised you after your mother died?"

"Foster families tried. But I was out of control. Ended up in Juvie."

Rick's story was so much worse than her own. Simone peered into his soft gray eyes and thought she could glimpse the terrified little boy he must have been. "How did you get to Oakhill?"

"Probation. Busted up a man in a bar fight. I've been in jail a few times for fighting. Figured Oakhill was better than prison. And something else." He shrugged and stared at hands that looked strong enough to crack walnuts. "I've tried to kill myself twice. I guess practice makes perfect." He gave a mirthless chuckle. "I don't think I want there to be a next time."

Children chased each other on the grass behind them, shouting and laughing, "We've only got a month," she said, shifting her position on the rock that suddenly jutted into her. "What will you do then?"

"I'll be okay. I'm not sure everybody will."

"I know. Like Marvin. He's such an innocent. This isn't a safe world for innocents."

"Do you put yourself in that category?"

Surprised, she searched his face for a smile, some clue that he was joking. "Hardly. I've had more lovers than Casanova."

"It isn't about sex."

"I guess not." She wasn't sure what defined innocence, but she knew that whatever the criteria, she didn't fit the category. "I colluded with my father against my mother. I'm definitely not an innocent."

"I'm not so sure."

"I am."

They watched the lake, the birds; the waning sun cast golden coating over trees and water. In contrast, her mind churned. Rick stretched again, and this time his shoulder brushed hers. He left it there, touching her. He wore a blue-and-gray flannel shirt, striped like the bars of a jail cell. Regardless of his reasons, going around beating people up was wrong. She scooted away just a fraction so that their bodies no longer touched.

"This isn't any of my business," she said, "but your story worries me. Did you manage to escape infection?"

"Depends on what you mean. I got infected with anger. But it was before AIDS, so I'm not HIV positive."

"Thank god. You can cure anger."

"Can you?"

"It seems like it. You're talking about your situation. That's the first step. You should discuss it at Oakhill tomorrow."

"Admit I was a prostitute?" He fingered his jeans.

"But you didn't do it voluntarily."

He made no reply, just tossed a small stone in the water. It formed ripples that spread further and further, a circle of small waves.

"You're not like me," she said. "No one was threatening me. I chose to leave the bathroom door open. I chose to call my rapist for a date. You did nothing to shame yourself." She picked up a palm-sized rock and squeezed it, pleased by its solidity and its rough edges. She squeezed harder.

Rick took her hand and gently lifted her fingers one by one. His fingers were rough, but his touch was soft. She dropped the rock. He released her hand. The damp smell of the lake eased the headache that had begun with her pledge not to hurt herself.

"Where do you live?" she asked.

"I have an old sailboat. It's just twenty-five feet. It's at a marina in Alameda. I live on it."

"Really? You sail?"

He flashed a rueful smile. "I want to. It's a fixer upper, but at least it floats. And I figure it's better to be stripping wood than hitting people. One of these days I'll sail it. I like living on it. At night, when the sun sets, everything seems so peaceful."

"I've always wanted to sail on the Bay."

"When the boat's finished, I'll take you."

"I'd like that."

"Might be a while. It doesn't have a mast."

"Details."

The sun set behind the surrounding hills; she shivered. Rick took off the flannel shirt he wore over his T-shirt and handed it to her.

"Won't you get cold?" She hesitated to put it on.

"I don't get cold much."

"Then why do you wear this shirt?"

"For protection." He smiled.

Simone wasn't sure she'd seen Rick smile before. She didn't know if it was his shirt or his smile that warmed her, but she was glad for both, though she could practically trip on the sleeves that hung far below her hands.

"Looks good," he said, smiling again.

"Feels good," she said, not smiling at all.

They made one more circle around the lake. The blackbirds warbled. Laughter sounded from a grill on a hill, the smoky smell of barbecued chicken tickling her taste buds. When they got back to their cars, she started to take off his shirt.

He held up his hand. "Give it to me tomorrow."

"Thanks." She buttoned it to the top. "And thanks for helping with Thomas."

"No problem."

"I wonder if Satch is safe."

"Hope so. You did all you could. You pack quite a punch. If you ever swing at me, I'll remember to duck."

They lingered by their cars, incoming fog casting shadows and chill around them.

"Want to get an early dinner?" he asked.

Part of her did, wanted to avoid being alone with all the thoughts and feelings that had come up for her, but she wanted to be home if Satch called. "Can I take a rain check?"

"Sure."

"See you tomorrow. And thanks again for the shirt."

"Any time."

They got in their cars, and she realized she should have driven straight home. It was six-thirty. Traffic would be jammed through the Caldecott Tunnel. Satch probably wouldn't call, but she needed to be there. Just in case.

At seven-thirty, Simone called Satch. The phone just kept ringing. She wished Satch had come home with her.

After a quick dinner and another unanswered call to Satch, she turned on the television and huddled on the couch, Rick's shirt wrapped around her. She didn't really focus on what she was watching; she kept thinking about Satch.

When there was still no answer at eleven, Simone decided to wait half an hour then call again. If Satch didn't answer, she would do something. Call 911. Go there. Something. She paced; it seemed only a few strides between walls. Watching the clock, she could swear she saw the minute hand move.

At eleven-thirty she called. Satch answered on the third ring. "Hello?"

"Are you okay?"

"Yeah."

In the background someone—presumably Thomas—played a mournful sax that filled her with loneliness.

"Don't call no more. I'm sleepy. See you tomorrow."

"You're safe? Thomas hasn't hurt you?"

"No. 'Night."

Satch hung up. It wasn't the conversation Simone had wanted to have—she would like to have talked to Satch about hitting Thomas and about her walk with Rick—but the phone line went dead and she replaced her receiver. Though she lay down and tried to sleep, the mournful tune from Thomas's sax haunted her, stirring images of empty city streets and littered cups rolling in the breeze.

Twenty-Five

Ringing shattered her sleep. It was six-thirty. Sunlight prodded the blinds. Simone grabbed the phone, fearing the worst. "Hello?"

"Morning."

At the sound of Satch's voice, relief washed over her. "You're okay?"

"Fine." Satch drawled the *i*, as if the long vowel sound would authenticate her words. "Gonna help my auntie move, so don't be calling. Thomas gotta sleep."

"You're not going to Oakhill?"

"Naw."

Simone listened closely to Satch's response, searching for anger or despair or anything else that might trigger her alarm.

"You gotta get Viola," Satch said.

"No problem." She recalled Satch's glum face when she refused to press charges, the defeated look in eyes so dark they reminded Simone of shadows. "You're sure you're okay?"

"Done told you I was."

She thought Satch's voice sounded heavier than usual, but she couldn't be sure. "You sound sort of down."

"Ain't slept much. Somebody call late last night."

"Sorry."

"See you."

"Satch!" Simone didn't want to hang up, to sever a connection that might keep Satch safe.

"Yeah?"

"I just..." She searched for the right words. "I really care about you."

"Uh-huh."

"I mean it! I do."

"I know."

"See you tomorrow?"

"Yeah."

"Be careful moving furniture. Don't strain your back."

"'Bye."

The phone clicked. Simone replaced the receiver and lay back down, musing about the call. It seemed too convenient that Satch's aunt allegedly needed her help the day after the incident with Thomas. Satch would know nobody would believe her if she claimed she had the flu. Simone suspected Thomas had hit Satch again, though he'd been serenading her with his sax the previous night, so maybe Satch was telling the truth, maybe all was fine.

Sunlight edged through a crooked blind, striping her fraying comforter.

A car pulled away from in front of the projects just as Simone arrived. Delighted with her good fortune, she parked and got out. Two men, older than the previous group, faced the street, hooded dark jackets shadowing their faces. They looked to her like Satanic monks.

She asked herself if she should be worried but recalled that previously the threatening young men had proven harmless.

She started up the walk; the men fell silent. She made eye contact with one whose eyes were like dark stones, and she looked back at the splotched pavement.

"Whooee," the other said. "Look what coming down the walk. White pussy." She looked up. He grabbed his crotch. "Gonna get me some of that."

Moving off the sidewalk, she gave the men a wide berth.

"Hey, I be waiting when you come back," one said. "Got just what you need, baby."

Laughter exploded from them, and she hurried up the stairs, noticing the stench of urine.

Darius opened the door to her, a pistol in his hand. He pulled the trigger, squirting her with water. Simone clutched her shoulder and pretended to stumble backward. "You got me."

Darius grinned. An unsmiling Viola took the gun from her son. Simone recalled the circumstances of Aisha's death and blushed.

"Where'd you get this?" Viola frowned in disgust.

Darius stuck out his lower lip. "Ryan gave it to me."

"Well I'm giving it back. You know we don't play with guns." Viola tucked in the upturned tag of her son's purple jersey. "Do you hear me, little boy?"

Straightening, Darius threw every inch of himself into filling out his shirt. "I ain't no little boy."

Viola squatted in front of him. "Even when you're all grown up and playing for the Oakland Raiders, you'll still be my baby."

"Aw, Mama." Darius put on a disdainful expression.

"Am I gonna be your baby, too?" Shona asked, taking her mother's hand.

"Always. My baby girl." Viola smoothed Shona's pink dress. "Give me a hug, babies."

Darius turned away. "I'm too old for hugging."

"There's no such thing as too old for hugs." Viola turned him toward her as Shona threw her arms around them and all three embraced.

Simone backed away. Her mother had never hugged her, not like that, not with that total, uncomplicated love. Never, she was sure of it.

A knock at the door startled her. Viola opened the door to the kids' babysitter and teacher, Eunice. After last-minute admonitions to be good, Simone and Viola left. To Simone's relief, the two hooded men were leaning against a car engrossed in a discussion with the driver.

On the way to Oakhill Viola read from a *Bible* study book. Simone puzzled over why her mother hadn't hugged her. If only she were still alive. Simone would like to sit down with her and talk, really talk. Probably everybody felt that way about parents who'd died. And maybe about living ones, too. It couldn't be often that parents and children talked openly, without walls or blame. Sadness stole over her. She marveled that it felt so sweet.

While Viola went on in, Simone stopped at a table with Regina, whose puffy face was wrinkled in concern. Marvin drooped, his head in his hands, his elbows propped on the concrete table. She didn't see his bears. "Where's Katrina and the others, Marvin?"

He covered his eyes.

"Been trying to get him to talk," Regina said.

"Did something happen to them?" she asked.

"Got pneumonia," he said, not lifting his head.

"Better take 'em to a doctor," Regina said.

Marvin didn't respond. Simone sat beside him and wrapped Rick's shirt around her against the chill. "Having a hard morning?" she asked.

"Yeah." He still didn't look up.

"Is there anything I can do?"

Marvin's glasses slipped down his nose. He didn't bother to push them back up. Simone glanced at Regina, who was clearly worried, too.

"You ain't hearing voices, is you?" Regina said.

"Only voice I hear be Evelyn's saying Oakhill closing." He dug his fingers into the table.

"We've got a month," Simone said, searching for some way to encourage him. "Maybe they'll change their minds and keep it open."

"Naw. Just like Katrina."

"Katrina?" She pictured the little bear, the one with the smile.

"The hurricane. Politicians don't care about no poor folks. Just leave 'em to drown."

"Morning meeting," Yvonne announced from the trailer door, her hand over her heart like she was about to pledge allegiance.

"I miss the bears," Regina said as they rose to go inside. "Bring 'em tomorrow?"

Marvin shoved his glasses back up his nose. "Maybe. If they better."

"I bet they will be," Simone said. "Bears bounce back."

During announcements in the general meeting, Muslimah reported that Satch wouldn't be in because she was helping her aunt, and Lonnie had gone to the Social Security office. After the meeting, Simone stopped Muslimah, whose gold dress reminded her of sunset.

"Did Satch sound okay?"

"Yes."

"You aren't worried?"

"Should I be?"

"When she called me this morning, she sounded down. I was afraid Thomas might have beaten her."

"Satch sounded perfectly fine. You need to focus on taking care of yourself." Muslimah glanced at her watch and walked away.

Clearly the woman didn't get it.

In her small group with Jun, Simone mentioned her fear about Satch, confident he would share her concern. He kept trying to steer her into a discussion of how she felt about the events of the previous afternoon. "Hitting him was more satisfying than sex." Surprised to hear herself say that, she wondered if it was how Thomas felt when he belted Satch.

After her own group, Simone attended Rick's, the first he'd ever called. Dressed in another flannel shirt—this one orange and red and green, autumn plaid—he kept his eyes hidden behind the hair that he let fall across them. In a halting voice he confessed his forced prostitution.

"Poor thing," Viola said, her voice like caressing hands.

"Can't imagine that," Marvin said. Without the bears, he wrung his hands.

"'Bout the age I was when my stepdaddy rape me," Regina said. "But it sound worse for you."

"It isn't a matter of better or worse," Jun said. "It was awful for both of you."

"It took guts to tell us," Simone said, and gave Rick her most encouraging smile. To her surprise, he smiled back, not a joyous smile but a frail one, his lips just curving up. She imagined trombones proclaiming Rick's triumph over his fears. She wanted trombones for Satch, too, but she kept hearing Thomas's sax, feeling a growing apprehension.

After Rick's group she decided that waking Thomas was the least of her concerns, and she called. No one answered. At lunch and before closing meeting she tried again with the same result. Leaving Oakhill, she told herself moving could take hours, but her logic didn't dispel her anxiety.

She drove faster than she should to Satch's apartment, flooring the accelerator at yellow lights, cursing every slow driver, every stop sign, every delay.

In front of Satch's she screeched to a stop and flung open the car door, then hesitated. What if Thomas were home? She opened the trunk and took out the tire iron. It felt brutal in her hands, hard, dangerous. She looked at it for a moment then tossed it back in the trunk, afraid he might grab it and use it, afraid *she* might.

The door into the building was again unlocked. The smell of fried onions followed her up the stairs she took two at a time. As she reached the gloomy third-floor hallway, she tried to formulate a plan, but all she could come up with was to barge in if Thomas opened the door and to pull Satch out if she did. She knocked, her heart louder to her ears than her fist. No answer. She pounded the door. She tried to convince herself her fears were groundless, that Satch was just out helping her aunt like she'd said, but she couldn't shake the dread in her bones.

She hurried back to the ground floor and hammered a door marked *Manager*. A woman answered, a cigarette dangling from her lips, her stomach dangling over her belt. Smoke half-concealed suspicious eyes. "Yeah?"

Simone explained that she had reason to be concerned about a tenant, and asked if the woman would please open the apartment door.

The woman put her hands on her broad hips and widened her stance. "You got a badge?"

"No, but—"

"You got a warrant?"

"No."

"Don't bother me." She shut the door in Simone's face.

Simone wanted to lunge through the door, but she suspected that only worked in movies, so she knocked again. When the woman didn't answer, she began kicking the door rhythmically—not hard enough to do damage, but too hard to ignore. *Thump. Thump.*

The woman opened the door. "Get outta here before I call the cops."

"Go ahead. But I promise you, I have a lawyer, and if my friend is in danger and you refuse to open her door, I swear to God I'll sue you."

The woman took a drag on her cigarette, studied Simone, and blew a small cloud of smoke in her eyes. Simone didn't flinch. Without a word the manager started down the grungy hallway with its stained wallpaper, keys jangling from a ring she clasped in her pudgy fingers, and lumbered up the stairs. Simone thought she could cut her wrist and bleed to death at the rate the woman moved. "Please hurry," she urged.

The woman ignored her. Simone followed close behind, catching whiffs of a rancid body odor that nearly choked her. When they got to Satch's apartment, the woman knocked. After a brief wait, she inserted the key, still knocking, and slowly turned the knob. Simone thrust open the door.

Satch was curled up tight on her couch in her orange sweats.

"Just asleep," the woman said.

Simone thought so, too, until she spotted the music box shattered on the floor, the ballerina broken in pieces. She rushed to the couch. Satch had a deep bruise under her right eye. Her left was swollen shut. Simone touched her shoulder, silently cursing Thomas. Satch didn't respond. "Satch?" She pushed her arm. Still no response. "Satch!" Nothing.

"Call 911!" Simone screamed at the manager, who stood there watching like this was a television program and she was debating whether to change the channel. *"Now,* damn you!"

The manager finally started toward the telephone. Simone held her fingers under Satch's nose. She couldn't feel a breath. She pressed trembling fingers to Satch's neck. Frantically searching, she discovered a faint pulse. Satch was alive. She glanced around the couch. A small brown bottle poked out from beneath the sofa. Simone snatched it up. Wellbutrin, an antidepressant. She didn't want to think about what Satch might have mixed with it.

Simone grabbed Satch's shoulders and hauled her into a sitting position. "Satch! Wake up!" Satch's head rolled on her chest. Her body remained limp. Simone slapped her. When Satch didn't wake up, she slapped her again.

Satch still didn't respond. Simone tried to pull her forward and up to a standing position, but Satch was heavy and limp, and her body kept sliding toward the floor. "Help me!" she yelled at the manager when she got off the phone. Reluctantly, the woman came over, cigarette still between her lips, and grabbed Satch under one arm while Simone took the other. They pulled Satch up; she remained unconscious. Her skin was still warm, but her body seemed boneless and unbelievably heavy, a ponderous slumping weight. As they tried to walk her around the room, her feet dragged the floor.

"She ain't gonna make it," the manager said, dropping her cigarette in a partially full coffee cup as they passed by; the cigarette sizzled.

"Shut up!"

The woman smirked but didn't say anything else. *Don't die,* Simone silently exhorted Satch. *Please don't die!*

They kept on dragging Satch until it seemed they'd circled her living room at least a hundred times. With each circuit her body felt heavier. Simone's back and shoulders ached from trying to keep Satch erect. The manager grunted, wiping sweat from her forehead.

Two paramedics burst into the room. Simone barely registered their ministrations as they tended Satch then strapped her in a neck collar on to a backboard. She hopped up in the back of the ambulance with Satch. A paramedic directed Simone to the padded bench beside the gurney. He put a small object on one of Satch's fingers; it looked like a Band-Aid with a wire and red light. It beeped—high-pitched and steady.

The siren shrieked. Simone wanted to. The ambulance sped away. The paramedic put an I.V. in Satch's arm and peppered Simone with questions about Satch, her identity and her bruises and about the Wellbutrin, how much and when. Simone had few answers. She felt submerged, could hear only vague voices, felt like she was drowning. She couldn't take her eyes off Satch's face. *Live,* she willed her friend. Satch had triumphed over so much abuse in her life, she couldn't give up now. The instant the paramedic signaled she could, Simone grabbed Satch's hand and held tight.

The ambulance rounded a corner and slowed. The high-pitched beeping of the cuff on Satch's finger began to drop ominously.

"She's destatting!" the paramedic in back called to his partner.

Simone froze. The beep slowed, deepened. The ambulance stopped. The driver leapt out. He flung open the ambulance door. They yanked the gurney out, punched a door code, and shoved the gurney with Satch through the first door of Highland Hospital then through swinging doors into the ER yelling "She's coding!"

Simone was right behind them through the first door. A bulky security guard blocked her way to the inner doors, which closed, cutting off her view of people rushing toward Satch.

"Can't go in there," the guard said.

"She's dying!" Simone lunged forward, trying to force her way through the swinging door, but the guard grabbed her and began pushing her back outside.

"You need to go to the ER waiting room, Miss," the guard said.

"Please! I have to stay with her!"

"Sorry. You got to go to the waiting area. Outside and around the front entrance."

The guard moved back. The door closed. Simone tried to shove her way back in, but the door wouldn't budge. Frantically she climbed up and over a rise to the hospital's front entrance, rushed inside, and followed the signs to ER waiting. She saw a crowd of seated people and a semi-circular desk where a lone receptionist spoke with a forlorn-looking couple. Another security guard blocked the hallway to the ER, which was again hidden behind swinging doors.

Simone hurried to the desk. "Excuse me," she said, intruding on the couple, "but my friend's coding! I have to be with her!"

The stoop-shouldered woman behind the desk looked at Simone with what seemed like genuine sympathy. "I'll be with you when I've finished helping these people."

"But my friend overdosed and she just coded and—"

"There's nothing you can do but wait, anyway. I'll be right with you."

Simone's gut knotted in a way it hadn't in weeks. For what seemed like hours she waited behind the couple, tapping her fists together in a futile effort to compose herself.

"Please," she said when it was her turn, "can you check on my friend? Satch Hughes." She grasped the desk's edge so tight she was surprised it didn't dent.

The woman behind the desk folded her hands as if moving slowly might settle Simone. "I can't leave my desk, but the doctor will be out as soon as there's anything to tell you. In the meantime you need to talk to the registrar."

"What?"

"About your friend." She had a look of compassion, but her words sounded almost recited, and Simone realized the woman must deal with frantic people all day long, that other people's emergencies were her routine. "After you talk to the registrar, you can wait in the family room." The woman indicated an area behind the security guard. "Next," she said.

A turbaned young man stepped around Simone; he held the hand of an elderly woman in a turquoise sari, her left eye blood red.

"Wait!" Simone said. "Can't you just check to see if she's alive? Satch Hughes."

"The doctor will find you."

The registrar who interviewed her was missing a front tooth and kept poking his tongue into the empty space. He asked her a slew of questions, most of which she couldn't answer. Did Satch have children, relatives, any known allergies, previous hospitalizations? Simone couldn't tell him much beyond the fact Satch attended Oakhill. When he queried whether there was anyone else who should be notified, she said no. Oakhill was closed for the day, she didn't know Satch's aunt's name or phone number, and Thomas deserved to be in jail. The registrar dismissed her and directed her to the family room, assuring her a doctor would talk to her "soon."

Simone entered the windowless family room: it was aptly named, she thought, because Satch felt like family to her. The room was so small she suspected people seated across from each other would bump knees. No one else was there. She tried sitting on one of the padded green chairs, squeezing her hands between her thighs, but she was too agitated, her stomach so knotted she could barely take in air. She leapt up and eyed the ER doors at the end of the hallway. For a moment she contemplated making a dash for the treatment area, but she sensed that might get her thrown out. Instead she crossed her arms, put her hands on her shoulders, and prayed.

Simone stood in the doorway, her eyes riveted on the treatment doors, for what seemed like the slowest moments of her life. Finally a young doctor in green scrubs and white coat came through the doors. His goatee was so short his chin looked like it had been dipped in ink.

"How is she?" Simone said, starting toward him.

"Are you with Satch Hughes?"

"Yes!"

The doctor looked down. "It took time to get her heart started beating, and we haven't been able to get her to breathe on her own. We're still trying. She's on a respirator."

"Oh no!" Simone covered her mouth with her hand and bit her palm.

"There's not much more I can tell you. We'll keep you informed." He turned and walked back through the ER doors.

Satch was drifting toward death. Tears stung Simone's eyes. She nearly fainted. The bare room seemed like a coffin. She yearned to call someone, didn't want to face this nightmare alone, but the person she most wanted with her was Satch. She struggled to think clearly. Meghan would never understand how much Satch meant to her. Viola had to tend her children. She couldn't reach Jun after hours. Her father still didn't even know she went to Oakhill. Rick might be comforting, but she didn't know his last name let alone his phone number. There was no one.

Simone stared at her watch, at the numbers in black bold digits, studied it as the seconds passed, each one feeling more like a minute, an hour, a year. Had Satch started breathing? Could she already be dead?

Finally the ER doors opened. The goateed doctor walked toward her. She tried to read his expression, but his face was impassive. "Her heart's steady for the moment. She's still breathing with a respirator." He cast her a furtive glance. "The next few hours will be critical. She may have suffered brain damage when her heart was stopped. That's not uncommon in these cases." He said something about moving Satch to ICU, but Simone's mind was stuck on the words *brain damage.*

The doctor turned to leave. "Wait! When can I see her?"

"Try the ICU in a couple hours. You can have five minutes every hour if they're not working on her."

"But you think she might be okay." She phrased it as a statement because she didn't want to give him an opening to disagree.

"I hope so."

She watched until he disappeared through the ER doors. It was 7:05. By nine, with any luck, she'd be able to see Satch.

At nine o'clock Simone pressed the intercom button in the tiny ICU waiting room. A voice came over it asking whom she wanted to visit, and she gave Satch's name. After a moment the door buzzed. She hurried through.

A nurse with peace-symbol earrings like Jun's and hair that brushed her shoulders led Simone to Satch's bed in a small glass-enclosed area and said she could have five minutes. Satch's color was ashen. Tape held a tube in place in her opened mouth. It led to a ventilator. A catheter tube snaked to a urine bag strapped to her bed. An I.V. in her arm connected to a bag suspended from a pole. Machines beeped and measured.

Simone gave Satch's hand a gentle squeeze. "You look like shit." There was no response. She had no idea if Satch could hear her. The words *brain damage* echoed in her mind. "Stay with us, Satch. Please don't die." No response. Not knowing what else to do, Simone rubbed Satch's hand. She wanted Satch to say something, do something, at least move her finger, but Satch just lay there breathing with the help of a machine.

After what seemed like mere seconds, the nurse beckoned to her that it was time to leave. Leaning over, Simone spoke in

Satch's ear. "Come stay with me. You don't need to go back to Thomas. I love you, Satch. Please live."

When she returned to the ICU waiting room, three people huddled together, sobbing, and she walked out because she didn't want to intrude on their grief. She thought about going home, but she couldn't abandon Satch even though Satch had chosen to abandon everyone who cared about her.

Eventually she returned to the ICU waiting room. The three grieving people were gone. Simone closed her eyes. She must have fallen asleep because she was startled by someone touching her shoulder. It was Thomas, dressed in jeans and a black leather jacket, wearing his yin-yang earring, his eyes full of sorrow.

"How's she doing?" he asked, and his voice broke.

She was dazed by his presence and his tears. "Unconscious but alive. For now." She wanted to scream at him, to curse him, to pummel him with blows and words, but his tears restrained her.

He wiped his eyes. "Why'd she do it?"

"You're kidding."

His voice was pleading. "I didn't hardly hit her."

She didn't want to talk to Thomas, didn't want to be on the same planet with him.

"Satch is always strong," he said, staring at his fists. "She always swings back. Not this time. She just stood there and let me hit her."

Simone's face flushed so hot she thought she could burn him with it. "What gives you the right to use Satch as your punching bag?"

Thomas opened his fists and stared at his long fingers. "It just seems like sometimes, I get so angry, I've got to hit somebody." He looked confused, puzzled by his own violence.

"Hit yourself."

He smiled for just an instant then his eyes teared up again. "She's gonna be okay, right?"

"They don't know. She might have brain damage."

"Damn." He looked away. When he finally turned back to her, tears slid down his cheeks. "Never O.D.'d before. Why'd she do it?"

"We found out the hospital's closing. Maybe that did it. That and your fists."

A look of anger flashed across his face. "That woman's been loving me a long time." He wiped away tears. "If you hadn't butted in, she'd be fine. You messed with her mind."

Simone's chest clenched. She stood and positioned herself so close to Thomas she could practically feel his breath. "If she recovers, I'm going to mess with her mind all I can to keep her from going back to you."

He leaned away from her. "I'll be back tomorrow. She'll be okay by then." He brushed his eyes. "Like I said, the woman was doing fine 'til you came along."

Twenty-Six

Satch had still not regained consciousness by eight the next morning. Another doctor told Simone it could be hours or days before they knew if she would. Simone decided she had to go to Oakhill. Since her car was still at Satch's, she took a taxi and practically sprang through the gate, ready to pounce, her mood made darker by the fog that partially shrouded the buildings. She entered the kitchen just as the weekly staff meeting—which was held where members, seated at an adjoining table, could listen—was breaking up. "Satch is in the hospital," she blurted out. "She tried to kill herself!"

"Oh no," Muslimah said softly, sinking back onto her chair, giving Simone the satisfaction of seeing the woman who had minimized Satch's danger shaken.

The members around Simone drew back in on themselves. Unable to contain her feelings, she slammed her palm against the table. Her hand hurt; she enjoyed the pain and raised her hand again.

Evelyn was instantly beside her, holding her wrist in the air, preventing her from bringing it down. "Stop! You aren't to blame."

How had Evelyn known?

Evelyn released her. "I need to meet with the staff. Simone, I want you to call a group with me. And I want you to promise me you won't hurt yourself again."

She was reluctant to agree until Rick moved beside her. "Okay," she mumbled. Jun touched her shoulder before joining Muslimah in Evelyn's office.

Several members clustered around her.

"Satch gonna be okay?" a teary-eyed Regina asked.

"I don't know."

Regina encircled Simone with her arms. Surprised Regina would risk contamination, Simone hugged her back. They held on to each other for one long desperate moment, then separated.

"How did Satch do it?" Rick asked.

His voice jerked her from her thoughts.

"What method?" Rick said.

"Pills."

"She didn't say nothing?" Marvin asked, clinching his bears.

"She was unconscious."

"Did Thomas beat her?" Viola said.

"Yes."

"Damn."

Coming from Viola, the word seemed like true profanity. Simone wondered how Viola had gotten to the hospital. "Sorry I couldn't pick you up."

"That's okay. Yule brought me."

The Christmas man, Satch had called him. The memory of Satch's teasing made Simone feel like crying.

Most of the members went outside. Regina walked to the sink and began washing her hands, over and over, pumping the lemon-scented soap. Simone didn't have the energy to stop her. Rick went to Regina, turned off the water and handed her some paper towels, which Regina used to dry her hands with the same repetitive motions she'd used to wash them.

Rick returned to Simone's side. "How are you doing?" he asked. He wore straight-legged jeans that bulged a bit around his thighs, giving the impression of muscled legs.

"I keep thinking of the things I did that I shouldn't have and the things I didn't do that I wish I had."

"Yeah. I do that." He took a notepad and pen from his autumn plaid shirt pocket, scribbled something and handed it to her. It was his name—Rick Stell—and phone number.

"I wanted to call you last night." Simone rubbed her aching temples, felt the exhaustion that seemed to seep into her with each word she said.

"Call any time," Rick said.

"Thanks." She slid his number in her wallet with fingers made thick by fatigue. She'd been wired through the night, but ever since Evelyn had stopped her from hitting the table, she'd felt soggy.

In the morning general meeting Evelyn spoke in her softest yet most resolute voice. "I know Satch's suicide attempt is upsetting. But remember that Satch is not you. Her choices are her own. We each have to shape our own lives." She looked right at Simone as she said that. Simone looked away.

"Talk about how you feel in groups and with each other throughout the day. Above all, do not go visit Satch at the hospital. You need to focus on taking care of yourselves."

Simone scoffed. Not visit your closest friend when she needed you most? What was Evelyn thinking?

She sat through four small groups. "Satch helped me to get strong," Viola said, tears welling in her eyes and falling down her cheeks. "Wish there was something I could do to help her."

"Maybe Satch right," Regina said in her group, wiping the tears from her eyes with tissue after tissue. "I'm wondering, why bother living when Oakhill closing, when you just be alone, when ain't nobody never gonna love you?"

"My mama's a ho," Lonnie said in his. "Wish that bitch kill herself."

Marvin held his teddy bears to his chest. Despite Jun's urging, he could bring himself to say little other than "I'm scared" in a voice so small it could have come from one of the bears.

When it was time for her group with Evelyn, Simone didn't know how to begin so she just sat there in growing anger, fingers gouging the fabric of the one stuffed chair.

"What are you feeling?" Evelyn spoke softly.

"Anger."

"At whom?"

"Thomas. The politicians who voted to close Oakhill. Myself."

"Why yourself?"

She felt the almost overwhelming urge to sob. "In my gut I knew something was wrong, but I ignored it. I should have left here early and gone to check up on her, should have realized how bad she felt. I just wish I'd gotten in my car and gone after her when she walked off down the street. If I'd been a better friend, she'd be okay."

"Do you really believe that?"

She stole a glance at the other members, waiting for one of them to confirm her guilt; all but Rick seemed lost in their own misery. "I don't know. Yes and no. Thomas blamed me."

Rick exhaled scornfully. "Right, like you're the one who beats her."

"Rick right," Regina said. "Thomas oughta blame hisself."

Simone straightened to make herself less susceptible to tears. She remembered the previous day, recalled hitting Thomas, his blood, her pleasure. And she remembered the defeat in Satch's eyes. "I sensed something was wrong, but I was too worried about my own problems to check on her."

Evelyn's eyes narrowed as if they were lasers she was pointing at Simone. "So you're mad at the politicians and Thomas and yourself," Evelyn said. "Are you mad at Satch?"

Simone's mouth practically dropped. "Of course not!"

"Why not?"

"She was only trying to escape her pain." Simone wished she had aspirin to relieve her own headache. After the group she would ask Jun for some. For once she was relieved not to be in a group with him. Jun's gentleness might serve to make her feel sad. Evelyn was just pissing her off. Anger made you strong, and that's what she needed to be, strong enough to help Satch.

"There were other ways she could have chosen to lessen her pain," Evelyn said.

"Like what?" Simone couldn't believe even Evelyn was saying such crap.

"Like pressing charges against Thomas. Like going home with you instead of Thomas. After all, you did urge her to stay with you."

"When you hurt so much, the pain blocks your logic. Suicide is an act of despair. When you have no choice."

"When you *think* you have no choice," Evelyn corrected, the skin between her eyes creasing into the shape of a quotation mark. "But Satch did have other choices."

"Not like I do." Angry that Evelyn was dismissing Satch's hurdles, convinced Evelyn's race and position diminished her empathy, she pointed her finger at the director. "Satch doesn't have an education or a good job or a safe place to live."

Evelyn didn't respond. Instead she glanced around the room, silently inviting the others to speak.

"She got you and Viola," Regina said. "Coulda stayed with you."

"And her aunt," Viola said. "I'm mad at Satch."

Simone felt the anger eke out, felt her body deflate. "I should have realized Satch was so desperate."

"You're missing the point," Evelyn said. "You didn't make Satch overdose. She chose to take those pills."

Simone's eyes burned with unshed tears.

"If you kill yourself, it's not because you have to," Evelyn said. "It's because you choose to. That's true for anyone."

"Right. It's all so *simple.*"

"It *is* simple, but it's not easy. I understand that."

Simone held her breath to stop her tears.

"Let yourself cry," Evelyn said, and this time Simone heard the consoling warmth in Evelyn's voice, saw it in her eyes. "You have a lot to cry about."

For the next several minutes, no one spoke. They just sat with her. She kept her breathing shallow, kept digging at the arm of her chair. Tears terrified her. She didn't want to be weak, vulnerable. When it was time for her group to end, she got up and hurried to the bathroom, where she splashed water on her face to dilute the few tears that had eluded her defenses.

After she left the bathroom, she made a quick call to the hospital. Satch's condition was still listed as critical. She hung up the receiver and clutched it, fearing that if she released it, Satch would drift away forever.

At lunch, Jun took the chair across from her. She hadn't eaten since noon the day before, and she hadn't brought lunch because she'd come directly from Highland, but she didn't care. The last thing she wanted was food.

"How are you doing?" Jun said, his eyes like hands reaching out to her.

"Lousy." She looked away. He made surrender too tempting.

"You're not eating?"

"Not hungry." Logically she knew she must be hungry, but she felt no desire to eat.

Jun peeled a hard-boiled egg and handed it to her.

"No thanks." She was embarrassed by his offer and scared by his concern.

"You need to eat. Don't be hard-boiled about it." He had a beautiful smile, open and zestful and inviting.

Reluctantly she took the egg and forced herself to eat it, slow bite by slow bite. Her stomach gurgled. Regina must have heard her stomach's noises, because she set half of her peanut butter and jelly sandwich on the table in front of Simone. Willy added an Oreo. Lonnie gave her a handful of potato chips, Marvin an apple, Rick a protein bar, Viola a stick of string cheese. She was red-faced, embarrassed by their concern and their sharing. But she ate everything given to her.

As she finished the last bite, Jun grinned like he'd just witnessed some sort of marvelous miracle. She had to admit that the food did make her feel better, which worried her. What if her improvement meant Satch's deterioration?

In volleyball she played intensely, smacking the ball as hard as she could, not caring where it went. Rick, her partner, graciously refrained from complaining. By game's end, though they'd lost fifteen to six, she felt significantly calmer than she had since discovering Satch comatose.

When Oakhill closed for the day, Jun made her affirm her contract not to cut and to eat well. She did, but she left before he could hug her. Rick and Simone took Viola home, then

Rick took Simone to her car, still parked in front of Satch's. A parking ticket fluttered in the fog-dampened breeze. Simone sighed, leaned back against the seat of Rick's van and closed her eyes. She wanted to rest, just for a moment.

"Guess you didn't get much sleep," Rick said.

"No." She liked the sound of his deep voice.

"You're going to visit Satch, huh?"

"Of course." Maybe Satch had regained consciousness. Maybe Simone could even think of some way to elicit a smile.

"You want company?"

Simone pictured herself at Satch's bedside, holding Satch's hand. She imagined Satch expressing her joy over being alive. It would be an intimate exchange that Rick's presence might preclude. "No thanks, but I appreciate the ride."

"Any time."

Simone opened the van door, which creaked the way her body felt. She bunched up the ticket and tossed it in the glove box. She would deal with it later. Chastising herself for delaying, Simone drove resolutely to Highland. The nearest parking spot was five blocks away. She told herself the walk would do her good.

Once she neared the hospital, Simone picked up her pace and rushed to the ICU waiting room, where several weary-looking women crowded together. They stopped their conversation when Simone entered.

"Satch Hughes," she said into the gray box on the white wall, pronouncing the name like it was holy.

"Just a minute."

Wait? She resolved not to inhale until the voice over the intercom returned to assure her Satch was alive.

"What's your name?" a metallic voice asked.

"Simone Jouve." No response. She felt like she needed to establish her credentials. "I brought her here yesterday. We're friends."

"She doesn't want to see you," the voice announced.

Simone leaned against the wall. The paint was chipped. "What?"

"She said she doesn't want to see anyone, especially you."

Simone's chest tightened, her cheeks flamed. She sensed the other people in the room staring at her. Her voice quavered. "She's okay?"

"She's stable."

"Is she breathing on her own?" she croaked, the tension in her throat making speech difficult.

"I'm sorry. I can't give you any more information."

The intercom went dead.

Still propping herself against the wall, Simone put her fist to her mouth. Unable to face the other people in the room, she kept her eyes on the scuffed linoleum. When she stepped outside into the hazy air, she breathed for what seemed like the first time since the intercom voice delivered its pronouncement, but it wasn't a deep breath. She couldn't breathe deeply.

She trudged to her car. A siren sounded faintly, growing steadily louder, closer, reminding Simone of a long-ago day.

The sun, rending aside winter, had spotlighted the newly bloomed lilacs that day, the sweet scent of the blossoms scattering about the yard. Simone, sixteen, and her father reclined on lounge chairs, rejoicing in the exquisite spring morning.

She remembered clearly the sound of the siren that murmured in the distance until it became a wail, a keening, then ceased in front of their house.

The officer explained that their loved one was critically injured, hovering between life and death, and escorted them to the hospital. By the time they arrived, Simone's mother was dead. Simone couldn't bear to see the corpse, couldn't stand to listen to the police officer explain to her father the details of her mother's accident. And so she'd remained on the other side of the glass. Blind. Deaf. Numb.

If only she'd been a better daughter to her mother, a better friend to Satch. She bit down on a knuckle until pain shot through it.

That night she stared at the swirling images on the television screen through long sleepless hours. Near dawn she dozed. She dreamed that her mother—skeletal—stood before her, her arms open. "I can't embrace you until you die," her mother said. "It's so simple. Just get behind the wheel and press down on the accelerator. I want to hug you. Join me." In the dream Simone drove a red Corvette. She kept pressing down on the accelerator, passing every car. She worried because she didn't want to take anyone else with her. The speedometer crept above 100 miles per hour. Suddenly a wall appeared before her. Simone didn't hesitate. She floored the accelerator.

She woke with a cry. Her heart pummeled her. She was terrified. And strangely exhilarated.

Twenty-Seven

Jun seemed to be crying. Seated in the beige general meeting room, he balled his hand into a fist and gently tapped his mouth. His obvious distress filled her with dread. Had Satch died? *Please God, no!*

Seated beside her, Viola took her hand. Evelyn rose. It seemed to Simone that even those people who usually slouched sat upright, rigid and fearful as a somber Evelyn moved to the front of the room. Simone shut her eyes. She remembered Satch telling her she looked like shit in moments when she had thought herself invisible. She wanted to hear Satch's "uh-huh," her "You don't gotta do nothing but die someday." She prayed that this was not Satch's day.

"This has been a hard week," Evelyn said, her teal silk blouse shimmering in the fluorescent lighting.

Afraid she was pressing Viola's hand too hard, Simone lessened the pressure; Viola clung tighter.

"I have more bad news," Evelyn said. "Marvin killed himself last night."

Simone's moan was echoed around the room. There were other sounds, too: the audible inhalations, the *"no's,"* a gasp.

"I'm sorry to have to be the bearer of so much bad news. I'd be happy to answer your questions."

Not Marvin, Simone thought. Childlike Marvin.

"How did he do it?" Viola asked.

"He jumped in front of a BART train," Evelyn said.

Simone imagined screeching brakes, screaming witnesses, Marvin's mangled body. Tears welled in her eyes. "Did he suffer?"

"No. He died instantly."

"Why he do it?" Regina's voice shook.

"He didn't leave a note, so we can't be sure," Evelyn said.

Simone half-listened through the rest of the meeting and roused herself to schedule a group with Jun, but she kept seeing Marvin: juggling his bears to make her feel better, waltzing with Katrina in the club, raising the little bear's paw to be her buddy that first difficult day. Above all she pictured Marvin in the drama circle, falling with so much trust, his face lit in a delighted smile she couldn't believe was gone forever.

The small group room was full, as it had been for others' groups, members attending as if by staying together they were holding one another, holding themselves. Rick sat on one side of her, Viola on the other, Regina beside Viola. Several others filled the rest of the seats.

"I have some good news," Jun said at the start of her group. "Satch is out of danger. I spoke with her doctor. She's been moved from the ICU. They'll be transferring her to Helms, their inpatient psychiatric facility, tomorrow or Sunday."

Simone wanted to shout her relief and she wanted to curl up into a ball and let the world go by.

"How are you feeling?" Jun said.

"Relieved but bad."

"About Marvin?"

"I can't believe he's dead." Marvin's innocence had at times comforted her; she gouged her chair with her fingers, determined not to cry. She wondered if Satch would cry about Marvin. "Satch wouldn't see me."

"You went to the hospital?"

Jun's tone was neutral; she was grateful for that because she was sure Evelyn would have reprimanded her. "Yeah."

"She'll get over it."

"I'm not so sure."

Jun gave her a smile so full of sympathy he almost broke through the barriers to her tears. "It looks like you're trying to hold back," he said. "Let yourself have your feelings so you don't end up hurting yourself."

"But Marvin was afraid to live without the hospital. His fear killed him. Satch despaired, too, and look where she ended up. How can you say feelings protect you?" Jun's eyes seemed bruised. Had he heard about Marvin's death before going to bed? Somber, shoulders down, he appeared exhausted.

"I think they didn't let themselves accept their underlying fear and sadness," he said. "My guess is they were trying to escape from them."

She wished Marvin had only tried. She pressed her hand to her mouth to stuff her tears back inside. "Did the doctor say how Satch was doing?" Maybe Satch would forgive her now that she was better.

"She's pretty down. Most people are after a suicide attempt."

"But there's no brain damage?"

"None," Jun said. "You look angry."

"I am. I'm angry that they're closing Oakhill, that the poor are invisible. It's wrong!"

"I agree, and I'm angry, too."

She imagined Marvin on a steel table, his taped glasses and frayed clothes gone, replaced by a white sheet.

"I wonder if there isn't more going on for you around the closing," Jun said.

It took a moment for her to realize that Jun had intended his statement as a question. Fingers steepled, chin resting on them, he studied her.

Her gut cramped. "What do you mean?"

"You said the poor are invisible. Maybe as a child you felt invisible, too."

She blew air through her lips dismissively. "No way. My mother saw me. In the bathtub. And my father saw me too much. I was the opposite of invisible."

"Did they really see you? Did they see your loneliness?"

"My mother was the victim in our family."

"Your mama didn't say nothing to your daddy?" Regina asked.

"She felt too left out. It wasn't just in the bathroom. He said inappropriate things to me lots of places."

"Regina's raised a good point," Jun said. "You were a child. Your mother should have spoken to your father if his behavior upset her."

She wrapped her arms around her body to keep from exploding. "But it upset me, too. Part of me at least, the part that knew it was wrong. *I* should have stopped him. Maybe not when I was little, but certainly when I was fifteen and sixteen."

"That's still little," Viola said.

She'd felt so adult at sixteen. Until her mother had fallen asleep and crashed her car. She had felt young then.

"You need to explore your relationship with your mother," Jun said.

She laughed. Not a humorous laugh. There was no humor in her or anyone else in the room. "You mean in all the time left before the hospital closes?"

"I'm not the one closing Oakhill," Jun said, a note of defensiveness in his voice.

"I know. I'm sorry."

"Start here. Continue with a private therapist. Don't look for a quick fix. And don't allow anger to block your other feelings."

Her anger ebbed; she felt herself bend, felt a raw sadness well up in her. For her mother. For Marvin. For Satch. For all the desperate people with nowhere to go and no one to hold them.

At closing it seemed every member wanted a hug from one or more of the staff. She waited in line. When it was her turn, Jun hesitated. She understood what he wanted. "I affirm my contract not to hurt myself."

He smiled, one of the few smiles she'd seen from anyone that day. "Good. And Simone, I strongly advise you not to see your father this weekend."

She'd forgotten all about her plan to see him Sunday.

"It's been a hard week," Jun said. "Make my day. Give yourself time to heal. And prepare."

She felt like an overused washrag—dried out and crusty. There was nothing left to wring from her. Jun was right. She would not go see her father. She'd seen more than enough of him already.

Saturday's *San Francisco Chronicle* carried an article about a "disturbed" Marvin Elliot, who horrified onlookers when he threw himself in front of a BART train. Simone felt sad but also angry at the paltry description. Marvin was so much more than that. She wondered what Satch would say and whether Satch still wanted to die. Sunday she would attempt a visit, hoping that Satch's anger would have subsided by then.

She sipped the coffee she'd prepared. It was as strong as Jun's but so much smoother, nutty rather than burnt. She'd loved coffee since her eighth birthday when her mother fixed her coffee milk for the first time, pouring a little coffee and a whole lot of milk and sugar in a cup for Simone, who had felt grown up to be allowed to drink the delicious brew.

Her mother had been in such a great mood that morning until Simone's father presented her with three dolls for her birthday. Her mother said that three dolls were too many, but her father retorted that there was no such thing as too many for Daddy's little girl.

After lunch her still-angry mother took Simone horseback riding for the first time ever. Simone's mother had been raised on a ranch; Simone imagined herself galloping her horse and jumping logs fearlessly, with perfect position. Her mother would throw her arms around her, amazed Simone was such a natural rider.

She remembered the events of that day well, even the name of her horse. Fury. But Fury didn't gallop or jump, just plodded. When she hit him with a twig to make him move faster, he bucked. Terrified, she dropped the reins. Fury lowered his head to graze. Her mother cantered back to her, grabbed the fallen reins, and jerked Fury's head up. "Don't let go of the reins, for God's sake! You've got to be boss."

Simone told herself she could do that and she straightened up. Her mother whipped her reins across Fury's haunches. He trotted forward. Simone began slipping.

"Hold on!" her mother commanded.

Simone grabbed for the saddle horn as her horse slowed. She tried to assume the correct position. Fury stopped. She was thrown up on his neck, and he thrust his head forward. Too late she grabbed for the reins.

"If you can't ride the damned thing, we'll just go back," her mother said, her voice crackling.

Simone drew her knees to her chest as she thought about how often her mother had been angry. At her father. At her. And no wonder. How many times had her mother heard her father say he should be married to "a girl like you"? It wasn't just the bathroom door Simone had failed to close. It was her father's mouth.

Despite his repeated professions of love, her father hadn't really seen her—her discomfort, her shame, her guilt. Jun was right. She'd been invisible to him. Forgiving her father had made it easy for her to forgive Spence and every other man she'd let violate her in some way.

Rage tensed her body. She had to do something. Maybe swimming would pacify her. She jerked on her suit and fled for the pool.

Someone's patio door was open, an old Bob Dylan song playing.

She strode forward, passing a lithe woman lounging on her patio applying Coppertone. It was her mother's favorite sunscreen.

"Look at me, Mommy!"

Simone stopped at the fence surrounding the pool. A small boy perched on a man's shoulders, the boy's swimsuit hanging low on his hips. "You're so tall!" a smiling woman said, watching him from the shallow end. The man heaved the child up toward the sky, and the boy flung his arms and legs in a thousand directions before he plummeted back into the water, hollering gleefully.

She had no husband, no child, and probably never would. In many ways she hadn't had a mother, either. Turning, she headed back to her condo, promising herself she would make her father admit his guilt. She would see him Sunday, demand he confess. Then she would go see Satch and plead for their friendship.

Dylan still played. The times might not be changing, but she certainly was.

Twenty-Eight

Her father's green Mustang was gone. She slammed her car door. Their rendezvous was for five o'clock. He was always punctual—or at least he used to be. She wondered if he and Claire had decided to stay an extra day and he just hadn't bothered to phone her; perhaps he'd forgotten his daughter as completely as he used to forget his wife. Well, it was only 5:05. She would wait.

Her mother always said that their tract-style house—white with green trim—reminded her of "constipated old ladies." The only saving grace in her mother's eyes were the lush, butter-yellow rose bushes framing the front door. Simone stopped to smell them, convinced as always that they would smell like roses should; they didn't. Still, she shared her mother's appreciation of the flowers. She'd always imagined the bushes as sentries and had told herself nothing bad could happen in a house guarded by roses.

She rang the doorbell, then let herself in and dropped her keys on the table by the door. Her gaze roamed to the Robert Wood painting over the fireplace of a stream in autumn woods; her mother had said it looked like a paint-by-numbers piece. Much of her art had been nonrepresentational, bold slashes of vibrant color that Simone's father thought simplistic. He'd dragged out that canard about how even a child could paint them, which just made her mother paint even more furiously. Had every item in the house been ammunition in a cold war?

She went to the kitchen, hoping to find some cold grape juice. Each refrigerator shelf was arranged by category and expiration date, every leftover container identified with a red plastic label. Closing her eyes, she pictured the refrigerator as it used to be when her mother was alive: dotted with crumbs, smeared with gravy or viscous red spaghetti sauce, the racks sticky with food, the insides reeking of spoiled leftovers. No wonder she'd hated to eat.

"Cleaning is your mother's job," her father had told a young Simone, flicking off the faucet lever over a sink of dirty dishes. He had forbidden her to clean the refrigerator, the counters littered with crumbs, the floors dotted with roaches that scurried for corners when the light was turned on.

"I need to paint," her mother would say to him over one of their scattered dinners. "Hire a house cleaner."

"You need to clean," her father would reply. "It's your job."

Simone would try to clown them out of it, with green beans hanging from her nostrils or with a joke she had looked up and memorized at school. He had house cleaners now. Of course.

There was no juice, so she swigged root beer from the bottle and smiled to herself as she pictured her father aghast.

In the hallway she looked up at the trap door that led to the attic, to what used to be the forbidden territory of her mother's art studio, and the one place her mother had kept immaculate, as she had witnessed on her illicit visits when her mother was out. She pulled on the rope that dangled from the trap door, lowering the stairs. She climbed up. The attic was cool—her father had run heater and air-conditioning vents up to it—and empty now except for layers of dust and an abstract stained glass piece that hung turning in the one window, sun streaming through the glass, streaks of red, orange and purple chasing each other about the attic like a rainbow playing tag.

She walked around the entire space, half searching for some overlooked object, some sign, to tell her why her mother had allowed herself to be trapped by a home and a man she didn't love. But all traces of her mother that she recalled from her own glancing moments in this space—canvas, paints, brushes, paintings, postcards from Paris sent by a friend living out her mother's dream—were gone.

She imagined herself as her mother, painting until her daughter came home from school. Though Simone had known not to intrude, she suspected the sounds of her entry downstairs would have fractured her mother's concentration like a tiny earthquake. Had her mother ever been glad to hear the door slam downstairs, her child singing to herself?

The front door opened below her. She hurried down the attic stairs, didn't bother to raise them. Her father was setting his suitcases on the floor.

"We betrayed her!" She hurled the words at him.

He looked up, his eyes baby-blanket blue. "Hi, doll. What did you say?"

"You shouldn't have come in the bathroom. You had no right!"

He hung his windbreaker in the closet. "What are you talking about?"

"You—"

Claire entered in pink pants suit, pink lipstick, and pink shoes, vanity case in hand. "Hi," she said, her face brightening.

Alone. She'd specifically told her father *alone*.

"Simone! I never knew Tahoe was so beautiful," Claire declared. "Have you spent any time there?"

Simone made herself answer. "Backpacking."

Claire put down her bag and took off her jacket. "Backpacking? How brave. I'd be scared of bears. Can you stay for supper? I'm making spaghetti."

Simone looked at her father, trying to make him see her urgency. "I don't... Let me help you carry the suitcases to your bedroom, Dad."

"They can wait. I need some ice water. Do you want some, honey?" he asked Claire.

"No thanks."

The three of them went to the kitchen. It was all she could do not to grab her father and shove him toward the door to the bathroom, the scene of the crime. He took several ice cubes from the freezer and dropped them, infuriatingly one by one, into his glass. She waited. Watched him drink it. Watched him refill his glass. It was as if he was deliberately teasing her with his nonchalance. Maybe he was.

"Can I get you anything?" Claire asked.

"No thanks." She'd become the guest, an outsider in the house she'd grown up in. It seemed appropriate. "Dad, I need to see you privately." She looked at Claire and cocked her head apologetically.

"That's rude, Simone," her father said.

"I told you when I called I have to talk to you. Alone." She kept her voice on the knife edge of reasonable, but it was difficult.

Claire looked from daughter to father. "Excuse me a moment." She left.

Simone didn't have long. "All those times you came in the bathroom when I was bathing—"

He smiled. "I remember. You liked to play with your little plastic horses. No rubber ducks for you."

Simone's shoulders went rigid. "I'm not talking about that."

His face had a dreamy expression. "We had such fun. You were just a little girl then."

Her throat tightened. "I wasn't always so little."

"Oh, well, you were always my little girl."

"I was a teenager, too. I had breasts, for God's sake!"

"You liked for me to wash your back. You couldn't reach it. What are you getting upset about?"

Unlike her own voice, his was even, unperturbed, and that made her want to slap him. "You'd stare at my breasts and tell me you should be married to a girl like me. How could you?"

He squinted. "I don't remember that."

"You said those things. You did. More than once." She wanted to cry. She needed him to affirm her testimony, to act like a father and confess he'd been wrong to say what he said, to wash her back, to stare at her breasts, but he looked clueless. Well, they had guilt to share. She willed herself to stay calm.

"You must have misunderstood," he said, his voice taking on a newly deliberate nonchalance. "I told you I loved you a lot because I did. There's nothing wrong with that."

She was lightheaded and for an instant felt herself slipping into his version of the story as if it were a mirror she could enter, into a different but familiar room, its bathwater warm and waiting. In that room, he might be at a sharper angle to her nakedness, only her prim back and spine in view. Maybe in that room he was saying he was glad he *was* married to a girl like her.

"I'm going to get Claire."

He pivoted from her, and in that action she knew she hadn't misunderstood him at all. She took four quick steps around him to block his retreat. "No!" Any louder and she'd be screaming. "You treated me like your wife. It was wrong."

His eyes widened. He stepped back, looked appalled. "I never touched you."

"You didn't have to. Your eyes and words did it for you."

A look crossed his face but passed before she could identify it. "You left the door open," he said. "It couldn't have bothered you very much."

"I was wrong not to shut it." She was ready for that. Her complicity would not be his defense. "How do you think Mom felt?" She made herself move closer to him.

He brought his glass down hard on the counter. "How do you think I felt with a wife who didn't love me?"

It wasn't the answer she'd expected. "If your marriage was so bad, why didn't you get divorced?"

"I wanted to. She wouldn't give me one. She believed it was a sin." His mouth tensed into a pout. "You have to remember that your mother was a selfish woman."

"This isn't about Mom," she said. "No matter what your marriage was like, it was wrong to treat me like you did! It messed me up."

A flush of embarrassment or indignation tinged his neck. "Why are you bringing all this up now? It was years ago."

"I blocked it out, and I didn't understand," Simone retorted. "I do now. Treating me like your wife was fucked!" Spit flew unbidden from her mouth. It didn't reach him.

"We don't use that language in this house."

"Fucked. It was fucked!"

Her father looked serious, maybe even angry, but somehow, gratefully, off balance. Simone let herself dwell for a moment in the subdued sunlight that streaked shadows about the kitchen. Her mother had loved to paint shadows, had chased light in her paintings. Light never held still.

"If I overly doted on you," he said, "it was because she'd turned away from me."

"*Doted* on me?" Saying he'd doted on her was like Spence saying he'd made love to her.

"I parented you. You *preferred* me, because your mother was unpredictable and angry. Don't you remember all the times she spanked you just because she was in a bad mood? Or banished you to the bedroom because you cried? And that's just the beginning."

"No. *You* made me choose you. Always. If you hadn't interfered, I'd have gone with her to the store and she'd still be alive." She was on the brink of sobbing.

"No she wouldn't." Her father's voice was curt, slashing.

"What?"

"She... It doesn't matter." He turned his shoulder to her as if to push past at last. "It was twenty-four years ago."

She barely registered Claire's entrance.

"Tell me."

She needed him to say what she suddenly knew: her mother hadn't fallen asleep that day.

"It's ancient history, Simone," he said as if he disapproved of her even asking. He started to walk around her, out of the kitchen, but she blocked him.

"I cut myself with razor blades. Deliberately," she said. He recoiled. "My thighs. My face. My stomach."

Fear filled his eyes. And pain. He moved his head as if to shake out her words. "Cut yourself?"

"I'm not teaching. I'm in a psychiatric treatment program."

He looked bewildered. "Why?"

"That's what I'm trying to figure out. I need to know the truth."

"But you're a great teacher."

"I was."

"I don't understand."

"I'm trying to. I need your help. I need the truth. The full truth."

He straightened up, wiggled his shoulders as if to shed the heavy cloak of her admission. "You're just lonely. You need a special someone in your life."

"Every special someone I date is a loser. No man has ever really loved me. She killed herself, didn't she?"

"But you're already hurting yourself." He spread his hands, gesturing nowhere. "How could this help?"

"Please." His eyes skittered away from hers as he seemed to debate what to say. Simone didn't move, afraid he was too brittle, that one little movement from her might make him crack like a hot vase in cold water and that her chance to capture the truth would vanish forever.

He raised his head, eyed her, and sent out words in little blasts of breath. "According to witnesses, your mother aimed at the pillar and accelerated. She killed herself." His eyes narrowed. "Don't you think that's the real betrayal?"

Her stomach seized. She was right. Her mother had committed suicide. She floated up and out of her shoes for a moment, then flashed to the other side of the glass from the policeman and her father, where she had stayed, maybe to protect herself from what she knew even then to be the truth.

"Your mother was a sick woman," her father said, his face screwed in anger.

She gathered herself, came back down eye to eye with him. "No. She was just betrayed."

He exhaled. His brow lowered to tighten his eyes on her. "Betrayed enough to kill her own daughter?"

Her heart seemed to stop beating. "What are you talking about?"

"You don't remember?" he shot back.

"Remember what?"

"She tried to get you to go with her."

Her stomach felt full of glass. She plunged back to that day—the sunshine, the lilacs. She and her father were lying on lounge chairs, talking trivia. Her mother had suddenly stood over her. "Come with me to the store," she'd said, reaching out her hand to her daughter, blue eyes pleading.

Simone hadn't wanted to leave the yard on that gem of a spring morning, but her mother's eyes brimmed with need. She started to rise. Her father uttered a loud "No!" He glared at Simone's mother. "Denise, you've been drinking."

"No, just one bloody Mary," her mother said. She extended one wavering hand to Simone.

The hand scared her. She waited until it withdrew, stayed in her chair, and listened to the door slam, the engine race, the tires screech.

Now, twenty-four years later, suddenly dizzy, she steadied herself against the wall.

"Why don't you sit down," Claire said, putting a hand on Simone's shoulder.

Simone was afraid that if she sat down she might not get back up. The accident had been no accident. But she didn't—couldn't—believe her mother had meant to kill her. "You don't know that."

"There is no doubt in my mind, not when you consider the way she treated you."

"You mean the way *we* treated *her,* don't you?"

"Simone, I don't know about... Maybe I... But I never did anything deliberately to hurt you."

He really hadn't. He was a man who didn't know himself, didn't detect the impulses that charged him, damaged her. She had to allow something for his unknowingness.

"Your mother needed help," he said. "I wish I'd seen that."

They'd all needed help. But all that mattered now was the possibility that her mother had hated her enough to kill her. Surely that wasn't true. Surely her mother's invitation had been nothing more than a plea for help. Simone tried to take a deep breath but couldn't. The air was thin in her father's house. "I've got to go."

"You shouldn't drive," her father said.

"Stay for dinner," Claire said.

"I can't." She started for the door.

Her father took her arm to restrain her. She couldn't bear to face him. "I'm sorry if I..."

"Okay." It didn't matter any more.

"Don't go yet."

"I have to."

"You've had a big shock," Claire said. "You're too upset to drive safely. Stay for dinner. I'll make whatever you'd like for supper. I could bake you some brownies."

"No, thanks."

"If you're not teaching, do you need any money?" Her father reached for his back pocket.

"No. I'm fine. I just..." She had to come up with an excuse so she could get out of this house. It was suffocating her. She forced a smile. "I have a date."

Her father released her, but he didn't look convinced.

"He's a teacher."

Claire also looked skeptical.

Her father said nothing for one long moment, but when he spoke his voice had the enthusiasm of a keynote speaker at a sales convention. "That's just what the doctor ordered."

She knew he didn't believe her but had decided to deny his disbelief. She'd learned her own habits of denial from a master.

"You need to live your life in the here and now," he said. "Don't get hung up on the past. And don't hurt yourself any more."

As if it were all as easy as saying so. She reached for the doorknob. Then she was outside, walking between the rose bushes.

"Simone," her father called.

She stopped.

"Your mother loved you as much as she could. I hope you know that."

His words stuck on the rosebush's thorns. Evelyn would say Simone hadn't been responsible for her mother's death, that her mother made her own choice. But Evelyn hadn't been there.

She walked on wobbly legs, fumbled with the lock until the car door opened. From behind the wheel, she saw her father and Claire watching from the doorway, their arms around each other, their faces somber. She started the motor. She wanted to cry and she wanted to scream and she wanted to grab a razor blade and start carving her wrist.

She drove to the freeway entrance ramp that her mother must have taken, the one closest to the house. Had her mother decided it would be her own exit ramp? Freshly tarred gravel clunked against her car. She rolled up her window to block out the smell and merged onto the freeway.

An overpass piling rose ahead of her, another not far beyond. Which had her mother crashed into, or was it a different one entirely? Had she chosen the first piling she saw, or had she been a comparison shopper? Simone smiled grimly into the glare. There was so much she didn't know about that day. She chided herself for not pumping her father for details. It didn't matter which piling her mother had chosen, not really, but she thought that if she knew the specifics—if she could say *that* piling, *that* section, *that* angle—perhaps she could survive the memory.

The freeway was rutted from winter, and she slowed, her car pulling to the right. Her wheels must be out of alignment, she thought. Not that it mattered. All that mattered was that her mother had wanted her dead.

In the freeway gloaming she saw rise before her an image of her mother's face, as if hurriedly painted there: dazzling blue eyes, cheeks colored like her pastels, naturally dark lips that so clearly signaled her moods. Each time Simone had come in the door, each time the attic stairs were lowered, her heart constricted: what mood would her mother's lips reveal?

The cars blurred into her mother's wavering hand, beckoning her.

A truck wheezed along in the slow lane, engine struggling to power its load. She gripped the wheel, her wrists twitching. With one spurt of gas and a sharp right, she could cut in front of it, cut herself in half, splatter like a bug on its windshield.

Jesus Saves read a bumper sticker on the car in front of her. Where the fuck was Jesus on the day her mother rammed her car into a freeway pillar?

Her mother's eyes had been so moist it seemed like they were melting.

Come with me to the store.

Maybe it was here her mother screamed, at this pillar, if she screamed. She wanted to cover her ears and scream, too.

The steering wheel vibrated in her hands. She glanced at the speedometer: eighty-five. A thrill shot through her, and she pressed down on the accelerator. A slow car loomed ahead. She accelerated and swung toward the fast lane.

A horn blared.

Cars were coming up on her left and right. She was only inches from the car in front of her with its rear window sticker warning *Baby on Board*. Its brake lights lit. She jerked the wheel left, stomped the accelerator to avoid the closing cars, and careened into the median strip.

Her car slid in the gravel. The rear end swung right, and Simone was borne by its velocity, flying across first one, then two, then three lanes of traffic, and she felt herself be stripped of all agency, giving up everything but her grip on the wheel and thus on the earth and her own curiosity about whether she would live, or die like her mother.

More horns. Horns? Her. They were honking at her. She considered lifting her hands off the wheel, letting her body take flight. Didn't. She managed to straighten her vehicle, slowed, and pulled on to the shoulder, kicking up gravel until she stopped. Her hands shook. All of her shook.

She had to see Satch.

Twenty-Nine

Simone got out of her car in the parking lot of Helms Psychiatric Hospital under a sky so smooth, so relentlessly gray, it looked like an ironed sheet. The air felt damp and she zipped up her jacket. From somewhere in the lot, a deep-throated dog barked, as if to give voice to the sullen sky. It was 7:20, the daylight draining. She had about forty minutes. If Satch would even see her.

She walked toward a drab cinderblock building: two stories, weedy brown grass, bedraggled flowers. A great place to send suicidal patients because here suicide seemed redundant.

Inside, the hospital was dark, the green carpet mossy, the walls scuffed. The jowly guard took the present she'd bought for Satch two days previously, opened the red paper, and probed its insides. Finding nothing suspicious, he handed her back the present, and she resealed its scars as best as she could. Once she passed through the metal detector and signed the visitor list, she looked for the staircase, which was in the far corner. She climbed to the second floor.

Would Satch welcome her, accuse her, or demand her eviction? Did she really want to find out? She opened the door. A guard in blue uniform stood in an office sealed behind a security window.

"I came to see a patient."

No response.

"Satch Hughes."

"You have to leave your purse and keys."

She handed him her belongings, and he buzzed her through a wire mesh door into a unit with brightly painted walls decorated with cheap prints. It radiated the artificial cheer of daisy decals.

Padded benches lined the walls. A few people sat alone, staring into nothing. Others were talking feverishly in pairs or trios. Simone walked by small bedrooms without doors, scanned benches, stopped at a large room with tables and a television, where several people watched *Ghostbusters*. Anxious, she feared Satch had killed herself but decided that was ridiculous. Suicide would be challenging on a ward without doors.

There. In a corner, on a bench, staring out the window, sat Satch.

"Satch?"

Satch looked over, her eyes taking a long three seconds to focus. It took all Simone's courage to move toward her. Satch watched her approach, then turned away, her face as impassive as the gray seamless sky. "What you doing here?"

Simone felt as if she'd swallowed sandpaper. "I miss you."

"Don't."

Satch's voice was the flat line on a heart monitor. Simone would rather Satch scream, spit, push, and kick her back to the guards' desk—anything other than this deadened indifference.

"Can I sit down?" Satch didn't respond. Simone sat on the bench across from her and groped to find words she wasn't sure she believed. "How are you?"

Satch poked her finger into a cigarette burn in the red Naugahyde.

"I've missed you," Simone said.

"Just gonna do it again where nobody find me."

"Why?"

Satch didn't bother to answer, or didn't have an answer. Suicide had to feel as right to her as breathing had. Silence fell between them, lengthened. The unit doors opened. An attendant pushed a meal delivery cart, stopping in front of the large room. People rose and trundled to the cart to take off trays that smelled of overcooked vegetables and gravied meat.

"Do you want to get dinner?"

"Naw."

"You're not hungry?"

"Food here don't taste like nothing."

"Think of the pizza and doughnuts and egg rolls waiting for you."

"That the Doughnut School of Therapy?" Satch turned to Simone and peered into her eyes, as if seeing her for the first time. "You look like shit."

"Yeah. Well. It's just…" She asked herself if telling Satch would further burden her or help take her out of her own very real problems, or if she could say anything that would touch Satch. "My mother killed herself." It was all she could bring herself to admit.

Satch didn't react. After a few moments she reached up and grabbed a handful of her own bristling hair.

"What's it like?" Simone asked.

"What?"

"Dying."

Satch shrugged. "Ain't like nothing. Just go to sleep and don't wake up. 'Less somebody stop you."

"I couldn't just let you die." Simone felt like a cloud inside.

"Yeah you could."

"I shouldn't have let you go after Thomas hit you. I'm so sorry. And I should have checked on you sooner."

"Ain't pissed about that. Pissed 'cause you ain't let me die."

Simone scooted forward, working to insert herself in Satch's line of vision. "What would you have done if you came to my place and found me overdosed?"

Satch glowered at her. "Ain't coming to your apartment without no invite. You didn't have none."

"Damn it, Satch! Don't tell me that. Don't sit there and tell me you're going to do it again, that I don't matter."

Satch sat as stiff as a textbook. "Ain't about you."

"Sure it is. At least in part. You're being selfish. You want to hurt the people who love you. I wanted to slap my mother, and now I want to slap you." Horrified by what she'd said, she pushed herself backward on the bench.

Satch crossed her arms, shoved out her lip, and stared willfully out the window. "Don't want nobody's love."

"It's too late for that."

Satch snorted.

"I do love you, Satch, and I'm mad that you tried to kill yourself, that you didn't care how your death would affect me or anyone else."

Satch just kept staring out the window.

"Damn my mother and damn you!"

Satch didn't stir. "What I'm gonna live for? Ain't got no home. No job. Car ain't running. Ain't got nothing." Satch's voice sounded rote, as if she were reading a list of names.

"Those are just things. Live for people. For yourself."

Satch looked at her. "Easy for you to say."

"Yeah, I've got more money than you. But right now I'm not even sure I'm going to make it through the night."

A flicker of doubt passed over Satch's face. "You telling me how I gotta live and you thinking how you gonna die. Why?"

"I have no family of my own. My mother drove her car into a cement pillar because my father and I repeatedly betrayed her. And my father said my mother intended to kill me, too."

"How he know? She leave a note?"

"No, but she asked me to go with her. What if he's right?"

Satch exhaled. "Saying something or thinking something don't make it so."

Simone frowned at this. "But if she was just asking for company and I'd gone with her, she might still be alive."

"Why you didn't go?"

Simone remembered the pleading in her mother's eyes, the trembling of her mother's hand. When she spoke, her voice was tiny. "I was scared."

"Of your mama?"

"Yeah." Her lip was trembling just as her mother's hand had. She felt small and lonely and frightened. The feeling was familiar.

"Why you scared? She beat you?"

"No." She thought of Fury and the fury in her mother's voice the day they'd gone horseback riding. Thought of the astringent smell of her mother's breath, still hinting of alcohol, that last day. "It's just, she was so unpredictable. And sometimes she'd get so angry."

"That why you scared when I get angry with you?"

"I guess so." Simone scrutinized the clouds, searching for one break, one seam. "I think I thought she didn't love me, that she'd have been happier if I hadn't been born."

"Yeah. Know what you mean." Satch squinted and seemed to think this over. "Your daddy, he love you? I don't mean when he was messing with you."

"I guess. He played with me a lot. Tucked me in at night. Read to me."

"So that's why you stay with your daddy. Your mama didn't love you enough. You ain't to blame."

"It feels like I am."

Satch grimaced. "Your mama drove her own self into that wall, Simone. You wasn't driving. Just like you ain't shoved them drugs down my throat. You ain't got that much power. Don't be blaming yourself for other folks' choices."

Maybe it really was that simple, Simone thought. She felt overwhelmingly tired, felt she could let go finally and sink into sleep right there on the bench.

Some patient behind her laughed abruptly, a hiccup of laughter.

"Do you ever blame yourself that your mother beat you?" Simone asked.

Satch looked back out the window at the smooth sky. "Maybe. Feel like that's how you love somebody, by beating on 'em. You ain't invisible. They got to see you to beat you."

A man shuffled by them, wearing a hospital gown and paper slippers. They both watched him pass.

"Thorazine?" Simone asked.

"Electric shock," Satch said. "Take a day to get over it."

"Not someone you'd want on your volleyball team. Remember that game when so many people played?"

"Damned crazy. Folks ducking. Screaming. Swinging after the ball hit the ground. Marvin and his bears."

Simone tried not to glance away but did.

"What? It's Marvin, ain't it?"

"Yes."

"He kill hisself?"

She nodded.

"Damn." Satch's eyes misted.

Simone felt her own eyes tear up and let them. "He lost it, I guess, with the hospital closing."

"Marvin, he like a little kid." Satch shook her head.

"Yeah. And Satch, when I saw you'd OD'd, when I heard them say you'd coded, I..." Tears spilled down Simone's cheeks. "I don't want to lose you."

Satch closed her eyes. Simone wanted to grab her, to make certain Satch couldn't block her out, but she was overwhelmed by her own tears. She cried for Marvin and Satch and her mother. She cried for herself.

"Get me out of here!" Both women jumped, turned around to see a teenaged patient screaming into a pay phone. Her wrists were wrapped in white gauze. Simone cringed. "These people are crazy! One guy shot himself in the stomach. Get me out or I'm going to jump out the window!"

A man with a wad of keys around a belt loop approached the girl, signaling her to lower her voice. She turned her back and screamed into the phone. The man clicked the phone to disconnect the call. The girl threw the receiver into his chest, and stormed into her room, the man following.

The young woman was so wrong, Simone thought. "These people" were her; they were Simone. They all needed food, shelter, medication, love. Without all those things, including that last one, they would all be wrapped in blame or guilt; they would all go crazy. When she looked up, there were tears on Satch's cheeks, too.

"Everything all right here?" a deep voice asked.

"Fine," Satch said. She looked out the window and so did Simone. Rain began. "Figure you can love somebody and not hurt?" Satch asked.

Simone wiped her eyes with her palms and blew her nose on a piece of shredded tissue she must have stuffed in her pocket long ago. Her voice was unsteady at first. "I guess not. There's always something. Sickness. Misunderstandings. Death. This sounds stupid, but to me it seems like a package deal. You go on the cruise, you get the full plan, like it or not."

"Ain't never gonna go on no cruise, but you right. Only way not to hurt is not to love."

"It's too late for that, Satch."

"You gonna keep your own self safe?"

"Does it matter to you?"

Satch's eyes followed the rain easing down the glass. Her silence pricked Simone's heart.

"Remember the day you come through that gate at Oakhill."

"You weren't real glad to see me."

Satch's lips turned up, just briefly. "Seem like you was everything I hated. A rich white bitch."

She wanted to say she wasn't rich, but she sensed it didn't matter, not really.

"Kinda funny. Got angry at you 'stead'a Thomas." She tugged on her hair again. "Then you took me home with you. In spite of all your carpeting and shit, then I just see a woman.

So if I live and you die, yeah, I'm gonna be sorry. And real pissed."

Simone felt like she could almost float away. "Live, huh?" She remembered the bird costume her mother had made for her one Halloween, spending hours cutting out feathers from iridescent purple fabric then sewing them on to black velveteen. *Your mother loved you as best as she could,* her father had said. Maybe he was right. Maybe the limitations were about her mother, not her. "Well, I will if you will."

Visiting hours are over, a voice intoned from above.

Rain spattered against the window. "Ain't supposed to rain in May."

"It might make the hills green."

"Just gonna get brown again."

"And green again after that."

"Shit."

Simone started to stand; the present she'd brought and forgotten slid to the floor. She picked it up and handed it to Satch.

Satch stared at it for a long time. Finally, slipping her fingers along the taped part, she loosened it. Hesitated. Then she folded back the paper and held up the gift Simone had searched four stores to find: an orange-and-purple swimsuit, size sixteen.

"I thought you'd like the colors. You can exchange it if it doesn't fit."

The man with the keys was circulating around the room, ushering visitors out.

Satch kept staring at the suit, not speaking.

"You can stay with me as long as you need to."

Satch buried her face in the suit. Simone touched Satch's shoulder. "Take care of yourself." She started toward the door.

"Simone?"

She turned back toward Satch.

"Ain't no telling what Thomas gonna do. You don't gotta take me in."

"As a wise woman told me, don't gotta do nothing…"

They finished the line together, "but die some day."

"Just not any day soon, okay?"

Satch held her gaze. The attendant gestured visitors near them toward the door. Simone started to leave. When she'd nearly reached the door, she heard a loud "Simone!" and turned around.

"You pick out these colors?"

"Yeah."

"Ain't bad for a white girl."

At the doors that led to the outside and the rain, Simone inhaled the piercing disinfectant a custodian was mopping on the lobby floor. It smelled blisteringly real. She watched the rain pelt the sidewalk, swirling into pools that multiplied the lights of departing cars. Rap music pulsed from a passing Chevy; it seemed to her to give voice to her own heartbeat. She stepped outside and turned her face up. Rain struck her head, her cheeks, and seeped beneath her collar. She inhaled the fresh scent of wet grass and thought that sooner or later the hills really would green again. Simone smiled and started walking.

Acknowledgments

So many people have influenced and sustained my writing, my life. I owe all of them my heartfelt gratitude.

Madelon Phillips for daily enlightenment and, with Mike Karpa, some eighteen years of encouragement and insight. Tarn Wilson for unwavering sensitivity. Writers group members Linda Anton, Anna Dabney, Margaretha Deresay, Jean Gregory, Catherine Conway Honig, Margaret Irving, Julie Klinger, Tracy Livezey, Patty Long, Amanda McTigue, Christine Myers, Sharon Noteboom, Bertha Reilly, Leticia Wiley, and Marda Woodbury for supportive suggestions.

Marilyn Baer, Lynn Beittel, Gini Carter, Dianne Elise, Joyce Marie Gray, Marcy Stites, Ron Stites, and Ruthann Taylor for critiquing and caring.

Joan Diamond for championing this book.

Kathleen Caldwell and the staff of Great Good Place for Books for shepherding me through the process.

Ernie Grafe for the website, infinite patience, and enthusiasm. Mark Rollins for the photographs.

Lydia Bird, David Groff, and Alan Rinzler for expert, enthusiastic editing.

Edora Stell and Jeff Mayfield for help with language.

Gil, Mike, Elizabeth, Richard, and Renee for all the lifelines. Randy McCommons and the late Sandy Stark for wise nurturing.

My brothers, Ron and Steven Stites, for sharing their memories and their love. Sandra Stites, John and Nobuko Felton for always being there. Ailea, Chris, James, and Sierra for delighting my heart.

Wally Lamb for unstinting generosity.

My husband Bert Felton for years of love, laughter, and wisdom. Without your help, this book would never have been born.

Thank you all.

Jan Stites taught screenwriting at San Francisco State and U.C. Berkeley Extension, geography in the Yucatan Peninsula, African literature in Kenya, and middle school in Missouri and the Bay Area. Jan has published in the *Village Voice* and other periodicals. She is coauthor of *Diver's Guide to the Caribbean,* and three of her film projects have been optioned. She lives with her husband in Oakland, California.

Visit the author's website at http://www.janstites.com

LaVergne, TN USA
03 April 2011
222651LV00001B/80/P